From the GROUND Up

BY

JENNIFER VAN WYK

BLUE TULIP
PUBLISHING

From the Ground Up
By Jennifer Van Wyk
Blue Tulip Publishing
www.bluetulippublishing.com

FROM THE GROUND UP
Copyright © 2017 JENNIFER VAN WYK
ISBN-13: 978-1544112091
ISBN-10: 1544112092
Cover Art by Jena Brignola
Formatting by Jill Sava, Love Affair With Fiction

Dedication

To my husband, Travis. You are the best man I know.
I love our marriage. I love you.

To Jill: You encouraged me every single day. Love ya, girl.

To: West Liberty Public Library

Jenif Van Yn

Prologue

Barrett

SEEING HER SITTING in the middle of this pickup, right next to me, just where she belongs, makes my chest swell with pride. After all this time, I still can't believe she's mine. I have several things planned for tonight, and I pray that it all goes as smoothly as I hope. It's all been in the works for a while now, and I want it to go perfectly – for her and me. We pull up to the first stop, an old drive-in movie theatre that's been around since… well, I'm not quite sure, but a long time.

She looks at me skeptically. I get it. It's the end of November in Michigan. Who goes to a drive-in, let alone one that is closed for the season? But I have connections. Connections being my best friend Josh's aunt and uncle, or something like that, own the theatre and said they'd help me out, for which I was eternally grateful. I back into a spot in the front row, not that it matters since it's completely deserted. Tess still hasn't said anything. I've learned this is her way, though. She's trying to figure out what's going to happen, but I truly hope she doesn't. It will take the surprise out of the evening, and I desperately need her to be surprised all night long.

"Stay here."

"Okay," she says quietly, quizzically.

I smile over at her as my nerves start to kick in. This is the first time I've been nervous about tonight, but I have too much riding on it. She deserves this night to be one she'll never forget. I retrieve the basket out of the small back seat that I filled before I left to pick her up, as well as the two heavy blankets. Not that we won't be sharing a blanket, but the bed of the pickup will be cold, so I figured we'd sit on one and cuddle up with the other. And it wouldn't be the drive-in if we didn't sit outside to watch the movie.

I arrange the blankets as well as the food. The meat and cheeses, some fruit, a big bag of popcorn I begged from the movie theater in town, M&M's, hot chocolate, and a couple bottles of soda — all those romantic staples. But I'm sure she'll get it. It will be romantic to her. And that's the only thing that matters. I have a bag of peppermint saltwater taffy hidden for later. It's her absolute favorite. I'm sure she has a couple pieces stashed in her purse anyway, but I want her to know I was thinking of her.

After everything is set up the way I want it, I walk around to the driver's side door and open it while extending my hand for her to slide out and into my arms. She giggles and shakes her head, looking a little confused, but follows me anyway. She always follows me. The trust that she has in me is enough to bring me to my knees.

I help her into the bed of the pickup and, right on cue, the movie starts up. When the opening credits to *The Princess Bride* begin playing, she squeals adorably and claps her hands together lightly before throwing her arms around my neck and kissing me squarely on the lips.

"Thank you," she murmurs. "You remembered? Our first

date?"

"Of course. How could I forget?"

"I love you. A whole lot."

"I know. I love you, too. More than you can even imagine. Now, let me feed my girl, that good with you?" I give her my biggest smile.

She looks down at the spread for the first time, and her smile grows even larger, which I didn't think was possible. "Barrett, it's perfect."

Her praise humbles me, especially considering the simple nature of the food I prepared. I didn't realize how much I needed her to approve of the plans I had for the evening until that very moment. We eat our picnic dinner while watching a movie that's sure to stand the test of time. A classic. One that I know one day we'll be forcing our grandchildren to watch, years down the road, of course. When she starts eating the popcorn and I remind her to add M&M's because "chocolate coating makes it go down easier," she laughs so loudly and hard I am afraid she will choke on the popcorn.

"Oh my gosh, Barrett. You're too much."

I scoff, "I'd like to think I'm just enough, fair lady." I smile cheekily at her.

She just shakes her head and burrows deeper into my lap while we continue watching the movie.

The final credits begin to roll, but the soundtrack is changed to one I know she'll recognize. I stand up and reach down. She smiles widely and places her hand in mine. The simple piano notes of "Can't Help Falling in Love" begin playing just as I pull her close to me. We sway slowly, her cheek resting just below my shoulder, and mine resting on top of her head. My hand is gripping hers, resting against my chest.

The song changes and moves into something more upbeat, faster paced. We separate just slightly and begin dancing, smiling and singing along. I dip her, the tip of her hair nearly touching the bed of the pickup.

"Barrett!" she squeals.

I lift her back up, chuckling. "What? You don't trust me? I'm offended, Tess. Really." I begin to fake pout.

"Ha! Nice try. That face doesn't work on me anymore. Besides, you know I trust you."

"Yeah? Prove it."

"How am I supposed to do that?"

"Oh, I have some ideas," I say, raising my eyebrows up and down.

"Not gonna happen, cowboy."

"Cowboy?"

"Sure."

"I can live with that. Why isn't it gonna happen though? It could. No one is out here." I look around at the empty lot.

"It's freezing! And yeah, you say no one is out here…"

"Fine. I'll give you the freezing thing, but no one *is* out here."

She pulls me back to her and snuggles in close. "I do like having you to myself," she murmurs into my chest, and, dammit it all, I start to feel emotional.

"I *love* having you all to myself."

"Mmm…" she says as the song shifts once again to a slow song, and we continue to sway under the stars.

After we've danced for several songs, I realize we need to keep moving. We still have one more stop to make. The most important stop. So, we pack up everything and climb back into the cab of the pickup. This time I don't need to tell her to sit next to me; she slides next to me on her own, sitting close enough that our thighs are pressed against one another's and she's nestled tightly into the nook under my arm.

"Good girl," I murmur and smile down at her then kiss the top of her head. She snuggles a little deeper in next to me and wraps her arm around my stomach.

"I'm a fast learner," she says with a smile in her voice.

The next stop is the big one. I drive over to the side of town that houses a park where we have spent so much of our time. It's a walking park, and, in the fall, it's beautiful, all woods and leaves changing colors. In the winter time, it's not quite the same but still gorgeous. The city comes in and clears walking paths from the snow, and a huge sledding hill sits in one section of the park that kids have named The Monster. But no matter what time of year it is, the park is special to us. My nerves start to come back as she realizes where we're going but still doesn't question me. She trusts me.

I park and we both climb out silently. I take her gloved hand and curse the cold temperatures. I want to feel her palm in my palm, her fingers laced with mine with no barrier. Nothing between us. I reach into my front jeans pocket with my left hand and feel for the object that will either make or break the rest of our lives. Feeling the small circular object, I make a fist around it, hoping that what it symbolizes will create the calm in me that it needs to.

There were flurries falling from the sky this morning, and the smell of snow is in the air. But for tonight, the ground is still mainly clear. We approach our bench, our feet making the last of the autumn leaves crunch beneath us. We sat on this bench at the end of our first date, and it's also the place where my lips first touched hers. She instinctively takes a seat, knowing that's where we were headed, and I follow suit. She's in my head more than I like to admit, just like I'm in hers. I can see the wheels turning behind those gorgeous bright blue eyes of hers. She can't hide from me. Never could. Never will be able to. And right now, she's probably thinking, *Why in the world am I sitting out here in the freezing cold? My butt is like an ice cube.*

I chuckle to myself as I look down at her.

"What are you laughing at?" she asks, smiling.

"You. You're not letting yourself just be. I know you're cold, and you're wondering what we're doing here, but just bear with me for a few moments."

"How did you know I was wondering that?"

My response is a raise of my eyebrows at her. Her cheeks are flushed in irritation with me — or maybe it's just the cold — which I find cuter than anything, and she looks away before mumbling that I was right.

I lean over and kiss her lightly on the lips; she tastes of peppermint, as I knew she would. I saw her bite into a couple of her favorite comfort taffies. "You always taste so damn good." I moan as I deepen our kiss.

"It's the taffies. I've been telling you for years they're delicious."

"Nope. It's all you. It's all you, my beautiful Tess."

She takes a shuttering breath then launches herself at me, wrapping her arms around my neck and taking over our kiss. She pulls me down toward her, causing me to rest one of my hands on the bench next to her while my other wraps around her back. Our tongues tangle, our breaths becoming one.

After several moments, I reluctantly pull away. Whether she knows it or not, tonight is about more than a hot make-out session. I rest my forehead against hers for a moment. "You turn me out every time, Tess. Every single time."

She smiles at me and giggles a little bit. "Yeah, I know the feeling."

I take a deep breath and stand from the bench, shaking my hands out slightly. These nerves are ridiculous.

She looks up at me questioningly. "Barrett?"

"Tess…" I begin as I drop to one knee.

Tears immediately flood her eyes, and she gasps, her right hand covering her mouth. Her left hand is in mine, shaking, trembling.

I stare into her bright blue eyes and begin the speech that I've recited in my head over and over again. The speech that I partially spoke to her father when I told him my plan, asked his permission. I will only do this once in my life and I must do it right, building our lives together from the ground up.

Chapter One

Tess

AT THE SOUND of my alarm blaring next to my ear, I groan and throw the leg off my stomach that had somehow managed to wrap around me all night long. After prying my stiff and aching body off the bed I look back to discover the leg that was wrapped around me was none other than the leg of Harper, our six-year-old. Of course. Still in our bed, she lies spread-eagle next to my still-somehow-hotter-than-the-day-I-married-him husband, Barrett.

Barrett's slightly curly, short brown hair is looking deliciously messy, and I so wish I could crawl back into bed, kick out the extra human, and curl up next to him. My fingers itch to run my hands through his hair. His shoulders peeking out of the covers are so tempting, strong and broad. He may not have that perfect six pack any longer, but his body is still better than any other forty-four-year-old man I know. It shows off the years of hard work he's put into building our family, that he's satisfied with not being a gym rat, but that he's still even fitter because his body has worked hard. But most of all, it shows that he protects our family with all that he has in him.

He's lying on his stomach, one muscled arm curled

under his pillow, the other reaching out to my side of the bed, Harper's head wedged underneath. I can just barely see a hint of the tattoo that wraps around his tricep, but I know it's there. It's one of the hottest things I've ever seen.

Somehow wedged around them lie our two dogs. Rex, our boxer, and Flash, our Jack Russell terrier, both think they're human. How the two of them managed — or all three, I guess — to make their way into our bed once again is beyond me, but not out of the ordinary. The last time I was able to share the marital bed with just my husband was, well, I guess I don't remember that far back.

The dogs have their own beds on the floor in the laundry room, but I know if we had a camera aimed at our bed, we'd see both sneak into our room at night and jump in with us. Harper, however, is a different story. She's not sneaky about it. She just barrels in at any hour of the night, even after she's been sound asleep in her own bed for hours. Her excuses are becoming less and less original with each night. Most of the time, she just mumbles incoherently under her breath or says something about a bad dream, then nestles in under the covers and falls back asleep within seconds. Bad dream my foot.

After wrapping my robe around my body, I slide my cell into the pocket, grab my glasses off the nightstand, and head to the bathroom. I look in the mirror after washing my face and gaze at my reflection. I can't complain, the years have been pretty good to me, even with turning forty a few years back. My skin is fairly clear and smooth, thanks to drinking tons of water, and probably sporting good genes too. My blue eyes are still vibrant, even with the few wrinkles that surround them, and my shoulder-length hair has some amazing highlights, but those are courtesy of Julia the Genius, making my hair a honey-blonde rather than the gross dirty-blonde it tends to lean toward without the aid of chemicals. My eyes are still tired, so I decide to leave my dark-framed glasses on until I'm ready for my contacts later.

I pad my way into the kitchen to where the coffee has already been made, thanks to its auto-brew setting. I grab a mug from the cupboard, add my favorite cream, and pour my first — probably of many, cup. I open the sliding door and close it behind me after I step onto the deck of our modest-sized story-and-a-half home. A chill in the air causes me to shiver, but my navy pajama bottoms and slippers that cover my feet help ward off some of it. When we were blessed enough to build our house right after Grady was born, we knew we wanted to be here forever. We both wanted our kids to remember this as their childhood home, and so far, we've been fortunate enough to stay put.

The wide, vertical, dark grey siding and rich ivory trim around the windows and doors was definitely something different from the norm when we built, but I couldn't be happier with it. It still screams home to me. Everything about this place is personal in some way, much of it handcrafted by Barrett and Josh, his lifelong best friend. When Barrett's father was still living, he made his living as an architect. He drew up our blueprints and helped design our home.

I smile when I hear the door slide open and shut and feel strong arms wrap around me from behind. Stubble scrapes against my neck, making me shiver, and a soft kiss lands just below my ear before I hear my husband's husky morning voice.

"Morning, babe."

It's the same way we've woken up since the day after our wedding. And lately it's the most physical touch we get with one another all day long.

"Morning, honey. How'd you sleep?"

"You mean with octopus legs kicking me all night? Excellent. You?" He has a sarcastic side I love. Even in my grumbly state for sleeping like crap all night, he still makes me chuckle lightly. Even through the depths of hell that can sometimes be day to day life, he still has the ability to make me laugh.

"We have to figure out a way to lock out the extras that seem to keep sneaking into our bed at night." I groan as I let my head fall back to his shoulder that I was basically drooling over just a few moments ago. Unfortunately, he slid a white T-shirt on over that tempting shoulder before he came out here. "Ugh, why did you put a shirt on?" I grumble, to which he chuckles. He knows my weakness for his upper body.

"Sorry, babe. It's cold out here."

"You tired?"

"What do you think?"

We're both exhausted, so when a kid comes climbing into bed at two o'clock, it seems much easier to just let it be. Fighting with her and dragging her back to her own bed all the way across the hall seems like way too much work and effort. Work and effort that would have likely paid off the next morning when we can barely move and have bruises on our bodies from being kicked all night long. A king-size bed seems huge until we have to make room for all the extra bodies.

"What do you have going on today?" his still sleepy voice asks as he looks out toward the landscape behind our home. The thick wooded area shows signs of fall with the many leaves covering the ground and the vibrant colors still decorating the trees. Barrett reaches around my body and takes a sip of my coffee, another thing he's done for as long as I can remember. He never wastes the time to prepare his own cup. After our private good morning moment is shared, he will, but it seems that he's eager to start our day this way. I can't say as though I mind.

He sighs contentedly, making me do the same. When we built our house, we were able to find a great deal on two lots, so even though we have neighbors, they aren't as close as they would have been had we not purchased them both. Barrett's grandparents left him a very generous inheritance that we put toward the asking price. Even with that help, we had years of financial struggle. Those years help us to remember to be grateful.

"I have just one appointment at eleven this morning. The couple took the day off work, so I assume they have lots of plans," I say as I raise my eyebrows.

He laughs. "What's with the brows?"

"I've just learned over the years that some couples tend to be more of a handful."

"And you think they might be?"

I shrug my shoulders. "Not sure. They sounded like they could."

"But that doesn't bother you," he tells me, rather than asking. He's learned over the years that more detailed-oriented couples don't get to me. I enjoy working with everyone.

"Nope, it genuinely doesn't."

"I love that about you," he tells me, making me smile.

I love being an interior designer, and the flexibility of owning my own business is perfect. I can work solely out of a studio by appointment only without having to adhere to standard work hours. While I know I could make my business more successful if I ran things differently, it's important it stays this way for now. With four kids and my husband being part-owner of his business, it's an advantage in juggling our various activities.

My clients seem to love my non-schedule, making it easier to find a convenient time to meet.

"After school Grady has football practice, Maggie has volleyball practice, and Harper has horse-riding lessons. I think I will put something in the Crockpot for supper tonight. I don't think I'll be back home until seven. What about you?"

"That sounds good. A normal day around here, huh?"

I chuckle lightly. "This time of year, for sure. What about you? What's your day like?"

"I have a couple meetings with contractors this morning, and I need to figure out what to do with Andy. As a project manager, he should know better than this." He sighs, much less contented this time around. Barrett and Josh started up their own general contracting business about fifteen years ago. Our businesses being closely related has been a huge help for both. We can each recommend the other, knowing well that if the recommendation doesn't pan out, we'll hear about it. It's made us better business managers. But now, Andy hasn't been showing up to job sites, leaving his guys to wonder what they are supposed to be doing most days. Andy was one of the first guys Josh and Barrett hired, so to say they're beyond disappointed in his behavior is a major understatement.

I nod my head in understanding. "He should. He does. Just keep on him, talk to him. Figure out what's going on with him and let him know it's not acceptable."

"I know," he grumbles.

He hates it when I tell him how to do his job. I suppose he has a point, but seriously. Men don't know how to manage things very well. At least this one doesn't. He'll want to have a beer with Andy, ask if there's anything he needs, and move on. He's fine with confrontation, but if he feels deeper stuff is lurking, he gets all squeamish, tucking tail and running the other direction. Since we have a feeling that what's going on with Andy has nothing to do with his desire to work or his ability to do so, but rather his personal life getting in the way, Barrett — and Josh in turn — have no desire to have that conversation with him. But they'd better sort it out soon because if they don't, they know that Lauren, Josh's wife, and I will be hauling his ass in by the ear and talking to him. They don't want that, and they know it.

"Good. You realize that if you don't talk to him today…"

"I said I know. I got it handled," he reminds me, his voice betraying his irritation with me, or the situation. Probably both.

Why I don't let it go is beyond me, considering I know this is a hot subject, but I can't seem to stop myself. "He's not doing his job, Barrett. You're paying him damn good money to work for you, and he's not doing it. If it were anyone else, he would have been fired a long time ago, and you know it."

"I do know that. I also know that it's our business. Ours, as in Josh and me, not you. Not Lauren. You two always stick your nose in our business when you have no clue what it takes, day in and day out."

"Excuse me? The business isn't mine or Lauren's? I'm sorry. I thought when we, as in the four of us, decided that you two would start up this business that it would be done knowing that we are all involved. We are all at risk."

"Don't you think I know that? And yeah, I get it. Andy's screwing up. He's in a jacked-up place in his head right now, and that's affecting his business decisions. I know this. I see it. Josh sees it. We also see that his stupid bitch-of-a-wife cheated on him with some guy she works with."

I can't control the gasp that comes out of my mouth. I didn't know that.

"Yeah. Didn't know that, did you? So before you start spewing your normal junk about who I should hire and fire, maybe get your facts straight. Andy's slacking, yes. He's also in a bad way right now after walking into his bedroom and seeing his wife reverse cowgirl her way to messing up their entire marriage. He walked in on them, Tess. In their bed. That screws with a guy's head, and I can't blame him for that. So yeah, we're gonna talk to him. See if maybe he needs to take some paid time off, because I'm not about to fire him and be a part of what makes him feel like even less than a man than he already feels after seeing his wife in that way."

"I'm sorry… I mean. First of all, why didn't you tell me? And second of all… dammit. What the hell is she thinking?"

"We just found out a couple days ago, and I don't know what she could be thinking, but hell if I'm going to give him a hard time about his lack of presence at work when in the past he's been nothing but a stellar guy to work with."

I'm a little irked that he hasn't told me until now when he knew a couple days ago, but I decide to let it go. "I didn't know…"

"I know you didn't. And that's the only reason I'm dropping this." He blows out a frustrated breath and shakes his head slightly. "Just… you and Lauren have got to put your trust in Josh and me, that we have the company's best interest at heart. Just like I put my trust into you with yours.

As much as you would like to think differently, you two don't know everything."

"We don't act like we know everything," I say, my tone a combination of being both lighthearted and a little annoyed.

He scoffs at me while shaking his head, but when he continues, he doesn't pick up on my lighter tone; rather, his is still lingering on the annoyed side. "Yeah, okay. Tess, you know there's plenty that goes on that you don't see and don't know about. And guess what? We manage just fine. Can you just back off?"

I flinch at his words. I can't help it; they sting quite a bit. Telling me to back off is not like him at all, although me backing off isn't like me, either. "I wouldn't have to put my nose into it if you guys would just tell us what is happening all the time. Yes, I have my business. You have yours, but how would it make you feel if I never told you a single thing that happened at the studio?"

"Honestly, if I don't have to hear about throw pillows and paint colors all the time, I'll be fine," he smirks, deflecting my snarkiness.

"Jerk!" I playfully hit his shoulder. Luckily his smartass comment is enough to stop our arguing, but it still hurts to know that he doesn't feel the need to share everything with me. I suppose maybe I come across as being bossy and maybe a bit nosy, but that's not it. I feel disconnected if he doesn't include me. It only gets harder and harder; we've been together for all of our adult lives and then some. To have this disconnect now is just… hard. And scary. And frustrating.

"I'm kidding, babe. You know that." He smiles at me and chuckles lightly but sobers quickly. He looks me straight in the eye and runs the back of his hand down my cheek. "And I'm sorry I snapped at you. I didn't mean to. I know

I shouldn't have told you to back off. That was an asshole thing to say. And it is *our* business, as in all of ours. It's just that when you question me like that, it makes me feel like you don't trust me. And, it's not that I don't appreciate you wanting to be involved, I *want* that. I want your opinions and suggestions, but like I said, can you please just show me a little more faith?"

"I know, but thank you for saying that. And I'm sorry, too. Sometimes I overstep because I can't help myself. I promise, I do have faith in you. A whole lot of it," I say as I reach up on my tiptoes and kiss his jaw.

The sound of my cell chiming a text brings another smile to my face and pulls me out of the funk that we were both gearing up to venture in to. Cole checks in every morning. He's our oldest but will always be my baby. No matter if he's twenty years old, 6'2", and has a good seventy pounds on me. When he left for college two years ago, I knew it would be hard, but having him check in so often, all on his own, makes life better.

Before I can check my phone, Barrett stops me. "We good?"

"Of course. We're good," I confirm.

He studies my face, and I can see the question still in his mind. "Barrett, I promise. You apologized, and we learned years ago that it doesn't help anyone or anything to hold a grudge. I promise. I love you. A whole lot. I forgive you."

He blows out a breath and says, "Thank you. I love you, too."

With our argument settled, I reach for my phone and pull it out to see what the morning has brought our oldest.

Cole: *Morning, Mom.*

Me: Hey bud. How are you?

Cole: Just woke up so ask me later.

Me: You have class at 9, yeah?

Cole: Yeah. Today's my busy day and I work tonight.

Me: I'm proud of you.

I tell him this every day. He knows it, but he needs to hear it.

Cole: Yeah, yeah, yeah. That's what you always say.

Me: It's true and you need to hear it. I also love you.

Cole: Love you too. Is Dad around today? I need to talk to him about something.

Because Barrett's nosy and was looking over my shoulder the entire time, he snatches the phone out of my hand, and I laugh as I watched his fingers fly across my screen.

Me/Barrett: Hey bud. Yeah, I'm around.

Cole: Figured you'd respond.

Me/Barrett: What? Your old man is

predictable? **scoffs**

Cole: **snorts** *just a little. Did you go out and greet Mom by hugging her and saying morning babe?*

Me/Barrett: ...

Cole: *Ha! Told you. You're as predictable as the sun coming up every day.*

Me/Barrett: *All right all right, I get it. I'm a boring old man.*

Cole: *I wasn't gonna say it but...*

Me/Barrett: *Now that you've officially hurt your dad's ego, what can I help you with?*

Cole: *I'll call you later. Just wanted to make sure you were around so I could. I have a couple questions I need to ask.*

Me/Barrett: *Sure thing, bud. Call me any time. Love you and have a good day.*

At that, he smirked, slapped my butt after handing me back my phone, and headed back inside.

Me: *Everything ok?*

Cole: *You're as predictable as Dad. I figured*

that'd be coming.

Me: *Well????*

No way do I care enough to have some witty banter. I'm not a helicopter parent by any means, but my instincts have always been spot on, and if I feel something is wrong, I'm not going to stumble around it. I am just going to ask.

> ***Cole:*** *I'm fine. Everything's fine. Life is good. I promise. Just needed to run a few things by Dad.*
>
> ***Me:*** *If you're sure.*
>
> ***Cole:*** *I'm sure. I gotta go — Justin and I are heading to work out.*
>
> ***Me:*** *Be careful. Love you.*
>
> ***Cole:*** *Love you, Mom.*

Chapter Two

Barrett

MY WIFE IS still gorgeous. How the hell is that even possible? Every day I look at her first thing in the morning, all grumbly and rumpled from her sleep. That soft lavender robe that she puts on every day, my hands have instinctually learned how to sneak underneath so I can feel the soft skin of her stomach. Every morning is the same, but it's the perfect way to start my day. Her stomach might not be as tight as it was when we first met, her curves more pronounced, but she's more beautiful today than she was twenty-two years ago.

Seeing Tess grow into the woman she's become has been the most wonderful gift she could have ever given me. Well, that and our four kids. Seeing her in her mom-role, some men might think boring. Some husbands see their wife's growing belly as getting fat. Never in a million years could I think that. It's the sexiest, most beautiful thing to see the woman I love more than I ever thought possible, care and love on our children.

I brush aside her messy honey-blonde waves to place a kiss on my favorite place in the world. It's where I feel at home, safe and so damn happy. That tiny crook of her neck, the delicate skin just below her left ear is the first place my lips ever touched her. It's where I could smell the light scent of her perfume that I inhaled so deeply it became a part of me. It's the place where, when I had to say good bye to my father after he lost his battle with time, I cried into, and Tess held me and didn't flinch at my unmanly act. It's where, after she gave me the greatest gift of becoming a father, I kissed then whispered words of love and thanks into her ear that only she could hear because it was only meant for her.

Every single morning since we said "I do," I have woken up and nuzzled into my happy place and kissed my beautiful wife. Some days, a baby was cuddling close as she was feeding him or her. Some days, it was done in a hospital waiting room while we worried over a loved one. Some days, it wasn't received with complete adoration, and some days, it wasn't done with as much affection as she always deserves, but it's one thing I will never stop doing.

Through the trials, tribulations, and arguments, we've never lost one thing. We've never fallen out of love. Never once have I wished for our lives to be different. Sure, it's more fun to always be happy. But that's not life. Life is ugly and messy, and marriages are hard. If it were easy all the time, no one would appreciate the wonderful times. It's in the messy that we appreciate the pristine. And the pristine that is Tess and Barrett Ryan is a beautiful thing.

After the argument with Tess, I was grateful for the welcomed distraction to speak with Cole. Well, speaking in his way. Texting is his favorite form of communication, but he knows we want to hear his voice, too. He knows that if he needs to talk to me about something later today, he damn well better pick up the phone and put it to his ear rather than using his thumbs to communicate. I have a feeling it's girl-related. Or job. Or school. Hell, I don't know. The kid is open with us, but he's also two hours away at school. I only know what he tells us.

"Morning, Dad."

I spin around to see Grady, our eighteen-year-old, walking into the kitchen. This last year, he really grew up. Being the oldest around here for his little sisters, he takes the role of protector very seriously. That, and his desire to get an athletic scholarship playing football. He's not allowing any distractions to enter his world, and when he's not focusing on his schoolwork, he's focusing on the physical aspect of his body. He's bulked up and, even though I will never admit it to him, is definitely stronger than I. He's always been a kid who loves the outdoors, though, so he doesn't spend his time in the gym. Rather, he and I built his own workout center in the back yard. It looks like something the Navy SEALS would torture their new recruits with. It feels like it, too, since he tortures me with it as often as he can.

"Morning, bud. How'd you sleep?"

"Eh. When I finally finished with my homework, good. I got a good hour workout in this morning though, so that helped wake me up," he says as he reaches into one of the dark-stained cupboards to grab a mug for a cup of coffee… something new.

"You know you don't have to kill yourself back there every day," I remind him, pointing to his makeshift torture chamber.

"Don't start. You know it's not just to get the scholarship. I love it," he says as he adds some creamer to his coffee.

"Whatever. I know all this is just so you can get Bri Jenkins to notice you," I said, teasing him.

"Nice." He barks out a laugh and shakes his head before

taking a sip of his coffee.

He's had a thing for Bri since he was ten years old. He was smitten when she intercepted the football right in front of him during recess. Since that day, they've been friends. Best friends, if you ask either of them, but I see the way they look at each other. What once was simply a deep friendship has grown into more. And the fact that neither of them date anyone else but continue to spend as much of their free time together as possible is a big flag in the *I love you but am terrified to tell you* book. He'll figure it out, but he knows I see it. He also knows I'll never stop giving him grief about it until he mans up and does something about it.

"One day, boy. One day some other schmuck is gonna walk into her life and recognize her for what she is, and you're not gonna know what to do with yourself."

"Dad. We're friends," he says, but I know he's saying it to remind himself as much as me. Meanwhile, his jaw ticks. It's obvious the thought of her with another guy doesn't sit well with him.

"Yeah. I've never heard of friends turning into more. Ever. Good luck with that." I chuckle and tip my coffee cup in his direction.

"He's so in love with her. She loves him too, though. Everyone at school sees it," Maggie, my fifteen-year-old, chimes in as she walks into the kitchen looking like a younger version of her mother. Beautiful.

I'm so screwed.

Grady groans and warns his sister, "Mags."

"Just sayin'," Maggie sing-songs. "Morning, Daddy." She smiles sweetly and leans up to kiss me on the cheek.

Harper is shuffling behind her, but considering that she barely slept last night — I should know since she chose to let me join the party and is definitely not a morning person anyway — I don't expect to hear her small voice for a little while yet. I give them both a kiss on the cheek and lean against the speckled tan, granite countertop and cross my legs. This is the second-best part of my day. Seeing our children, hearing their relationships with each other. Harper slides onto one of the benches that flanks the kitchen table I made when we first moved into our house and lays her head down on the table, causing me to roll my eyes.

Maggie pours herself some orange juice and starts peeling a banana, but I can see the wheels turning in her head already. I smile as I watch what I know is going to be a fun exchange of the *shit or get off the pot* speech that Maggie is undoubtedly about to give Grady. She's Bri's biggest fan. Well, aside from Grady, obviously.

"Just keep quiet. You know I can't go there," Grady says with irritation already lacing his voice. He starts gathering the ingredients to make himself a protein smoothie and lifts his eyebrows to Harper, no doubt knowing she'll ask him for one anyway.

She nods in her own sleepy way and gives him a small smile. "I don't know why not. I swear, Grady, you know how the other guys at school look at her. You have to just suck it up and go for it."

Called it.

"She likes you. Not just as a friend. You know she does," she huffs, clearly disgusted by her older brother's reluctance. "Besides. If you don't go for it, you know Dawson is going to. He's been flirting with her all school year. He's so gross and creepy, though."

"I don't have time for a girlfriend," Grady mumbles, ignoring pretty much her entire speech. He presses the button on the blender, but it doesn't deter his sister from continuing.

"Newsflash, you already have a girlfriend. You two just haven't crossed the line."

He fills his own cup and then one for Harper. He slides it across the table to her and winks. "How do you know we haven't," he smirks, hoping it will shut her up. Apparently, he doesn't know his sister well at all.

"Right. And she looks so satisfied because…"

"If we had crossed the line, she'd be satisfied!"

His defense makes no sense, but I let it go, though I do swallow down a laugh because he's flustered by just a couple simple remarks from his little sister.

"Satisfied about what? What does that mean? And what line?" Harper's innocent question cuts through their conversation. She may not be a morning person, but growing up with three much older siblings has made her know way more than she should… and a nosy little turd.

And that's where dear old Dad has to step in. "Nope. This conversation just took a wrong turn." I look behind me to Grady and give him a pointed look. "You'd better not be crossing any lines or satisfying anyone. Got me?" I say with my eyebrows raised. I'm not oblivious. My kids aren't always going to be innocent, but in no way am I condoning anything.

"I got it. Dad, I was just messing with her."

"I know that, but don't disrespect Bri that way. You know better," I tell him and raise my eyebrows.

Grady has the common sense to look a little ashamed but still smiles as he nods his head and replies with a quick, "Yes, sir."

"Good. Now that we have that settled," I say, clapping

my hands together and rubbing them. "Who's making their dad breakfast?"

At that, the kids laugh and walk out the kitchen door. I'm really not sure what was so funny about that.

Chapter Three

Tess

*T*WEET TWEET. THE sound of my phone tweeting makes me giggle. My husband, the idiot, loves to change my ringtones and my text alerts often. So often I usually have no clue that it's even my phone alerting me to someone trying to reach me. But he finds it hilarious. Because he's a weirdo.

I put down the fabric swatch I'm looking at for the Simpsons, the new couple I'm working with. They chose light grey, navy blue, and white for their living room — it's going to look amazing. Classic. A large area rug covers part of the beautiful wide-plank cherrywood floor and the floor-to-ceiling stone fireplace will be the central focus of the room, but we still need to decide on furniture, accent pieces, and window treatments.

I love my job.

When I was in high school, I took a home economics class my freshman year that touched on interior decorating, and it became something I loved. I took every home ec class I could, hoping to learn more. My mother was a homemaker when I was growing up, and she loved do-it-yourself stuff. Then Mom got sick. It was the summer before my junior year when she was diagnosed. Breast cancer nearly beat the life out of her, but she fought. She fought hard. And she beat cancer's ass. But throughout her battle, the only thing that kept her happy was decorating and making the house a home.

She couldn't get out as much as she liked, so making the house look a little more appealing was a simple thing we could all do. But me, especially. I guess that's where my passion and love for it came from. I love taking the plain and jazzing it up. I fell in love with the entire process of going through our old stuff and reworking it to make it fresh and new.

When the chemo and drugs sank Mom to her lowest and she couldn't get out of bed, she and I sat together and poured through catalogues and magazines. I went to the library and picked up books. This was before the Internet. Before Pinterest. She had stacks and stacks of magazines by her bedside, some dog-eared, some with slips of paper sticking out of them. When she had a good day or two in a row, we put some of those ideas into action and created. Together.

When Barrett saw them all stacked by her bed and all over the living room one day when he came to visit her, he instantly drew up the plans to make her a shelf.

"Mom, what about this one? Isn't it pretty? Something like that would look great on the dining table," I say to my mother, pointing to a picture of a centerpiece arrangement.

"It is, baby. I think we could do that one easy."

"I'll put it in the pile."

"The pile is getting a little out of control."

"It is. We need a new system," I tell her just as I see Barrett walk into the room carrying two glasses of water.

"She's right, Mrs. Cole. It is getting a little… cluttered in

here."

"Barrett Ryan. What did I tell you about the Mrs. Cole thing? It's Debbie, Deb, or Mom, you understand me?"

Barrett smiles and looks down at his shoes. "Yes, ma'am," he says, his tone teasing and light.

My mom giggles and shakes her head. "What am I going to do with you, kid?"

"I'm fun, right?" he asks before his tone turns a little more serious. "But seriously, Debbie. You need a better system than this. Your magazines and books are just falling over."

"There's a method to my madness," she tells him, smiling, but I can see the wheels in his mind turning as he nods his head and continues to survey the bedroom and books and magazines.

It was the first thing he made on his own. No help from anyone. It had cubbies and slots of all different sizes and one large section on the right that was backed by corkboard so Mom could pin up her favorite pictures and ideas. I didn't ask him to do it. My parents didn't ask him to do it. He did it because he's an incredible man who loved building things for people, even at a young age.

I look back now and wonder if that was part of the appeal to me for Barrett. When we were in high school, I took a shop class, and he was in it. We both loved designing, creating, building things. During the summer before our senior year, Barrett helped a local contractor, and he decided quickly that's what he wanted to do for the rest of his life: see a person's home being built from the ground up or a room renovated to what they envisioned for their family.

I love being able to make someone smile just by changing a room to look the way they envisioned it, and most of the time, not even how they envisioned it, but better. He loves building something that is going to make someone's life easier, better.

Just call us Chip and Joanna.

> **Barrett:** *Cole called me.*

> **Me:** *And?*

> **Barrett:** *Just telling you.*

The little shit. He knows it will be bugging me all day long to not have a clue why Cole needed to call, and now he's gonna hold out on me?

I don't think so!

> **Me:** *Tell me tell me tell me tell me.*

> **Barrett:** *Oh, you wanted to know what he wanted to talk to his dad about?*

This conversation will be much quicker than our old-people hands can text out if I just call him. Not to mention the amount of deleting and retyping it takes. And don't get me started on the autocorrect. When I told Cole to check my love box for a pair of gloves instead of the glovebox, I was certain that he would need therapy for life. And seriously, why does everything turn dirty? I honestly don't use the words masturbate and penis in my texting endeavors, but my phone seems to think they're words I use consistently. I need to hear his voice anyway. The last client I had has me in a tizzy, as he calls it, and Barrett's the only one who can calm me down.

"Hi, babe." I can hear the smile in his voice when he answers on the first ring. Like he was expecting my call and didn't even have to look at the caller ID. Dang. Cole is right. We're so predictable it's a little ridiculous. I hope predictable doesn't also mean boring.

"Don't *hi babe* me," I reply.

He laughs. Laughs!

"Barr-rret! Just tell me. You know it's killing me, and those clients who took the day off? They were the definition of high maintenance. I need a distraction." My voice almost comes out as a whine.

"Usually high maintenance doesn't bother you."

"Yeah, well considering that they both have separate — and I mean completely separate — ideas of how each individual room of their six-thousand, yes, six-thousand-square-foot home should be decorated, the level of high maintenance-ery is a little over the top. Now, tell me why our firstborn son had to talk to his dad and couldn't talk to his mom. And please tell me he sounded good. I haven't heard his voice in a week. I need to know he's eating healthy. He's not drinking — well, too much. I'm not an idiot. He did drunk text me the other night, which was funny, but I'm his mom and don't need to read that, or see the video he accidently sent me of him doing some whip dance. And for that matter... damn texting. I should take it off our phones..." I'm rambling, and he needs to shut me up.

"Babe!" He chuckles into the line. "He's good. I promise. He did have a couple questions for me and didn't want his mommy to read too much into it."

"A girl."

"I swear. One day I'm gonna crack that mindreading code you have. No. Not a girl. The girl. Or at least, he seems to think it might lead in that direction. They're only talking and dating casually for right now, but he sounds serious about her. Way more serious than in the past."

"More serious than *her?*" I practically sneer the word her.

Her is in reference to Simone. Simone was nice. Pretty. Until she thought Cole was going to be her meal ticket, considering he's pre-med. Then she hooked her nasty claws into him, announced a fake pregnancy — at eighteen — and tried to trap him. Luckily, I'm an intuitive person. And no one messed with my kids. Simone isn't in the picture anymore, but he had fallen hook, line, and sinker for her, so it was quite the blow to his heart when he found out what she was like.

"Not even close. First of all, his eyes are wide open. Second, he said she's not at all impressed about his pre-med status."

"Really?"

"Really," he says in a weird Scottish accent.

"Ok, Shrek. What's her name?" I grin at my own lame joke, and his.

"He said he wasn't ready to tell me her name, but that he will be bringing her home for Thanksgiving, if that was all right with us. Her family isn't going to be around for the holiday, and he didn't want her to be alone…"

Oh, my heart. I know he's still talking, but the fact that my son is courteous enough to know that someone shouldn't be alone for the holidays makes my heart swell — and, apparently, my ears to close up. Well, to some that might not seem like a big deal, but he's twenty. He's not necessarily intuitive yet.

"Yes," I respond when I realize I've gone off into my own little world while Barrett was still talking, but now there's silence, so I figure he must have asked if that was okay with me, and of course it is.

"Well, I never asked a question, dream girl." He chuckles. The smart ass.

"Oh, whatever. What did you say?"

"Nothing to worry about. We'll talk tonight."

"You sure?"

"Positive." He assures me.

"Love you."

"Love you."

My afternoon and early evening consist of shuttling Harper to and from horse-riding lessons. Luckily, Grady has his license and his own car and can take care of getting home from football on his own. Typically, he picks up Maggie from volleyball as well, but since his coach asked the guys to stay tonight so they can watch game tape for the Friday night game, one of her friends is dropping her off at home.

By the time we all shuffle into the house, it's a little after seven, and no one has eaten supper, started their homework, or managed to say more than a few words to one another. As we sit around the long, dark-stained, and well-used farmhouse table Barrett made for us when we first moved into our house, eating chicken tortilla soup I had put in the Crockpot that morning, we fill each other in on our days. The kids seemed to have fairly typical school days — a few months into their school year, and things are going smoothly for each of them. It's still weird to me that Cole isn't sitting in his seat, even though it's been a while. We had just gotten used to him being home again this summer, and then *poof!* he was gone again.

"Did you get your clients sorted out today? The ones with the enormous house?" Barrett asks, bringing me out of my thoughts of Cole.

"Sort of. I guess. I don't know. They have several projects they both want to do, but neither of them seems to agree on anything."

"That sounds like fun." Barrett's sarcasm always makes me chuckle. "I mentioned something to Keri about your new clients, and she said she knew them. I guess she grew up with the husband or something and had seen that they'd bought this new house. She said they posted something about finding this incredible interior designer and couldn't wait to get started going through all her amazing ideas."

Even though it was nice to hear that my clients were excited to be working with me, my mind was stuck on Keri. Who the hell was Keri?

"Keri?" I ask, somehow keeping my voice even; meanwhile, I wanted to screech the bitch's name at the top of my lungs and demand to know who the hell she is and why he's talking to her.

"Yeah. Keri. The new office manager," he says like I already know this.

"When did you hire a new office manager? And where did MaryEllen go?"

"Babe. MaryEllen retired three months ago. We had a party for her. We hired Keri before MaryEllen left so that she could train her."

"MaryEllen retired? You had a party for her? How did I not know any of this? And where did Keri come from? How old is she? Is she married? Does she have kids? Why haven't I ever seen her before?" I ask as I frantically look around the table, sure that the rest of my family would be as clueless. Unfortunately, they're looking at me like I'm the clueless one.

"Yes. We had a party for her. She worked for us from the moment we started the company, so of course we had a party. You were gone. Remember? You said you had to go to that design show and that we could handle it. How do you not remember any of this?"

"I don't… I don't know. Honestly, how do I not remember this?"

"No clue," he says with a large amount of annoyance in his voice. "And, by the way, you've never seen Keri because you haven't been by the office in over four months. No, Keri isn't married. No, she doesn't have any kids. She's about twenty-five-years old, I think," he tells me, his voice a scary brand of Barrett I haven't heard in a long time. He knows what I'm thinking. He knows that I'm questioning him. And, truth be told, I guess I am.

"How do I not remember any of this?" I ask again, still looking around the table at every single family member who is looking at me like I'm ten shades of crazy. Which, again, I guess I am. I somehow missed something huge that happened in Barrett's world. How did I not realize these things: One, MaryEllen retired? Two, he has a new office manager, a female, who I've never met. Three, it's been four months since the last time I was at his office?

I feel like the crappiest wife in the history of crappy wives.

"Babe. Relax. It's been a crazy few months. No worries," he says and shrugs his large shoulders. From the look in his eyes, it's clear he's placating me so we don't have a huge argument in front of the kids at the dinner table.

"Yeah," I mumble. Still, I'm more than a little perturbed by the fact that he has an office manager that I've never met and that she's young, beautiful, has the perfect body, laughs at all his jokes… always listens when he talks. Just perfect.

Well, Fudgcicles.

My mind is running away from me, and all I know is her name.

Shortly after dinner is eaten and the dishes are cleaned up, Grady and Maggie both disappear into their bedrooms to take care of their homework. I settle onto the couch with a load of laundry with Harper next to me cuddled close. I've just started folding a second load when she panics and realizes that, even though I had already asked if she had homework and she said no, she does, in fact, have a page of spelling words to tackle.

"Dad! I forgot I had homework!" Harper says, her voice at a high-pitched level only bats could hear. It's also her accusatory tone, as if it's his fault that she forgot she had homework.

"Harper! I forgot Mommy asked if you had homework just an hour ago!" Barrett responds in his own high-pitch voice, mimicking and mocking her, for which she shows no appreciation. I almost snort while listening to them.

"Dad! Stop it," she says with a foot stomp. "What am I gonna do?"

"Well, Harps, probably your spelling homework."

"Da-a-d," she whines, not appreciating Barrett's sarcasm.

"Go get your backpack and meet me at the table. I'll help you go through them. Won't take long. Just relax."

Back to the table Barrett and she go while I try to

continue to work through the mountain of laundry. Another load folded and another shriek is heard through the house.

"Mom! Where's my Friday shirt?" Maggie yells from somewhere in the house, sounding like Cher from *Clueless* asking Lucy where her white collarless shirt is. Why would Maggie have remembered that she needed that one specific shirt to be washed and cleaned and ready for Friday before now? That would take all the fun out of the evening. I suppose using the word *fun* might be a bit of an exaggeration.

"Come in here and talk. No need to yell through the house."

A moment later she appears looking frazzled. "Mom. My Friday shirt. Where is it?" She asks me like I should have a clue what her Friday shirt is, in a tone of voice I don't appreciate. She has too many school-pride shirts to count, which is usually what she wears on Fridays, so I haven't got a clue what she's talking about.

I raise my eyebrows to let her know that I don't care for the way she's speaking to me and she, in turn, mumbles, "Sorry, Mom. Do you know where my Friday shirt is?"

"What shirt, baby girl?"

She huffs at me for not reading her mind and knowing what she's talking about and replies, "Cole's old football sweatshirt that I cut up? That one."

Barrett's voice booms through from the kitchen moments before he appears with his hands on his hips and a confused expression covering his face. "You cut up one of Cole's sweatshirts? Why on earth would you do that?"

"Um… because it was too big? And besides, it's way cuter this way. I cut the bottom hem so it's shorter," she tells us as she points to her belly, which we can only assume means she shows part of her stomach when she's wearing it.

"And if I turn my shoulder just right, it falls off the side." She goes on to explain like that's a completely normal and logical explanation. To her credit, she does a fabulous job with clothes. She has a sense for it and is always making her own creations. I would be shocked if she didn't go into something with fashion when she graduates from high school.

Barrett's eyes widen, and eyebrows shoot to his hairline. "Not a chance," he says and starts to turn around as if the discussion is settled because, it appears that he's never met Maggie and forgot that she's stubborn and determined.

"What? Why?"

He stops in his tracks, turns back around, and stares right at her. "Why? You wanna know why? Want me to get Grady out here to answer that question too?" he asks her, to which she shakes her head adamantly that she, in fact, does not want her big brother, who is quite overprotective, to be brought in the conversation.

"Right then. Not. A. Chance. You're fifteen. Need more reason?"

"Dad, don't be…"

He cuts her off before she can dig herself into a deeper hole. "Nope. End of discussion. First of all, it's against school policy, thank the Lord above for that," he says as he looks to the heavens, and I know, without a doubt, he is truly thanking God for blessing us with a strict school dress code policy. "Second of all, you don't need to be searching for reasons for boys to notice you. You're beautiful enough as it is when you're fully covered."

"But…" She half-heartedly tries to argue her position again.

"I said no. End of discussion."

"But, Dad, it's not to get boys to notice me! The shirt is

cute!"

"I have no doubt the shirt is cute. I also said no. Besides. School. Policy." He grins widely, knowing he's got her there. He'd gladly make her wear a nun costume to school every day if he could, but having the school policy as backup makes his argument that much easier.

She throws her arms up in the air and screeches, "Inconceivable!" before stomping away. It's possible we may have made her watch *The Princess Bride* one too many times.

Barrett roars with laughter at her response, smiles my way, clearly satisfied with the way his end of the discussion went, and turns on his heel, heading back to the kitchen to help Harper with the rest of her spelling words.

By the time eleven o'clock rolls around, I'm exhausted and so is Barrett. We've both had long days, and tomorrow will be the same. Tomorrow night, we get to cheer on our boys under the Friday night lights while they work to continue their undefeated season. As we crawl into bed next to one another, alone for once, we take one look at the other and almost weep. It is so rare for us to be able to climb into bed at the same time, and we almost don't know what to do with ourselves when we do.

Unfortunately, once again, exhaustion and questions over tonight's dinner topic trumps sexy-time, and soon we're both lying next to one another in silence, but at least we're together and touching. Touching means more than sex at this point in our lives. Touching is intimate, and we are desperate for the intimacy. At least I am. I have no idea if Barrett feels the same way or not. We would have to be able to have a conversation for more than fifteen minutes a day that doesn't center around something involving the kids in order to understand what the other is thinking. I hear

Barrett's breathing start to slow, but there's so much we need to discuss before I can sleep.

"Babe."

"Hmmm?"

"You awake?"

"Hmm-mmm."

"Babe. We need to talk. Wake up. Earlier today. On the phone. What else were you saying?" I lightly push on his shoulder to help him fully wake up.

"Huh?"

"Open your eyes. This afternoon when we talked about what you and Cole discussed. You were talking…"

He interrupts in his sexy sleep voice, eyes still closed, "And you were in your dream world and not listening."

"Yup. That time. What were you saying?"

He sits up in bed and rests his back against the pillows resting against the headboard. His naked chest looks so inviting for me to rub my hands over as he scrubs his face to help wake himself up, making the muscles in his arms and shoulders bulge and contract.

I raise up also and sit cross-legged on the bed facing him.

"I was trying to tell you we talked to Andy. He's going to take a few weeks off so he can focus on figuring out where to go from here. He says he can't trust her now and has no desire to stay with her, or stay in the house she did the nasty in with some other dude, so he's moving out. No reason to stay for the kids since the boys are in high school now, and, from what he told me, they know everything. They're pretty pissed at their mom. They want to stay with Andy, so he's trying to find a place to live for all three of them and all the junk that goes along with it.

"Anyway, he was grateful that we offered him some time

off, but he seems surprisingly good. Obviously it messed with his head, and he needs time to work out the logistics, but he's moved on to the angry phase of grief, and he has plenty of it directed at her. It seems to be working for him."

I open my mouth to speak but Barrett holds up his hand to stop me. "Don't even start. He needs to deal with it the way it works for him."

"You're sure? If he needs a place to stay, you know he's welcome here. We don't necessarily have an extra three bedrooms, but we can make it work."

Barrett nods his head in agreement. "Yeah, Josh and I both told him that already. But thank you for saying that, too. Means more to me than you know. I'm sorry I blew up at you this morning. I guess I've just been feeling on edge lately."

"Me too."

"Yeah?"

"Yeah. And apology accepted. And I'm sorry, too, if I ever make you feel like I don't trust you to lead this family. You've never once steered us wrong, and I do have faith in you. I love you. You're a great husband and father."

"Thank you. You're not so bad yourself at the whole wife-and-mother thing."

"Gee, thanks," I say and playfully punch him in the shoulder.

He gives me a huge cheeky grin in return. As much as I want to ignore it, I can't. We need to talk about something else tonight before I'll be able to fall asleep.

"Barrett, the MaryEllen and Keri thing. I can't believe you haven't mentioned it more until now. Why?"

"Why what?"

"Seriously? Why haven't you talked more about either of

them? Either MaryEllen's retirement or Keri's job?" My voice comes out accusatory, which I didn't mean but… maybe I did.

"Probably because you didn't ask. Probably because it didn't seem to be top of your mind. Lately, if it's not something that directly affects you, you never ask or care to know more," he says, voice a little harsher than I'm used to. "That's why I get so frustrated when you suddenly act like you should have so much input in the business. You never ask, never want to be involved, and then suddenly you think I'm screwing something up so you have all these ideas and plans. It's frustrating as hell."

"Barrett, I care. You know I do, right?"

"I know that, Tess. But you haven't seemed very interested lately, so I've just not brought up anything going on there, aside from the Andy thing."

"I'm sorry, Barrett. I don't know what to say."

"It's fine. Well, it's not. But it will be, right?"

"Right. I promise. I'll make sure to be more active and stuff."

"Well. Don't try too hard." He chuckles.

"Nice." I laugh. I pause, twirling my hair in my fingers a little, nervous to bring up my next question, but I have to, so I just pull up my big-girl panties and do it. I lick my lips and run my teeth over my bottom lip and muster up the courage to ask my next question. "So, Keri?"

"What the hell, Tess? Are you kidding me right now?" he says as he sits up straighter, his voice low and angry, one he rarely, if ever, uses on me.

"What?"

"Are you seriously accusing me of something going on between me and Keri?"

"No! I mean... I guess I don't know. You've never mentioned her. And things between us, they've not exactly been rainbows lately. What's she like?"

"I can't even believe that you're questioning me about her right now."

"Why won't you answer the question then?"

"Because the question doesn't deserve an answer! And neither does the accusation!" He stands up and runs his hands through his hair. He's frustrated with me, and I can see why. Barrett has never, not once, given me a reason to question his love or devotion for me, yet here I am, feeling a little uncertain about us and immediately jumping to conclusions.

"Tess. She's the office manager. I don't know. She's in her mid-twenties, like I said. No, she's not married, but I think she has a boyfriend. The only reason I know this is because she sometimes talks about a guy, and she randomly gets flowers. That's the extent of my knowledge of her personal life."

"Is she pretty?" I ask, because I'm an idiot and can't stop myself and evidently don't listen well.

"What the... Tess. You're starting to piss me off. She's Keri. I honestly don't look at her in any way but as our office manager."

"Barrett, I'm sorry. I trust you." I plead with him as I wring my hands together. "I promise I do. It's just that lately, I don't know. We've been... off. You have to admit that. And I don't know, I'm just so exhausted all the time, but I feel like we're slipping. I hate this feeling," I finally admit, the tears starting to build behind my eyes.

He blows out a deep breath and runs his fingers through his short hair again. "Me too, Tess. I know what you mean."

"You do?"

He gives me a look and furrows his brow at me. "Of course I do. And I forgive you for being an idiot and thinking that I could ever, ever look at another woman the way I look at you."

"Yeah?"

"Yeah. Tess. See, when I was seventeen I fell in love. And I never fell out. I was lucky."

"No, Barrett. I was the lucky one. Still am."

Before I have a chance to say more, he climbs back into bed and crawls near. When he reaches me, he grabs the back of my neck and pulls me in for a kiss. Apparently not feeling quite so tired or upset anymore, he flips me onto my back as he simultaneously rolls over on top. Even though emotionally I feel we're a bit off, physically we have been too. Having this connection is important to us and without it, the rest of what I was feeling was amplified. It's been so long that I can't remember if we were missing each other physically first and the rest faded away, or vice versa.

"Maybe we both got lucky, yeah?" he says as he looks down into my eyes, his own eyes shining a little darker than his normal hazel shade.

"You may be right," I say quietly as I graze his cheek with my hand, the stubble coarse against my fingertips.

His weight on top of me is a welcome feeling as his hand trails down my ribcage to my stomach. His fingertips graze under my camisole and move up toward my breasts, all the while his lips never leaving mine. His tongue invades my mouth, claiming me once again. As if I wasn't already always and forever his.

"Mom!" The sound of Harper's screech, followed by footsteps coming across the hall, is like a bucket of ice water dumped on both of us.

Barrett rests his head on my forehead while mumbling curses and reluctantly rolls off me with a groan. He reaches up and presses the heel of his hands into his eyes, clearly as frustrated as I am.

Harper comes barreling into our bedroom, jumps onto the bed, and curls her body up to mine before we can even speak a word to her.

"Harper, baby, what's up?" I ask, my voice raspy.

"Bad dream," she mumbles before drifting off into a sleep as quickly as if we'd given her a tranquilizer.

"This is ridiculous. She's six years old. Why is she still coming into our room almost every single night?" Barrett grumbles.

"It is ridiculous, and I don't know why she does it, but right now I'm too tired to fight it because I know if I bring her back to her room, she'll fight it and be awake until who-knows-how-long, and then we'll be in for a bigger fight before school in the morning."

"I'm too something right now, but tired isn't it." I giggle at his grumpy attitude, but mainly because I know exactly what he means, and I get it. I really do. It's a stupid vicious cycle that I know we need to pull ourselves out of, but we can't figure out how. Unfortunately, he's not as quick to let go of his grumpiness.

"I'm serious, Tess. This is ridiculous. Why are you acting like this is not a big deal?" He whispers to not wake up Harper, but it's angry, definitely not the sexy whisper.

"What do you suggest I do, Barrett?" I reply, my giggling mood now gone and, in its place, frustration and anger — all directed at him, whether he deserves it or not. Our earlier fight still rings in my head.

"Oh, I don't know," he replies with irritation lacing his voice. "Maybe bring her back to her room? Maybe put your foot down and don't allow her to join us in our bed that's supposed to be for two?"

"Well, excuse me. I didn't realize your frickin' legs were broken! I wasn't informed that you weren't able to walk your tired ass across the hall and bring her to her room, or that this was all on me, and I was the one who screwed up our marital bed all on my own," I whisper shout back to him.

"Tess." He growls, ready for a fight but I don't have the energy for it.

I turn my body away from his, my sign of *go away.*

Brat. Brat. Brat. Going to sleep angry isn't a good idea. I know this. But my feelings are hurt, and I'm irritated. Why is it only my fault that we don't communicate? Why is it only my fault that we never have time alone? I have what feels like a million questions about our marriage right now and don't seem to have a single answer.

When Barrett and I first got married, we always made time for each other. It was easy. It was just the two of us, and there were no kids. Our commitments began and ended with our jobs, so when we weren't working, we only had each other to focus on. Neither of us could go all day without talking to each other, seeing each other. Barrett would surprise me a few times a week to take me to lunch or with a coffee. I would do the same. We never parted without a kiss, ass grab, hug, whatever we felt like. If we watched movies, we sat together. We played cards, danced under the moonlight in the back yard, cooked together, walked around the house naked. It sounds cheesy as hell, but it was our early years in marriage.

Then Cole came along. Adding Cole to the mix was

never a problem. Adding all the kids was never a problem. No matter how hard it is now, we would never change that. The problem came when we forgot how to be Barrett and Tess, husband and wife, and only focused on being Barrett and Tess, Mom and Dad.

No more going for Sunday afternoon walks, no more Saturday morning sleep-ins. Going out to dinner alone seems like a thing of the past; having a schedule that doesn't revolve around our kids is next to impossible. Definitely no more walking around the house naked. It's not that our life is bad. It isn't. It's wonderful. I'm blessed — we're blessed. We have a happy and healthy family. But damn it all if I don't miss the way it used to be.

I don't remember the last time that Barrett surprised me for lunch or made plans for just the two of us to do anything that didn't involve us putting on the school colors and attending a sporting event. When had he last grabbed my hand and pulled me outside to dance under the stars or pulled me down next to him while watching a movie or even kissed me goodbye? Not the peck on the lips, have-a-good-day, babe type of kiss. The bend-me-over, show-me-what-he-has-in-store-for-me-later type of kiss.

I love my husband, but I miss him.

Barrett

GREAT. THE TYPICAL sign of *go away* from Tess as I'm trying to fall asleep. Just fabulous. Little brat. She knows how much it pisses me off when she just flips over and ignores me. This also means tomorrow morning is going to suck ass. Waking up the day after a fight is the worst. I don't get how we got here. Not just tonight. Tonight has become something all too familiar, though. And even though I realize I could haul my ass out of the bed and get Harper back into her own bed, lay down the law, and tell her that she needs to keep her cute little butt in there, I also know that it won't make a difference. She'll still prefer her mom over me in the middle of the night. She'll still weasel her way back in here somehow, someway, at some time. And I'll still be frustrated. With both of us.

Tess used to show up at my work at the most random times. She brought me a soda or a coffee and something from one of the bakeries. She surprised me with my favorite meal and served it to me in just an apron; dessert was always first on those nights. We slept in on Saturdays, went for walks on Sunday afternoons. She snuggled up to me on the couch rather than lying in one of the kids' rooms at night and falling asleep.

She sometimes called a family member and found a place for the kids to spend the night so we could have a night in alone and always kissed me goodbye in the morning. Not the distracted type of kiss. The type of kiss that turned into more, or showed me what her plans were for that night.

We used to talk. Not just about the kids' schedules, what was happening at work, or house stuff. We found more about our lives to talk about. We had each other to focus on, to love on.

Lately what I receive is barely a peck on the cheek and a mumble goodbye as she shuttles herself and the kids out the door for school. I don't remember the last time we've had dessert first, or the last time she's surprised me at work just to say hi. I don't remember the last time she made my favorite meal, and I don't remember the last time she listened when I put on music, which used to be the only cue she needed to know that I wanted to dance with her under the stars.

I love my wife, but I miss her.

Chapter Four

Barrett

"WHAT'S UP YOUR ass today, dude?" my partner Josh asks me in an equally irritated voice.

Do I tell him I haven't gotten any from my wife in what feels like forever? He's my best friend. Well, aside from Tess. But since Tess and I lately can't seem to have a conversation that doesn't either lead to arguing over just about anything or involve the house or the kids, I don't have room to be picky about who I divulge my horniness — or the fact that Tess and I are just off — to. Although, I suppose Tess should, in concept, be the one who knows about it first.

"I'm so damn horny!" I blurt out like a teenager, last night's epic distraction still playing on repeat in my mind. Not to mention how pissed off I was that Tess even insinuated that Keri was anything but an employee. I decide to keep that part to myself and allow Josh to focus on the fact that I can't seem to get any with Tess. And like a good friend does, Josh laughs. Hard. No, he wheezes, and I'm pretty sure he spit out his soda. "Shut up, prick! You have no idea what it's like right now! We don't have a moment alone, and I need more than five minutes!"

Josh is still laughing, granted, but at least now he can

talk. He takes a deep breath and makes a big show of blowing it out slowly while wiping the tears from his eyes. Then he adds in some ludicrous hand gestures — probably insinuating that I jerk off and take care of business on my own — which causes him to start cackling at himself, of course. I start laughing because he's such a jerk, and if the situations were reversed, I'm sure I would be doing the same.

We're sitting in our shared office, each behind our own desks that face each other. When we started our business together fifteen years ago, we were young and cocky, thinking we had the contracting business by the tail. We had worked for a local contractor for a few years and decided we wanted to try to make a go of it on our own. The first seven years were rough. Financially, emotionally… it was a strain on everything, but we've made it a successful business over the years and truly love what we do. When we first started up, we each wanted our own office, each trying to stake our claim as king. We soon realized that if we wanted to work together and make joint decisions, sharing an office was a necessity. It was the best decision we ever made. Surprisingly, we don't get sick of each other either.

I throw a pen across my desk at him, which hits him square in the chest. "Screw off, man. I don't want my own damn hand. I'm married for shit's sake. I don't use my own hand anymore unless she's involved and doing…"

He holds his hand up and stops laughing abruptly. "I'm gonna stop you right there. I've known Tess as long as you have, and she's like a sister to me, so I don't need detail on your sexcapades."

"Or lack thereof," I grumble.

"Dude," Josh says, his tone suddenly serious, "what's going on?"

"I don't know." I stand up and rake my fingers through my hair. "Dammit! When did I turn into a chick and talk to you about this instead of my wife?"

"Um… apparently when you grew a vagina and stopped getting any?"

"Argghh!" I stomp out of the office toward the back room, but not before kicking the trashcan in our office for good measure. I didn't realize how frustrating this was to me until this very moment. We have a couple of boxing punching bags set up in the back of the shop area for this purpose. Well, not this purpose exactly — the sexually frustrated part. The rationale behind our idea to have punching bags is because the guys tend to be, well, guys, and sometimes need something to take their mind off whatever is bothering them, and this is it for most of us.

I quickly change into some basketball shorts and tape up my hands with gear I keep in my office for such occasions. I take all my frustrations and aggression out on the punching bag, remembering Tess questioning me about Keri and our lack of closeness lately. I still can't believe that she accused me of anything with my office manager. The more I think about it, the more pissed off I get. I have to remind myself of our morning talk before I get too worked up again.

"Barrett, I'm so sorry for last night. I guess I was just feeling a bit vulnerable or something. I know you. I know you'd never do anything with another woman, emotionally or physically. It's just — we haven't been ourselves lately, and I can't decide if it's because of our lack of a sex life or if we were drifting apart first," Tess admits with a hitch in her voice. *She has tears built up in her eyes, and a few have trailed down her cheeks.*

I pull her close and hug her tight. I hate seeing her cry, hate seeing her upset for any reason. I'm glad to hear her apologize to me for accusing me of what, I don't know — but it is still hard to hear. I must have done something to put that thought or fear into her mind.

"I don't know either, pretty girl, but we can't fall apart. I can't have you questioning my every move. Trust me? And even more than that, trust what your heart is really telling you, not what you're letting your imagination conjure up."

"I know. And I do trust you. I promise."

Hearing her say that allows me to be able to breathe easy again. I hate it that she even had those thoughts flitter through her mind, but knowing she trusts me and isn't questioning that anymore makes it better.

"We need time together," I say, even though she obviously already knows it.

She sighs deep and heavy, and the sadness hasn't fully left her face, which bothers me more than anything. "I agree," *she says but is interrupted from saying anything else by the kids coming into the kitchen ready to start their day. Of course.*

After kicking, hitting, and punching until I'm out of breath, I have sweat dripping down my face. Josh moves off the wall he'd been leaning against while watching me. He comes over with a towel and water bottle and hands them over wordlessly. Neither of us are sentimental saps, but we know when we need each other, and usually what it is we need. And right now, I just needed to kick the hell out of something because I'm beyond frustrated that my time with Tess is just not as simple as it should be, or once was.

"Dude. What the hell was that about? That's way more than pent-up frustration over you guys not being able to have wild monkey sex lately."

I look around the shop because there's not a chance in hell I want my business to be spreading to our employees.

"Tess and I are going through something," I state simply.

"No shit?" he says sarcastically. "Come on, man, give me more than that. You just went ten rounds with Mike Tyson's tiger, so it's obviously something big."

"Alright. Ah, hell. I don't even know what exactly is happening, but we're drifting apart. Last night at dinner I mentioned Keri, saying that her friend was Tess's new client — you know how she mentioned that to me yesterday when we were standing by her desk?"

He nods his head that he remembers, so I continue on, "Well, she acted like she didn't have a clue who Keri was. She forgot that MaryEllen retired. MaryEllen! Who's been with us from the beginning? All because she was so damn wrapped up in her own life at the time and couldn't make it to her retirement party." I air quote myself like a douche. "Then she basically accused me of — well, I'm not entirely sure what she was accusing me of, but something bad with Keri." I say the last part as quiet as possible just in case anyone is around listening.

"Whoa."

"Yeah. I don't know what the hell is happening to us, but her accusing me of stepping out of our marriage is something I never expected."

"You told her about Andy, right?"

"Yeah, why?"

"I don't know. Do you think she was just being overly sensitive because of his situation? None of us ever saw that coming with Andy and Heather. At least we sure as hell didn't. They were always the picture of happiness — I think Andy thought so, too. Maybe her questioning you was only a result of hearing about what happened to them."

"I'm not sure. It's crossed my mind, and I have a feeling that's part of it. What pisses me off the most is that she forgot all of that and acted like I'd been keeping it from her. If I had forgotten something major like that, I'd have blue balls for months. Or, bluer balls for even more months, in my case."

"Barrett. You need to fix this. You need to make sure that Tess has absolutely no reason to second guess you or to question anything in your marriage."

"Tell me something I don't already know," I grumble.

"Well, you know Lauren and I are here for you guys. And you'll fix this. You two are perfect for each other. You just need to get back to that," he says in a rare moment of showing his own possession of a vagina.

"Thanks, man. I know. I'm just frustrated. We'll sort it out. There's no way I'll not get us sorted out."

"I get that."

My phone beeps, stopping our conversation from turning into even more girl-talk. I almost feel the need to reach into my shorts and check to make sure that I still have my balls.

Josh must sense it too because he clears his throat and slaps me on the shoulder before taking a few steps back, "Alright, I'm gonna go to the back room and check that my nuts haven't hibernated, maybe chew some tobacco or something like that to get my man card back."

I grin at him and chuckle. We're so much alike it's scary sometimes. And he's right. None of this is unfixable; we just need to figure out how to fix it. I have a feeling we need to get back to the basics and move forward from there. I check my phone and my grin spreads.

My Girl: *Can you pick up some cut up*

vaginas for after tonight's game?

I laugh out loud. I can't help it. I'm fairly positive that she didn't mean cut up vaginas. Well, I hope not, but still. Texting and my girl are not the best of friends, but they make my day, none the less.

Me: ...

Me: I think I'm gonna go with a NO on that one.

My Girl: Why not?

Me: Pretty girl, did you read your text before you hit send?

My Girl: WTH! Autocorrect, you asshole!

Me: LOL – so no to the cut up vaginas?

My Girl: Obviously. I meant veggies. Clearly texting and I need to break up.

Me: Please don't. Your autocorrect fails are usually the highlight of my day.

My Girl: So glad I can be of service.

Me: I'll tell you how you can service me...

My Girl: Service me, I service you.

Me: *Tonight?*

My Girl: *Please yessssssssss!*

Me: *So, I'm not the only one horny as duck?*

My Girl: *LOL — well I don't know how horny ducks are, but sure…*

Me: *Dammit!*

I assume she's gone as I wait for another text. Then I hear the familiar ping of my cell.

My Girl: *So, the v-e-g-e-t-a-b-l-e-s?*

Me: *Hahahaha, funny girl. How long did it take you to type that out? Yeah. I can grab some on my way home before we head over to the field.*

My Girl: *A long damn time and thanks, babe. I love you. Tonight. Xxxxxxxxxxxx*

My Girl: *In case you misunderstood that, that was me raining kisses down on you.*

Me: ****strips in anticipation****

My Girl: ☺

Me: ☺ ☺

And just like that, we are back to ourselves. Well, almost. As long as we can keep the extra bodies out of our bed and actually stay awake long enough to do something about it.

Chapter Five

Tess

"OH MY GOSH, I'm gonna throw up." I stop talking for a few moments and take a deep breath, choke down a little bile, and spray water from the spout on my water bottle onto my face. "Nope, false alarm. I'm good." I take a deep breath and blow it out before continuing. "Can I ask a serious question, please? Who the hell invented burpees? And wall sits, and knee lifts, and friggin' mountain climbers? Seriously. What sadistic jerk thought of these workouts? Who thought it was awesome to jump and then fall to a push up then start all over again?" I mumble to Lauren who's been coming over to my house to work out together for years now.

We used to go to a gym, but when it became clear that neither of us could do jumping jacks or jump rope without peeing a little, we thought it best to move our workouts to a more private location. Only, just recently, we've decided to jump on the CrossFit bandwagon, but do the half-assed workouts at home rather than torturing ourselves with medicine balls and kettle balls and heavy weights at the gym. So basically, we're doing schoolyard workouts, but it makes us feel like we're at least doing something. Plus, doing it together gives us the motivation to keep going.

I assume Lauren doesn't want to look like a quitter just as much as I don't. And it's more fun. We can laugh together (and at each other) and have girl time. It's perfect. Or, it has the potential to be if we were in yoga pants and drinking wine rather than wearing yoga pants and pretending to work out.

"Someone with a major complex who enjoys watching people puke just trying to get in shape."

"Clearly. This is ridiculous." I groan as I roll over onto my back with my arms spread-eagle.

Lauren is next to me, lying prostrate on the ground. She lifts her head, looks my direction, and gags a little bit. Pretty sure she just swallowed her own vomit. No judgement, though, since I fought it off just moments ago. The stupidest part of it all is that we do this crap voluntarily. Voluntarily! But it's either that, or Grady will give us his own WOD to follow, and I'm absolutely positive that would be worse.

Maybe.

Probably.

Not exactly sure which would be worse at this point in time.

I try to stand up on wobbly legs, moaning and groaning like a big baby the entire time, and failing miserably as I fall back to the floor. Lauren snickers up at me until she tries it, then she moans and groans the same way and decides to stay down.

Back away from the brownies and wine, ladies.

"The most ridiculous part is, now I want to eat. All. The. Food. And I'd probably throw up anything that I put in my mouth, but I'm so damn hungry. Still, anything I want to eat will make everything we just did a *moo,* not moot, point." Lauren laughs at her *Friends* reference. "I just need to get a pair of plaid pregnancy pants and be done with it. Or borrow Monica's lavender tunic. Then it won't matter if I work out or not."

"Definitely not the paste pants. Those won't hide a thing."

"So true."

"Not even if I… Pivot!" I exclaim in response for some unknown reason and shove my fist in the air. We both lie there and laugh at our *Friends* references and continue making them for a solid five minutes before our stomachs start growling at us. "If you think I went through all that work just to eat some weird carb-free, flaxseed, protein, imitation muffin, you've got another thing coming. I'd eat one of Rachel's meat trifles at this point. I'm so hungry. We're going to Christine's, and I'm ordering a latte and one of her cream-cheese-frosted cinnamon rolls," I say with authority.

"There's a reason you and I are best friends."

"So what's new with you?" Lauren asks as we sit down to have lunch.

We came straight from my house, so I can't imagine what we both look like. A hot sweaty mess, more than likely. We are at our favorite coffee shop, the one belonging to Christine, Bri's mom, but she doesn't seem to be working today. It was her dream, and when her husband passed, she discovered that he had been setting aside money for it. It was hard for her to accept at first; she felt like he should have been the one to help her set it up. After several months, though, Barrett and I helped her to take the leap and start Dreamin' Beans.

"Same old same old. You?" I respond and shift the focus to her quickly.

"What's wrong?" Lauren asks immediately. "I can tell something's up. You know you can't hide anything from me. How long have we known each other?" she asks. However, she doesn't give me a chance to respond before she continues. "I've known you since I was seven years old, Tess. There's nothing we haven't been able to take on together. You know I won't think any differently of you."

She's so right and, at this moment, even though I should probably be talking to my husband about this, I decide I need my best girl's perspective. I lick my lips and then roll them together to muster up the courage to talk it out with my best friend. "Something's going on with Barrett and me," I blurt out.

"Bullshit. You two are like the perfect couple," she defends immediately.

"You only see us on the outside. Not that I'm trying to present this *'Oh we're the perfect couple and my husband is perfect and my kids are perfect'* but…"

"I get it. Your troubles are your troubles. No need to air them because that's your business and your business only. But… tell me what's going on." She prods anyway.

I know it's not her being nosy. It's her caring. Which is a big difference.

"I don't know, to be honest. It's like we're both so damn tired all the time. We argue over little things that normally don't even faze us. Oh! And I can't believe I'm about to admit this because you're gonna think the worst of me, and speaking of, not sure why you haven't mentioned it…"

"Tess, you're rambling, and stop twisting your hair!" she

says with raised eyebrows and a chuckle. She knows I ramble and twist my hair when I get nervous.

I release my hair from around my finger and drop my hands to wrap around my coffee cup. "No judgement, right? This is bad." I pause, trying to gain some strength to admit everything. "Lauren, I forgot MaryEllen retired and had no clue who Keri was. I questioned Barrett about Keri, for pity's sakes. I know better. I know deep in my heart that he would never step out on our marriage," I tell her, then lower my voice. "I think I was just a little on edge because of finding out about Andy and Heather, you know? I guess I just never imagined they would split, or that she'd cheat on him. Hearing it just scared me with how distant we've been with each other lately. But most of all, we're both so hard up in the bedroom that I swear I'm about ready to start sitting on the washing machine or break out Mr. Rabbit."

"Holy crap, Tess. I feel like my mind is spinning with all this information. Let's break it down." She takes a sip of her coffee and then puts the cup back down on the table. Looking me dead in the eye, she goes for it. "How in the hell could you ever think Barrett... Barrett of all people... would ever even look at another woman? And seriously, haven't you noticed Keri sitting at MaryEllen's old desk? Don't you remember we had the retirement party for her?"

I groan into my hands, mortification of my selfish behavior lately setting in. "Truth? And this is where it gets worse. Way worse," I tell her, pleading with my eyes to be understanding. She circles her hand in the *get on with it* gesture, rolling her own eyes. "Ok, don't judge me. I had a design trade show the weekend of the retirement party. I remember asking Barrett if I needed to do anything for it, and he seemed a little, I don't know, indifferent. Now that

I look back, he was probably pissed that I was choosing the design show over him, and, truth be told, he has a right to be pissed. And the reason I haven't seen Keri is because I haven't been to the office in four months." I mumble the last part quickly as I begin to take a drink of my coffee and divert my eyes from hers.

"Say what?" she asks, her eyes squinting at me, eyebrows bunched together.

I set my coffee cup down and clear my throat and tell her a little more clearly this time. "I haven't been to the office for four months."

She looks at me blankly then blinks a couple times. "How is that even possible?"

I shrug my shoulders in response and look away, tears building in my eyes. I'm ashamed that I've let our relationship come to this. I don't think either of us even realized it, to be honest. It just kind of happened. We both started letting things slip and slide until it got to this ugly point.

"Tess. Sweetie, this isn't like you. You used to show up unannounced at the office all the time. Trust me, I know this all too well," she says with raised eyebrows, no doubt thinking of the few times I've walked in on her and Josh in the middle of gettin' some.

"Yeah, I can never un-see that, thanks very much."

She grins, unashamed, and shrugs her shoulders. "Tess, you need to end that. Make sure you go and meet Keri. She's super sweet, and she has a boyfriend — a boyfriend she's planning to marry as soon as he proposes. There's nothing you can do about the past four months, but you can change the present and future."

"Right. But the guilt…" I shake my head and scoff. "It's killing me. I feel awful for the way I've been allowing myself to get so wrapped up in life that I forgot he has his own things going on, too. It's been four months since I've been to the shop. Four months, Lauren. That's a long time. I feel bad enough for that, but the Keri-thing. I can't believe I accused him of even looking at another woman that way. What was I thinking?"

"You weren't. Your emotions are getting the best of you." She gasps dramatically and puts her hand to her chest before whisper shouting to me, "Do you think… Are you going through the change!?" Her voice is a mix of horrified and teasing.

"You're such a brat," I say, to which she smiles.

"You love me. But, I'll repeat, there's nothing you can do about the past. You can make the rest up to him. Get back to your roots. Now, I'm gonna ask… Why is it that you're both so hard up? I've seen you two around each other. You don't seem the type to be low on sex drive."

"It's definitely not lack of sex drive that's the issue. Well, sort of. The desire is there, but we're also exhausted, or we have Harper barging into the bedroom. Or Grady coming home at whatever time of night from Bri's or Brandon's house. Or so many other things that seem to keep popping up that we're deeming more important that I know aren't. We need… I don't know. I was going to say a break from life, but neither of us are willing to miss the kids' games and just… Gah! I'm whining. What's up with you?" I shoot her a fake smile to stop my own rambling.

"You are so weird." She chuckles while shaking her head at me. "First of all, that's not whining. That's venting to your best friend. You could have ranted on BookFace. *That* would be whining and trying to get everyone's sympathy." She grins cheekily.

Lauren — and our husbands — have a huge pet peeve with Facebook. The guys started calling it BookFace because they'd rather take a book to the face than engage on Facebook. But in her opinion, no one is ever honest in their posts. The way she sees it, everyone has to make sure they look perfect, only show their kids in their best light and their husbands doing awesome things. They never mention that it took them twenty practice shots for the selfie to turn out just the way they wanted it to, that they had to bribe their kids with ice cream in order for them to behave for the picture or video clip. Never admit that the husband was bribed with some lovin' just so he would cook dinner or go to the grocery store. But they still post the picture for all the world to see so they have proof that their family is better than yours. Her words, not mine.

She's probably fairly on point in her opinion, but it still cracks me up. I think the only reason she even has a Facebook profile is so that she doesn't miss out on what fiction — again, her words, not mine — everyone posts. It's hilarious. And it's one of the reasons I love her so much.

"Come on, Lauren. Tell me what to do. I'm being serious now."

"I'm being serious, too. Exactly how long has it been since you've had a chance to bump nasties, do the oompa loompa, the horizontal mambo, gotcha some, hit a home run, played a little slap and ti—"

"Oh my gosh!" I interrupt her and look around to make sure no one heard us while my face is flaming red. "Shut up! You're so ridiculous," I say, barely able to hold my laughter to a dull roar.

"What? Saying 'When was the last time you ma-a-ade lo-o-vve' is so boring and so nineties," she somehow says with a straight face, meanwhile making an obscene gesture with her hands, since, apparently, we're sixteen again.

I laugh so hard I almost pee. "You're such an idiot. Where do you come up with this stuff?"

She taps her temple and proudly says, "It's all stored up here. Awesome, right?"

"It's something, all right. I can't even have a normal conversation with you," I tell her.

"Sorry." She visibly shakes her body like she's shaking out the crazies. *Good luck with that.* "So are we talking weeks? Months? How long, babe. Give me a timeline so I know if we're in like a DEFCON 3 situation, or if it's a Charlie Brown problem."

"So it's definitely more serious than a Charlie Brown problem, whatever that is, but I'm assuming you mean not serious. But it's not as extreme as calling in the National Forces. I don't know. It depends if you're including the number of times we've tried but couldn't get any downtown action happening because we got interrupted." I sigh.

"It's been a few months, huh?"

I wish I could lie and tell her she's wrong. It's not like we haven't tried. The interruptions seem to be endless. Tears threaten to build in my eyes, which is stupid. It's sex. But obviously it's more than that. It's not just the sex that I miss. It's him. It's us. We don't get time together like we used to, sure. But that's no different than any other married couple with active kids. We're all busy. I get that. That's also why I feel stupid whining about it, but I can't help it.

I want a marriage that's about more than the kids' activities and our work schedules and what needs to be done at the house. And who's going to get the cut-up vaginas from the grocery store. *Geesh.* That was one for the record books.

I nod my head and look away. I'm ashamed to admit that to anyone, including myself. Two months. Sixty-six days, to be exact. And what we had for a few months before that wasn't anything to write home about.

"Well, think of it this way, when you finally have sex again, you'll be tighter than a nun. You'll be re-virginized!"

A snort-laugh bubbles out of me because, damn her, I've actually thought that! I need help. We both do. I drop my head to the table and bang it a few times.

She giggles lightly and grabs my hand that's dangling lifelessly at my side. "You, Stella, need to get your groove back, and the rest of it, the stuff that's just as important as the sex stuff, will fall into place."

"How many of these do you have, exactly?" I groan and glare at her, even though she can't see me since I still haven't lifted my head. She really is the definition of ridiculous.

"What, witty remarks that help you forget your vagina is lonely? Hundreds. No. Probably thousands, but I'll stop. I'll be honest…" She pauses until I look up and make eye contact with her. "…two months is a long time, yes. But it could be worse. And remember, life has been insane lately. First things first. Harps has got to stay in her bed. Do what you have to do. At this point, you need to be above good-parenting skills and hit up the BookFace variety. Bribe her with a new doll or riding boots or whatever you can think of, but seriously, she needs to keep her scrawny horse-riding butt back in her own room."

She gives me a stern look, and I nod in agreement. I know this. I'm not an idiot.

"Second. You two are going away. For a few weeks at least. Obviously, Cole can't come home and stay with the kids, but Grady and Maggie are old enough to take care of things, for the most part anyway. Call your brother. They adore Uncle James and will love to have him come hang out for a while. He works out of his house anyway, unless he's traveling to a different restaurant, and you know he'd be there in a heartbeat. The volleyball and football seasons are almost over. We'll help with the kids too. You know that."

She's right. James will be here in a second if he knew we needed his help. He works with restaurants that are going under, revamping their menu, décor, staff. He loves everything about the food industry, including cooking, so at the very least the kids will eat incredibly well while he's there. If we asked him, that is.

"I know that. And, truth be told, it sounds like a really good plan. Two weeks seems like a little too much, but I agree that we need to get away."

"But…" She ended speaking with a lilt to her voice.

I blow out the breath I'd been holding and watch the barista frantically filling orders for a few moments. Admitting the no-sex fly zone that had inhabited our home for the last two months was one thing. Admitting that I was afraid my husband didn't like me anymore was a whole other thing. Of course, I know he loves me. But like me well enough to be alone, no kids, no distractions, for two weeks? I don't know. I'm terrified to find out, though.

"Talk to me, Tess. What's the problem here? This is Barrett and Josh's slow season. Or slower season. You can say no appointments for a few weeks. James will come help. I'll even help you find a place to stay."

"I know all that. Those details I have no worries about. I'll miss the hell out of the kids, but as long as I can still check in with them every day, I'll survive."

"What's the issue then?" she presses. I know she won't

back down, either. It isn't her style, and, to be honest, it isn't mine. Neither of us would ever let the other sit quiet over coffee when there is something clearly weighing down the other's thoughts.

"What if Barrett doesn't like me anymore?" I murmur, saying the words out loud for the first time. *Geesh, my hair hurts.*

"Come again?" she asks, her eyebrows raised in my direction.

"I know he likes me. I know he loves me. But what if we are too into our boring routines of our humdrum life that we can't focus on each other and put the rest of it behind us? What if we've become one of those couples whose relationship is built solely on the kids and everything else? I can't tell you the last time we made out like teenagers on the couch just because. Or even cuddled. I miss the intimacy. I miss the innocent touches. I *really* miss the sex…" I groan. I was feeling borderline pathetic at this point, and I prayed that she understood what I was trying to say.

"Oh, hon. I get it. I promise, I do. You two have just lost focus of why you fell in love in the first place. We all miss those butterflies we get from the early moments in relationships. You're not alone there. But don't think for one second that Barrett isn't one-hundred percent in love with you," she said, holding up a hand to stop my argument.

"And, yes, in like with you, too. He likes you a whole lot more than a little." She laughs.

"I KNEW you saw that on BookFace, you dork."

"I admit it. That was a good one. Cute little penguin. But, trust me. That man's as smitten as he was in the beginning. Life is just getting in the way of the woo."

"Ugh. The damn woo. I swear the damn woo is gonna

be the death of me. Or lack of, anyway. I can't remember the last time I felt wooed," I admit and choke back the tears. "It's just been so long since Barrett showed me more, you know?"

I see the look on her face. The look that said I had confided in the right person. The look that said she had ideas rolling around in her crazy head, ideas that said that Barrett should probably block her number. I know she and Josh haven't always had it easy either. But they are basically empty nesters already. Their twins, Brandon and Mia, are Cole's age. Brandon works for the guys, and Mia is at the same college as Cole. With no kids distracting them at home, they're like sex-starved hippies, willing to do it anywhere they see fit. I think they've been caught either well on their way or in the middle of doing it at the office at least a dozen times.

I can't say I'm not jealous. I'd kill to have that sort of sex life once again. The sound of that damn tweety bird chirping brings me out of my funk once again. I look at my phone and instantly feel lighter, happier. It's a picture of Barrett. At Costco. By the giant boxes of condoms. I knew he needed to grab some supplies for the shop as well as the vegetables I'd asked him to pick up for tonight, and, by the looks of it, he got sidetracked.

> **Me:** *What the…*

> **Barrett:** ☺

> **Me:** *I don't even want to know.*

> **Me:** *Do I?*

> **Barrett:** *Oh yeah, pretty girl, you do.*

Me: *I fold. What are you doing in the condom aisle?*

Barrett: *Looking at condoms. Duh. Seriously, pretty girl, I thought you were more perceptive than this, darlin'.*

Me: *Oh my gosh. No, you dumb ass. I realize that you're looking at them. What I wonder is WHY?*

Barrett: *If I must spell it out for you…*

Me: *You must.*

Barrett: *We haven't done it in a… well, a really long time.*

Me: *I'm aware :/*

Barrett: *And when we finally do it, I want it to last more than eee errr eee errr.*

I almost spit my coffee out on the table. He's such a dork. Man, I love him.

Me: *That would be most desired, yes.*

Barrett: *So, I figured a layer between us will offer me some help in that department so I don't blow at first contact.*

Me: *I think that's the sexiest most romantic thing you've ever said to me.*

Barrett: *IKR?*

Me: *Did you just say IKR?*

Barrett: *I did. I'm hip. I'm all down with the lingo these days.*

Me: *I don't think saying you're down with the lingo these days qualifies as being hip but I'll give you points for effort.*

Barrett: *As long as those points can get tallied for tonight, I'm ok with it.*

Me: *Definitely.*

Barrett: *I miss you.*

And now I'm crying. In the middle of the coffee shop. Because I miss him, too. I look up at Lauren who's watching me closely. She reaches into her purse and hands over a tissue. I gratefully take it and laugh lightly before replying.

Me: *Me too. Tonight?*

Barrett: *Tonight. Xxxxxxxxxxxxxxxxxxxx*

Barrett: *That's me raining kisses on you,*

too. Even your special place ;)

Me: *I'll prep.*

Barrett: *Much appreciated, madam.*

Me: *Did you get the cut-up vaginas? ;)*

Barrett: *Yup — funny thing. They were next to the condoms.*

Me: *LOL I love you.*

Barrett: *Love you too, don't ever forget it.*

Me: *Never ever.*

Barrett's reply is a bunch of kissy-face emojis and a series of what I think is supposed to be several that turned dirty in his mind, but I can't be sure. Either way, his text is all it takes to bring me out of my funk. I'd talk to him about going away, and maybe I will pull on my big-girl panties and talk to him about the woo. As much as I feel like I'm missing out, I know I've been clearly neglecting him in that area too. But it ends. Tonight. I hope. Man, do I ever hope.

"By the smile on your face and the blush in your cheeks, I take it Stella's getting her groove back?" Lauren says with a smile that matches my own.

"Oh yeah, as long as the stars all align just right."

"Oh, come on. You're his lobster," she says, smiling and hooking her fingers together. We really need to lay off the *Friends* talk.

"Ha! I suppose you could be right about that."

"Of course I'm right."

I hope she is, too.

Chapter Six

Barrett

W HEN I WALKED into costco this afternoon, I honestly had no intentions of buying a year's supply of condoms. But a guy doesn't buy just three condoms at Costco. He buys a box large enough to supply the football team. And as much as I have no desire to have that layer between me and Tess, I know I'll need it. Just thinking of her this afternoon is getting me hard. I don't think I've ever been so hard up for sex with Tess in my entire life. Even after the kids were born and we were reduced to that damn six-week ban, we still made good on our time together. I would diddle her; she would take care of me. We made it work. But now. Well, two months is a long damn time to go without.

"I'm home!" I yell into the quiet house. The fact that there were no vehicles in the driveway when I pulled in tells me that the only ones to greet me will be of the four-legged variety, which is weird that I was yelling that to them, but I'm not going to question myself. The sound of dogs running on the hardwood floor makes me smile. I have no doubt our two guard dogs were sleeping peacefully on either our bed or the sectional in the sunken living room — Tess's favorite part of the house because she wanted one ever since she was little. They both come traipsing into the kitchen, begging for my attention immediately. I drop to my knees and allow them to shower me with affection before I open the back door and let them out to relieve themselves. They bound down the stairs off the deck after running through the door, Flash getting distracted immediately by a bright red leaf that blows passed him before it looks like he remembers his initial reason for being outside in the chilly autumn temperatures of Michigan.

I know Grady won't be home until after his game tonight, and I have no doubt that Maggie will only be home for a few moments after volleyball practice before she heads out to the game, hopefully not changing into her Friday shirt that almost caused me to have a heart attack last night. Tess will be home any minute with Harper, who goes to the studio with her after school.

It's become a tradition since Cole played football that our group of friends each take turns hosting our families after the games. Whether we are celebrating another win or licking our wounds from a loss, we've come to truly enjoy having time together postgame. Not to mention the ton of food that our teenagers usually end up stopping by for at some point. Sometimes, we'll pull out games like Catch Phrase or Cards Against Humanity, depending on our mood for the evening. It's like our version of tailgating, only it's after the game.

Tonight is our turn to host, which means we supply the feast. We found it easier that the host family provides all the food rather than us all trying to figure out what to bring to someone's house weekly. Takes the guess work out of it. Tess prepared most of the dishes this morning, so I check the few items that are in Crockpots. The barbecue pulled pork for sandwiches and buffalo chicken dip are cooking nicely. I place the tray of cut-up vaginas, er… vegetables in the fridge and notice that she set a tube of salami and block of cheese in there. I take care of slicing it up and put it on a platter before placing it back in the fridge, knowing it will help her. She also made two pans of brownies this morning — it seems she was busy — so I cut those up, too. I need to start doing more things like this again for her. It may seem small, but it has always seemed to me like it's the little things that matter more than the big things. I know I've been slacking in that department. Making her feel cherished and appreciated. After ensuring everything is as it should be, I head upstairs to take a shower before the game.

Just as I'm stepping out of the stall, my beautiful wife enters our en suite bathroom, turns, and locks the door. The look in her eyes makes me rise to attention immediately as she saunters over to me.

"Hi, babe," I say, the corner of my lip turning up. I'm not even trying to cover myself or hide the fact that just her mere presence while I'm naked is doing things to me.

"Hey," she replies in the sweetest voice ever heard. As much as I'm not ashamed of presenting myself to her, she's not ashamed of staring at what she wants. And what she wants is obviously me. She walks over and rests her slender fingers on my chest, slowly dragging them down, teasing me with a promise that I can't wait to see her fulfill.

As her hands continue their slow descent down my stomach and into the promised land, I can't help but to shift my hips and press myself into her. She doesn't hesitate a moment and grips me in her small hand, causing me to groan and drop my head back. She exhales as if she's missed touching me just as much as I've missed her touch. I reach over to her and pull her closer, not even caring what time it is and that we need to leave to get to the field to watch Grady kick some turf ass.

"Where's Harper?" I ask, somehow able to have a rational thought.

"She's with Maggie. They're both changing clothes and getting ready for the game."

Her answer is all I need to hear to get me even harder. "You don't want to start something you can't finish, pretty girl," I say as I capture her mouth in a kiss. Oh hell, her mouth. Her taste. She's so perfect, it still surprises me over twenty years later.

She pulls back slightly, tilting her head to the side to give me access to her neck. "Who said I can't finish? I figured maybe we could do something now… and later?" she asks softly, like the tease that she is.

"Hell yes," I grind out.

And because the universe, or our kids, hate us, we hear Maggie and Harper both yell that it's time to leave. We both whimper, and I think I feel a tear threaten to escape my eye, but the heat in her gaze as she looks at me is a promise of finishing later. Now I can only hope my hard on will go away so I don't look like a creepy douche at my son's football game, sporting a boner like a pubescent teenager.

"Bloody hell," I groan in a horrible British accent, but I need something to lighten my mood. It was the first time Tess had her hands on me in far too long, and my children were cockblocking me from getting some. Again.

She giggles adorably, obviously loving all my botched accents, before she releases me and responds to the girls. "Yeah, yeah, yeah, we're coming!"

"I was trying to, anyway," I grumble. I'm not even going

to apologize for my bad mood now. My grumbling causes Tess to burst out into laughter before she tells the girls to make sure the dogs have food and water before we leave, then shuts the door to our bedroom so I can change, giving me a few moments to get myself back under control.

I walk into our bedroom and pull on a pair of boxer briefs — half tempted to go commando just so she knows how easily accessible I am the entire night and maybe drive her a little crazy — a pair of faded jeans, and a school T-shirt and hoodie. I slide my feet into a pair of sneakers, and I'm ready. Not the most stylish, but it's a high school varsity football game. In southeast Michigan. In October. Style isn't a factor — warmth is.

I look over at my wife who is dressed similarly, but somehow she still looks gorgeous. Her shoulder-length hair is in its usual soft waves that I know will smell like coconut when I lean in to kiss her neck, which I do. Because I can. Simple as that. She has on a dark pair of skinny jeans that hug her ass as if they were made for her alone. I won't be able to keep my hands off her ass all night.

I walk over to where Tess stands in front of the mirror in the bathroom, reapplying some makeup and fixing her hair, and wrap my arms around her. She turns to face me with one cheek blushed and the other not. I smile at her because I can't help it. She looks so goofy with her makeup half done and her big, beautiful innocent eyes staring up at me. She leans up and kisses my chin and tries to spin back around to face the mirror, but I stop her with my tight grip on her waist.

"I miss you," I say.

Her body sags against me, and tears immediately form in her eyes. She's always been an emotional sap, but I know it's more than just her normal emotions getting to her now. She feels it too. I need to do something about it, and seeing her to the point of tears breaks my heart. She should never feel that our relationship will cause her tears.

"Don't cry. Please, Tess. It breaks my heart. I can't take the tears."

"I'm sorry." She sniffles. "I can't help it. It's not just the sex. Yes, I miss it terribly, but it's you. I miss you, too. We have to find a way to get back to ourselves."

"Come on now, I know it's really just my magical penis that you miss," I tease her.

She looks up at me with a watery smile and says through her chuckling, "You know it."

"Pretty girl, I feel it, too. We're gonna fix us, you hear me? Surely the kids are old enough to live on their own, yeah?"

My weird comment hit the mark exactly where I intended it to. It lightened the mood. I get the smile back from her that we both needed. We can't be heading off to cheer for Grady in a sour mood. It just won't do.

"Come on, stud. Let's get this show on the road." She playfully smacks my butt then pinches it for good measure. She's always had a thing for my butt. If she were a guy, she'd be an ass man. She's so weird. But I'll do squats until I'm ninety to keep my gluteus maximus tight if it means she'll keep wanting to touch and squeeze it.

"I don't think I've ever not wanted to have our postgame gathering as little as I do tonight. Would it be bad if we put a table outside with the food, drinks, and plates with a sign that says 'Help yourselves and wait outside'?"

"Let's make sure to add the scarf to the doorknob. I'm sure they'd probably figure that was a little odd, but I'm game."

"Tonight," I promise... once again. I think I'll lose my shit if tonight's promise is broken to either of us.

"Tonight," she promises back, a big smile covering her face.

Chapter Seven

Tess

GRADY'S TEAM WON. They've only lost one game this season, and that was when five of our starters were out because of a major case of food poisoning. So, to say that game is a bit of a sore spot for everyone on the team is putting it mildly. Even with winning almost every game, they're still pumped after a win. And by pumped, I mean lots of chest bumping, jumping around, and hitting each other on the helmet, and a few butt slaps.

They're also all ravenous after their games. We make our way home to get the food ready with a convoy of our friends' vehicles following us. After we all have made our way inside, the women begin getting the food lined up on the kitchen island while the men get the basement ready for the onslaught of teenagers who are about to invade the home. Simple tasks, like bubble-wrapping the walls, screwing down furniture, that type of thing.

The door between the kitchen and the attached garage opens, making me smile just knowing who is coming through it. Only a few people aside from those who live here use that door.

"Hi, Tess," Bri's sweet voice calls out to me. She's a part

of the family, and ever since she and Grady were in seventh grade, she's called me Tess, a departure from the ma'am or Mrs. Ryan that she had previously used. I love it. I want her to be comfortable in our home. She'll be my daughter-in-law one day, even if she and Grady won't admit it.

"Hey Bri," I reply, smiling at her. She's wearing Grady's red game-day jersey, dark skinny jeans, a pair of camel-colored Ugg boots, and has black painted under her bright green eyes with her thick dark hair up in a ponytail full of curls. She looks adorable. If I was judging by looks alone, there would be no question as to why he has a crush on her. Her olive-toned skin and green eyes with dark hair make her look exotic, but her personality and the dimple in her left cheek makes her appear like the girl next door.

"Anything I can do to help?" she asks. Such a good girl.

"No, sweetheart. We got it. The men are downstairs getting the basement ready. You're the first here. You can hang out here with us until the rest of the kids get here, or you can wait in Grady's room. Up to you," I tell her and smile her way.

"I'll wait here. I'm hungry anyway," she says a little shyly and shrugs her shoulders. Another thing I love. She eats! She's like the unicorn of teenage girls. She eats more than just salads in front of the boys, talks to parents, and isn't attached to her phone.

"Hi, Mom," she says as soon as she sees her mom, Christine, walk into the kitchen. She's such a mini version of her mom it's almost eerie at times. Christine is spunky and adorable. The main difference in their long, dark, almost-black hair is that Christine has a couple red streaks through the front, setting off her bright green eyes. She does yoga almost every day to keep her petite five-foot frame in better shape than most forty-something-year-olds, and recently she got a tiny diamond pierced into her nose. If it didn't match her personality so perfectly, I'd think she was going through a mid-life crisis. She's one of the most beautiful women I've ever seen in real life with her flawless skin. She's so incredibly sweet and likable, I probably hate her just a little bit. Plus, she feeds our coffee and sweets addiction, so there's that.

"Hi, honey. How are you?"

"Good. Did you go to the game? Did you see Grady's last touchdown?" Bri beams with pride for her *friend*.

He started a tradition after he scored his first touchdown on the varsity team where he taps the top of his helmet twice then presses his right fist into his chest over his heart before he points to the stands. He won't tell anyone why he started it and what it means, but we all know that Bri is part of it, considering it's always pointed in her direction. I don't push or ask. But I want to.

"I did, and of course I saw it," Christine says and grins as she winks at me.

The door to the garage opens again, and this time it's Grady making his presence known. He throws his gear bag down in the wooden lockers that Barrett built into the house before kicking off his shoes and walking into the kitchen.

"Ladies," he says in his loud voice, arms spread wide like he's the king announcing his presence. His good mood after his win is infectious and has all of us smiling and shaking our heads. His short, dark-blond hair and broad shoulders remind me more and more of his father every day; he could be Barrett's eighteen-year-old twin. I briefly wonder if Grady's hair will turn light brown like Barrett's did over time. His hazel eyes sparkle with green flecks, and his smile shows off his straight white teeth that came from years of living with braces that he finally got off last summer. He's definitely not lacking for confidence or charm, also much like his father.

All the ladies in the kitchen say hello to Grady, barely looking up from their tasks of setting the food out. A few say "good game" to him but, other than that, they're immune to his charming ways.

"Hey, B," he says, a smile evident in his voice. He immediately walks over to Bri and places his hand on the small of her back before leaning down to whisper something in her ear.

She smiles but rolls her eyes, clearly amused by whatever he said to her. "Of course," she says quietly in response to whatever he whispered.

"Good. Hey, Mama C," he says to Christine and gives her a side hug. Grady has always been an affectionate kid, but he has a soft spot in his heart for Christine.

"Hi, kiddo," Christine says as she returns his hug.

He walks over and hugs me and lifts me up, his favorite way to embrace me. Then he looks down at the counter. "Awesome. Pulled pork. Thanks, Mom." He kisses my cheek and then turns to Bri and says, "Wanna get some food and head downstairs?"

"Yeah. I'm starving."

"Me too."

They pile plates full of food, grab a couple of drinks from the fridge, and make their way to the basement. I hear the door to the basement open, and loud laughter and teenage voices fill the house. The kids tend to use the basement door when coming and going, one thing we have to monitor regularly. The other moms and I share a smile as the dads all quickly make their way upstairs, almost knocking over Grady and Bri in the process, desperate to get their food before the kids demolish everything in their path.

Less than an hour after the kids have all invaded the home, they're all heading back out, their own convoy of lights leading the way. Grady and Bri are the last to leave, and he tells her that he'll follow her to her house so she can drop off her car and get in with him.

"Bye, Mom. Bye, Dad," Grady says to us, kissing me on top of the head before he heads out the door.

"Bye, son. Bye, Bri. You guys be safe, and Grady, don't let Bri out of your sight, got it?" Barrett instructs.

Bri's dad passed away from cancer three years ago, and, with as close as she always was with Grady, it was natural to welcome her into our fold even more. Christine is doing the best she can, but sometimes a girl needs a dad. While Barrett might not be her dad, nor does he try to be, he definitely shows her that he's there for her and loves her like his own.

The kids are going to a field party, typical for after a Friday night football game for our small town. They don't hide the fact of where they're heading, but they also don't plan to divulge all the details of the party, either. But we trust Grady; he's focused and dedicated to staying on the straight and narrow.

"Hadn't planned on it," Grady replies, looking into Bri's eyes and placing his arm around her shoulders.

She blushes slightly but beams up at him.

"Bye everyone," they both call out, and the parents all say their goodbyes.

Chapter Eight

Barrett

Everyone has gone home from our after-game party. Maggie is spending the night at a friend's house and, miracle of all miracles, so is Harper. Well, she's staying at Lauren and Josh's house. I have a feeling I know how that came to play, but I'm not gonna even bring myself to care that I know Tess discussed our lack of sex lately with Lauren. Hell, I talked to Josh about the same thing. And they're good friends. They've been there once upon a time. Plus, they love Harper and her energy. They seemed excited to have her overnight.

I walk into our bedroom and notice that Tess has candles of all colors, shapes, and sizes lit around the room. I wish I had thought about doing that. I've been so focused on getting to the sex part that I've neglected the rest of it. She deserves the world, and I know I need to step up my game. I scroll through my phone and find some music to help set the mood that she'd already begun. After finding what I'm looking for, I place it on the docking station that doubles as my charger and alarm clock.

I'm stripping down to my clothes, just what the song is telling me to do, when my beautiful bride walks into the bedroom from the bathroom. Naked. Now, she could have slid on something sexy, like a nighty or lacy thing that pushes her boobs up, but any man will tell you this is way better. So much better, in fact, that I'm suddenly naked. No idea how I managed to get the rest of my clothes stripped so quickly, my clothes flung all over the room. I briefly think that I hope I didn't throw anything on a candle, but a quick sniff tells me nothing is on fire — except for the spark that ignited between us the second I caught sight of her. She's beautiful. Even better, she's mine.

She's had my heart since I held her hand the day she let me take her home from school when I was just seventeen years old. I was a goner then by that one touch. Then, the next night on our first official date, when we were crossing the street to go to the movie theater, her letting me hold her hand was all it took for my heart to race and my mind to go foggy.

"C'mere," I command, knowing my girl loves it when I'm a little more demanding in the bedroom. She complies quickly by sauntering over to where I stand next to the bed. I pick her up and throw her playfully on the mattress. She laughs loudly, the sound a direct line to my quickly growing hardness, but it dies quickly when I crawl over top of her and press myself closer to her, not entering her just yet. I know as soon as I do it will all be over.

My mouth descends on hers, and I quickly slip my tongue into her mouth. Mine. I pin her hands above her head and grind myself into her, my message clear as to where this is going.

"Please." She breathes out when my mouth moves from hers down to her neck, her collarbone, her bare breasts. They've gotten bigger, fuller over time. They're amazing, and I prepare to ravish them.

"Not yet, sweetheart. You know I won't last," I mumble around her soft skin and grab her wrist when I feel her hand gliding down my stomach to where I want her the most.

Her back arches off the bed, pressing herself into me even farther. "Just… do-o-o something, Barrett. Please. I need you. So bad…" Her voice is a whimper and she wraps her legs around me, holding me to her.

"I need you, too. But first I'm going to take my time with you."

"After. We have all night. I just need to feel you first. We'll go slow next time."

I can't hardly argue with that. Still straddling her, I reach into the nightstand for a condom. Yes, I bought them. I wasn't joking with her when I said I won't last and, even knowing we have all night and we aren't going to be a one-and-done couple tonight, I'm not about to let this end after thirty seconds. She raises an eyebrow at me when she sees the little foil package, and we laugh as we both fumble around with it like it's our first time. We've been married for over twenty years now. We haven't used condoms for over twenty years, but I meant it when I said I want this to last, and it might help to not be skin on skin right away. After retrieving the condom from its gold wrapper, she lifts her body up and takes it out of my hand before sliding it over my…

Ring… ring…

"Who the hell is calling!?" I shout my frustration.

"Ignore it," she pleads and reaches for me again. But the damn thing will not quit ringing. As soon as it quiets, it seems that the caller picks back up again and calls right away.

I look over at my phone and see Cole's name lit up and immediately my heart sinks. I grab the phone off the dock and quickly hit Go.

"Cole? What's wrong?" I answer in lieu of hello.

That gets Tess's attention. She sits up immediately, worry lacing her beautiful face, her body still exposed to me.

"It's Grady," he chokes out. Two words. That's all it takes. Our evening plans long forgotten, my heart now sits in my stomach.

Tess's eyes are burning into me, apparently wondering what it is that has me in such a panic, and, more than likely, she notices that the blood has run from my face.

"What is it?" she asks, her tiny hand resting on my forearm to gain my attention. I put the phone on speaker so whatever I'm about to hear come from my firstborn's mouth is nothing that I have to repeat.

"Cole. What's going on?" I ask, staring into Tess's worried eyes.

"There was… dammit. Dad, he was in a fight. Brandon just called me. I guess some dill hole — that Dawson kid? Well, he tried hitting on Bri. Which would have been fine, I suppose, if he had kept his hands to himself. When he got a little too handsy, and when I say handsy, I mean the prick *actually* hit her when she pushed him away, well that's when Grady lost it. Brandon said he wasn't drinking, which isn't shocking since he never drinks, but also is beside the point, and, at the same time a good thing, considering everything else. Anyway, when he heard what happened and saw the red mark on Bri's face from where this little punk hit her after she told him no, he lost all sense of reason. It took Brandon, Matt, and Nick to pull him off him. As far as I know, Dawson's fine — just beat up, which the little punk deserved — but, Dad, the police were called. He's at the police station. They arrested him for assault."

Chapter Nine

Tess

PARENTING IS HARD. Whoever said that it is the hardest job a person will ever have, well, they knew what they were talking about. As Barrett and I walk hand in hand into the police station, a place where I never imagined I would be entering, especially to pick up my son from being arrested, I am plagued with the vision that we will forever have burned into our memory. After talking with the front desk, they bring out the arresting officer who explains that Grady was arrested but that the victim wasn't pressing charges.

Little punk. I know my kids aren't perfect. Far from it. But I also know that Grady would never assault someone who didn't provoke him in some way. And messing with Bri was the number one way to get his attention, to get a rise out of him. While I'm grateful that he's not pressing charges against my son, if what Cole told us is true, I will have a hard time not encouraging Bri to do so. I don't want him thinking all he's going to get is a beat down for doing that to an innocent girl. But I need to get my facts straight before I let my mind continue to wander.

When we see Grady sitting in a jail cell, head in his hands, elbows on his knees, I can't hold back the sob that escapes me. When he hears our approach, his head shoots up, and the regret that is plaguing him is evident all over his face. His eyes are red, his left eye looks to be developing a nice reminder of his evening, and his hands are shaking… and bloody. Or what looks like dried blood. He looks broken. In more ways than one. Upon seeing us, he gives up the fight and releases the tears and flood of emotion he, no doubt, has been holding in since the cell door closed behind him.

"Grady."

"Mom. I'm so sorry, Mom. I'm so sorry." He continues to repeat how sorry he is until I step closer to the cell and wrap my hands around the bars. He does the same, resting his head against them.

"I know, baby. I know. We're gonna get you out of here, and when we get home, we'll talk about it. Just relax. We're just waiting for them to have the paperwork ready for us to sign. They let us back here to see you first."

Barrett has been quiet, not breathing a word since we received the call from Cole. I know the questions are rolling through his mind. *Why didn't he call us first? Why Cole? Why didn't the police call us? Or Grady? What could have caused him to intentionally hurt someone?* One of the questions he did voice and get answered from Cole after he told us that Grady had been arrested was that Bri was safe. Since Brandon was at the party, he called Cole first, figuring that Cole will be able to explain things best to us. He also let us know that he and Mia were on their way home, and that Brandon took Bri to her house, Bri insisting that she didn't need to see a doctor. She did, however, make sure to let Dawson know that if he so much as gave one thought to pressing charges against Grady, that she will happily return the favor.

After signing all the appropriate paperwork and waiting

what felt like forever to be able to hold my son again, he was released and in my arms. No matter how old my children are, I will always want to hold them and fight for them. I will always hold their hand and let them cry on my shoulder when needed. Which is what Grady is silently doing now.

We collect his things, including his phone, which we discovered now has a cracked screen that happened during the fight, and both Grady and I climb into the back seat of Barrett's pickup, and Grady immediately leans his head on me. The ride home is… well, interesting. Barrett is still quiet. Not angry quiet. Just quiet. The events of the night finally taking over, first the winning game, Bri's attack and getting arrested — it's all come to a head for Grady as he lays his head on my shoulder, his own shoulders shaking and holding me around the waist tightly. It's all enough to bring any teenage boy to his knees, and my Grady is no different. He is powerful, strong and brave, but put him up against the force of someone threatening to hurt the person he loved most in this world and it is all too much.

Barrett pulls into the driveway and parks, and we all somberly walk into the house, not quite ready to share our individual thoughts, one of which being, what will happen when his coach and the recruiters who have been calling find out. But that's neither here nor there right now. Tonight, we need to comfort our son.

"I need to call Bri." Grady's timid voice breaks through the silence as we all stand in the kitchen, none of us moving toward our bedrooms quite yet.

"She's fine, honey. Brandon got her home, and Cole checked on her," I reply with a soft voice.

"No, Mom. I need to call her. I need to hear her voice, to hear from her that she's fine. I know I got there in time, that he just—" He chokes on his voice and bites out his next words. "—hit her. But, Mom and Dad, you have no idea…" His voice trails off, and I can just see how much this is affecting him.

"Grady, I'm exhausted. This is by far not what we had planned for tonight, and before we sit down and hash everything out, I need sleep. I'm afraid I won't be the best listener right now, so I think it's best for everyone's sake if you go to your room, call Bri for your peace of mind, but don't talk long. Get a good night's sleep, and we'll talk in the morning." My husband's gruff voice sounds scratchy and tired.

And as much as I want more explanation from Grady right now, I have to admit he is right.

Whatever Grady hears in Barrett's voice makes him realize he better not argue. "I will, but, Dad, I know I said this, but you've gotta know… I'm so sorry. I would never hurt someone on purpose. I can't explain it, but I lost it. It's just seeing Bri, she's…"

"I get it, son. Bri. That's why I get it. You understand? That's also why I'm not yelling my lungs out right now, but it's never a good excuse. I want you to go to bed. Think about it. Think long and hard about your actions. We'll talk first thing in the morning. Don't make any plans tomorrow."

"Got it," Grady replies with a single head nod and hard swallow. The dark bags that have already developed under his eyes are the physical evidence of his own exhaustion, and cuts that cover his hands tell a story I'm sure none of us want to relive anytime soon.

"Grady. Shower first, yeah?"

That gets a small smile out of him. "Sure thing, Mom."

"Love you. Get some sleep."

"Love you, too."

Barrett walks over and gives Grady a hug before stepping back, keeping his hands on Grady's shoulders. "Love you, son. Never forget that." His voice is now less scratchy and far more firm.

"I won't, Dad. Love you, too. And again, I'm sorry. I know this isn't at all what you expected from tonight." Grady gives us another small smile then heads downstairs to his room and the bathroom he's claimed as his own.

Barrett's large frame sinks onto the kitchen chair as soon as Grady is out of sight, and his head goes straight to the table with a loud *thunk*, causing me to giggle. Probably not the right response right now, but the night has been one I never expected.

"Ahhh, hell, Tess."

"I know."

"What a screwed-up damn night. How do I even begin to discipline him for something that I would have done too?"

"What do you mean?"

"If that were us… if it would have been you being attacked by someone? I know I would have beat the shit out of him, too. Without a second thought. And probably not felt a damn bit sorry about it."

"I know, babe. I know. And I agree with you. But it doesn't make it okay."

"No. It doesn't." He sighs deeply and rubs the scruff on his face. "I wonder what kind of conversation Dawson's having with that prick of a father of his tonight."

"Oh crap. I didn't even think of him. How long do you think it will be before he beats down on our door?"

"Well, I guess it depends on what Dawson tells him. If he tells him the truth, then he won't show up. If he admits who beat him up but doesn't tell him the why, then he'll be showing up any time. My guess, though, is that even though Dawson's dad is a supreme asshole, he won't stand for him attacking a girl, so he's probably withheld that little tidbit of information."

"Well, if he shows up, he'll find out. No way am I gonna be able to hold back and not let him know what his son did."

He grins at me, shaking his head. "I know, mama bear. I know."

I roll my eyes at him. "Let's go to bed. I'm exhausted. You're exhausted. And if I know my sons, Cole will be here first thing in the morning, and Grady will be up at the crack of dawn, ready to explain."

"Sounds like a plan."

Chapter Ten

Barrett

I'VE HAD SOME crazy things happen as a parent. But none crazier than hearing my son was arrested at the same time I was about to finally have sex with my wife. If anyone ever says being a dad is easy, he's lying. Maybe deserves to have his nuts in a vice. Some days parenting sucks. It's hard as hell, frustrating, both discouraging and encouraging, but it's all worth it. It is. After last night, I have to remember why it's so worth it. Never in my life did I expect to receive a phone call like that.

It seems weird, but I almost have to be grateful. At least he had a decent reason to beat the crap out of that punk. Bri is like a daughter to me. The thought of someone doing anything to hurt her in any way angers me enough to make me want to go over to his house and have a few not-so-kind words.

After an insanely fitful night of sleep, I drag my old ass out of bed, feeling about ten years older than I did yesterday morning, and walk into the kitchen to start the coffee. A full pot. We are definitely going to need it. I turn my head when I hear shuffling feet moving across the dark wood floor and see my beautiful wife, sleep rumpled and stressed. She immediately walks over to where I'm impatiently waiting for the coffeepot to fill and wraps her tiny arms around my waist. She lays her head on my chest and sighs heavily.

I lean my head down and kiss her on my spot. "Morning, babe."

"Morning. That had to be the crappiest night of sleep I've had since we had infants in the house."

"Yup," I reply, no further explanation needed.

"Thanks for starting the coffee, honey."

"Any time. I have a feeling we're gonna need it today," I reply.

Just then the door to the basement opens, and not only Grady appears, but his older brother Cole as well. Not surprised. He probably headed out at the crack of dawn, getting here as soon as he could for Grady. And us, too. He's such a good kid, and I have no clue how that happened.

"Cole!" Tess excitedly runs over to her firstborn. He lifts her up slightly and hugs her close. He's my height now, and seeing her around her two boys, she looks so tiny.

Cole's dark hair is a little longer than normal, and he's grown an impressive amount of facial hair, sporting a full beard. He has on a plain, dark blue T-shirt, but what I keep focusing on are the many tattoos that are trailing down his arms. He's been busy, it seems, adding several more since he's been back in school. He'll be the scruffiest looking doctor.

I glance over at Grady to see him leaning against the doorway watching the two of them. The weight of the evening before is obviously heavy on all our hearts. The nervousness comes off Grady in waves as he shifts side to side on his feet, crossing and uncrossing his arms.

"Hey, Mom," Cole says as he clings tightly to her. He murmurs something to her, more than likely telling her to go easy on Grady, before releasing her back to the ground. She beams up at him, and I know her well enough to know that even with the reason he's here, she's still so happy to have him home.

The second Tess is on her feet she steps over to Grady, takes his face in her hands, and reaches up on her toes before kissing him on the cheek. "How are you, baby?"

"I'm good, Mom," he says, a slight smile to his face.

"Explain," she replies simply.

"I talked to Bri. She's good, she's not mad at me… just hearing her voice last night helped me relax. I know she's still upset about what Dawson did." He clenches his jaw, and I can see the anger boiling up inside once again. He shakes his head slightly and continues on. "I texted Coach last night already so he will see it first thing this morning. He texted back already. He's coming over here later to talk it all through. He'll get on the phone with the recruiters who have been calling, too. We'll get a plan together, but I wanted him to find out from me rather than through the chain of gossip that will be sure to fly around."

The pride I feel over the maturity my son has shown in the situation swells in my chest. I know this situation isn't good or ideal, but I'm glad to see he's thinking with his head. Unfortunately, I also need to be bad cop here. He needs to understand that fighting is never the right thing to do.

"Grady, have a seat, son. We need the details on last night. As happy as it makes me to hear that you've talked to Coach Mac already, there's more important things we need to worry about."

"I know, Dad," he says with a bit of annoyance in his voice.

"Do you? Do you understand what you did? You could

have ruined your entire future by acting before thinking. Why couldn't you have just left well enough alone?"

"You mean if someone had assaulted Mom at a party, and when you got to her she had a red mark on her face from him hitting her and was crying, that you'd 'just leave well enough alone' and walk away? Screw that. That's such bullshit, Dad, and you know it!"

"Hey, watch your mouth. And no, that's not what I mean. I wouldn't just walk away, but beating him to a pulp isn't the answer either. You could have pulled Bri away from the situation, away from Dawson…"

"Right. Just pulled her away from that prick and never said a word. Never even defended her? Do you realize what he could have done to her if I hadn't stepped in? What it looked like he planned to do?" His voice is pained, and I wish I could take away what he clearly keeps seeing in his eyes, his memories not fading away in the slightest.

"Grady, sweetie, what your dad is trying to say is there's always another option. Fighting isn't the be-all-end-all. I get that you were upset," she says but is interrupted by Grady's scoff, indicating he is a little more than upset. "But…" she says and gives him the eye, "…the main focus needed to be getting Bri away from Dawson."

"Yeah, I did that. I made sure she was safe. I put her in my car and had her girlfriends with her. I tried to get Brandon to stay with her, too, but he wasn't having it. He saw the whole thing go down, too, Mom. The prick got what was coming to him. I'm sorry you guys feel that I should have just walked away, but you have no idea what it was like there. No. Idea. He hurt her. He hurt my Bri. And yeah, I know exactly how that sounds, but screw it. I'm tired of not being honest about my feelings for her and, on that note, I'm not sorry that I hit him. There's not a chance in hell I'm going to apologize to the douche nozzle after what he did," he says with absolute certainty. He stands up, angrily shoves his chair back into the table, and storms off down to the basement.

We sit in silence, trying to fully understand what just happened. Grady seemed calm and relaxed and, suddenly, he stormed off. Damn teenagers and their hormonal ways.

Chapter Eleven

Tess

THE REST OF the day is… well, it's weird. Between the constant slamming doors by Grady, being graced with Eric, Dawson's horrible father's presence, the visit from Coach, and Bri not answering Grady's phone calls for some reason, we've had all the fun we can handle. Cole tried his best to be Switzerland. If he wasn't trying to stand up for Grady, he was trying to get him to understand our point of view.

The day goes back and forth from wonderful to crap and back to wonderful again.

Dawson's dad hadn't been told the entire story, no shocker there. When we politely informed him of the truth, he was less than impressed with his son's actions. Of course, he didn't believe us at first, but after a few phone calls, he got the picture, especially when he saw a picture of Bri and what his son had a hand in.

I should be used to the love I have for my husband, but seeing him stand toe to toe with that horrible man, standing up for our son — and for Bri — not backing down an inch, only made him even sexier, and I fell for him all over again. Something about my man going to bat for our children… it's just hot: his shoulders broad and strong, his square chiseled jaw clenched, those bright hazel eyes dark and stormy. My goodness, if the situation wasn't so serious, I would knock him down and straddle him right then.

When Maggie and Harper came home after their sleepovers, they were beyond excited to see Cole home. Harper jumped into his arms and has been clinging to him like a spider monkey since. Maggie hasn't left his side either, which means that all four of our kids have been stuck like glue to one another all day long, since Cole hasn't separated from Grady since they woke up this morning.

Grady called Maggie and explained everything to her, but we kept the details from Harper, only telling her what she needed to know, that her big brother stuck up for his best friend. She's not old enough to understand all of what has happened, and she adores Bri like a sister, so we didn't want her to worry. Grady wanted Maggie to hear it from him, not only knowing how much Bri means to Maggie, but also because word will be around school on Monday, and probably sooner, thanks to social media.

Barrett left for about an hour today to get Grady's screen replaced. While he was at the cellular store, he was informed that we could update ours. I think he needed the break away from the house and all the drama, a chance to clear his head, so I told him to go ahead and switch ours over to the newer versions, knowing it would give him more time away from the house. Of course, no doubt because of our old age senility, we messed things up during setup and now somehow keep receiving each other's texts. We are both way too technically challenged, as is obvious by our texting issues. I'm sure Grady or Maggie can figure out how to get our phones back to normal, but for today, I'm just too wiped out to care, and we both need to focus on the family. Besides, it's not like either of us have anything to hide, so receiving each other's texts isn't that big of a deal. Stupid Cloud. Who understands it anyway?

This evening we are having a family night. A much-needed, long-overdue family night. We order pizza, grab a bunch of snacks and some soda, and head into the family room, where Harper and Maggie have already picked out a couple of movies for us to watch. Barrett sits down on the large, dark brown sectional in one of the seats that doubles as a recliner. Maggie saddles up next to him while the boys stretch out in the other recliners. Harper makes herself comfortable on Cole's lap, still not letting the poor guy out of her sight for more than a few minutes at a time, and I sit on one of the corner seats. Barrett and I are nowhere near each other. Again.

The first of the two movies comes to a close, and Harper didn't make it to the ending credits before falling asleep. She's dead on her feet, so Cole picks her up and carries her to her bedroom. Barrett glances over at me with raised eyebrows and says, "See how easy that is?"

Is it right to want to gut check your husband? Probably not, but that's my initial reaction. I'm sure he didn't mean it to be rude or hurtful, but hurt doesn't even begin to describe what those five words do to me. I don't even know why. It's true. It's not hard to bring Harper to her room. What hurts is that he acts as if it's all on me.

Just last night we were back to ourselves, and now it's like we took a hundred steps backward. How can we go from forgiving and loving toward each other to this? The day has been a bundle of stress, but that's when we should lean on each other, not pick each other apart.

"Did *you* see how easy that is?" I smart back.

I notice Maggie and Grady are looking back and forth between us and can see the concern flashing in their eyes. We know the kids need to see a real marriage, which includes disagreements, but what they don't need to see is their parents being plain nasty to each other, so before it can escalate into something far worse than those few words, I turn my attention toward the TV and try to focus on whatever family movie the girls chose for round two.

After we've finished watching the movies, the entire family stands up to head to their rooms. I know Grady will flip his top if Bri doesn't answer the phone soon, so am not surprised in the least when he asks if it's okay if he and Cole head out to check on her. Maggie says she's tired and heads to bed, and Barrett says he's going to let the dogs out, leaving me to clean up the empty pizza boxes, chip bags, soda cans, water glasses, and all the paper plates and napkins. Apparently, no one had a single thought of possibly helping good old mom out.

I finish cleaning up, check the coffeepot to get it ready for the next morning, and shuffle my way to bed, only to be greeted by Barrett's light snoring. Just great.

I get ready for bed, which takes way longer than it used to. Some nights I'm so tired and dread the thought of all that it entails to get ready: washing my face, brushing my teeth, applying ointments and creams and lotions. It's like a strange science experiment I have to conduct on my face every night. In the middle of my bedtime regimen, I hear my phone chirp with an incoming text, so before I settle into bed for the night, I check my phone, only for my heart to nearly stop.

Thanks to somehow goofing up our sending and receiving of texts, I received one of Barrett's. Only I am fairly positive this one I'm not meant to read. So much for neither of us having anything to hide.

> **Keri Office:** *Thought you'd like to see what you were missing tonight.*

Followed by a picture of who I assume is Keri, since I've never actually met her. But now I've seen her. Naked. Well, basically naked. It's of her with no top on, her one arm stretched over her chest barely covering her perky bits. Her slim, toned stomach on full display, and I'm sure if the camera view would have allowed it, I'd have gotten a good look at her southern region too. Yay.

I stare, dumbfounded. My eyes well with tears before I can stop them. A loud sob erupts from my throat that I don't even try to catch. With shaky hands, I put my phone down and stare at it.

What the hell do I do?

That question flits through my mind for about 0.4 seconds before I pick my phone back up again. Then with some clarity that comes from somewhere magical, I walk over to the door to our bedroom and lock it so Harper isn't able to sneak in. Then I turn back around and chuck the stupid phone at a sleeping Barrett's chest. I watch as he hastily wakes up and looks around the room in complete confusion as to why he was just pelted with a cell phone during his sleep.

"What the hell?" he grumbles.

"What the hell? What the hell? I'll tell you what the hell! Look at the phone, Barrett! You had the balls to sit there and tell me that she was nothing but an office manager and that!? What the hell is right!" I whisper scream, my voice coming out like that of a pubescent teenager, my words barely making any sense.

He sticks a finger in his ear and wiggles it a bit. "Tess, when you scream in such a high-pitch voice that only dogs can hear, I don't understand a word of it. Now, what the hell is going on?"

"Look at your phone you… you… you liar!" Nice one. "Remember how we have been receiving each other's texts all day? Well, it totally screwed you over, buddy." I cross my arms to keep my pounding heart from exploding through my chest, which it feels like it could do at this very moment, as upset as I am.

He glances down with confusion then swipes my phone to wake it up. I hadn't cleared out of my messaging app, so it's right there for him to see. He drops the phone like it's acid and quickly scampers away from it and is in front of me faster than a man of his size should be capable of.

"Oh shit, Tess," he says reaching for me.

I shrug away quickly and cross my arms tighter. "Oh shit is right."

"No, you don't understand. Not oh shit that I got caught — oh shit that it was absolutely not meant for me. I guarantee you I have never, ever, ever received or sent any texts to Keri like that. Go through my past texts from her. I promise. You'll see nothing but work related stuff." He reaches back onto the bed and picks up the phone before shoving it at my chest so I'm forced to take it. It feels like hot lava in my hands.

I look up at Barrett, stare into his hazel eyes that are brimming with concern and, dare I say, honesty. He takes a deep breath and holds my face in his big hands. "Tess. You know me. Look in my eyes. You know my heart. It holds you.

It holds the kids. That's it. You know how my mind works. Trust yourself. There's no way I could ever possibly have eyes for another woman. I swear. I swear on our kids' lives, on your life, on our lives together that never has anything inappropriate happened with Keri or anyone else. It has to be a mistake. She had texted me earlier today about being able to find some sort of special stamp made for the mailers we send out around Christmas."

"Barrett, I'm just…"

I'm interrupted by my phone chirping and see another text from Keri come through. I look down at my phone with panic racing through my entire body. I feel like there's hot pokers slicing into my skin and fire in my veins. With freakishly steady hands, I lift my phone and swipe it to open the message just as it chirps five more times in a row.

> **Keri Office:** *OH MY GOSH! DELETE DELETE DELETE DELETE I'm SO SORRY – DELETE, please!!!*
>
> **Keri Office:** *I'm so embarrassed.*
>
> **Keri Office:** *Please tell me you didn't see that. I meant to send it to my boyfriend Kade. I have no idea how I sent it to you.*
>
> **Keri Office:** *I'm SO SO SORRY!! Did you delete? Please tell me I'm not fired.*
>
> **Keri Office:** *Please tell me you didn't see it and also that I'm not fired.*

> *Keri Office:* *Did I mention that I'm sorry? And super embarrassed?*

Well, she's either scared that I will see the text first, or she genuinely screwed up and accidentally sent the text to Barrett. Just as I'm about to open my mouth another text comes through.

> *Josh:* *Ummmm ok, I'm gonna do my best to pretend this never happened.*

> *Keri Office:* *I'm so embarrassed.*

> *Josh:* *You mentioned that.*

> *Josh:* *Honestly, Keri. Forget it. Barrett and I won't mention it again if you don't.*

> *Keri Office:* *Deal. Barrett? Maybe you never saw it. **crosses fingers***

I start to hand over the phone to Barrett with a huff and a roll of my eyes when I see his slightly smug expression on his face. He moves to his nightstand and grabs his phone to text her back, and I watch as his fingers move across the screen. Because my phone is still receiving everything, his reply comes through on my phone as well.

> *Barrett:* *It's ok, Keri. Never happened. Deleted and forgotten*

> *Keri Office:* *Thank you. I'm so sorry, again.*

I swear that was an accident

Barrett: *Figured as much. No worries*

Josh: *See? Nothing happened*

A few seconds later another text from Josh comes through the screen. This time, not from the group text that I didn't realize it was earlier.

Josh: *Holy shit. How am I supposed to look her in the eye on Monday?*

Josh: *Oh bollocks! I hope that Tess didn't see that and it cause problems for you two after she was already questioning who Keri was.*

Josh: *She'd know it was an accident, right?*

Barrett looks up at me since I'm still reading everything on the screen. I roll my eyes again and mutter, "Fine. You were right. I'm sorry. But I had reason to question."

"You're right. You did. But you also didn't. Tess, do you have that little trust in me?"

He quickly fires off a text to Josh saying that they will talk later and throws our phones on the bed before shifting his focus back on me.

"I'm waiting, Tess. Do. You. Not. Trust. Me? I've only been one-hundred-percent faithful to you for... oh, I don't know, twenty-seven years now. It's probably been my fault. What with giving you so many reasons to question my loyalty and all," he says irritably.

"I'm sorry, okay? I know I jumped to conclusions, but with everything that's been happening over the last week, do you blame me?"

"Truthfully, yeah, I do," he says, looking and sounding irritated. "Tess, what does this say about us if you immediately assume the worst? That you don't even take the time to ask me what that could have been about?"

I blow out a frustrated breath just as I hear a loud bang against the door and the soft whimpers of a child. I open the door to see Harper sitting on her butt, staring at the door and holding her forehead.

"Why is your door closed? And locked?" she mutters, looking up at the both of us from the floor. She looks adorably frumpled.

Barrett steps around me and swiftly picks her up and starts walking back to her room. "Because, baby girl, you need to stay in your own bed. Mommy and Daddy need to talk… about your Christmas present."

The liar. But it must work. I hear him murmuring softly to her followed by the quiet click of her door shutting. Soon he's coming back into our room and shuts the door again. His shoulders lift as he takes a deep breath and blows it out before turning around and facing me with his hands on his hips. He looks enormous. And angry.

"Tess. I'm going to ignore this. I'm going to do what Keri pleaded with us to do and forget it ever happened. I'm going to get back into bed, pull you close, and go back to sleep. You know why I'm going to do that?"

I shake my head from side to side, frozen in my spot.

"I'm going to do that because if I don't, all we're going to do is argue. And I'm tired of arguing over the same damn thing all the time. I'm tired, Tess. You know the truth in your heart. Reach for it."

"You're right." I sniffle. "I know I'm just being paranoid and letting trouble in."

"You are. And it ends, now. Alright?"

I take a deep breath and nod my head as I reach for him and wrap my arms around his waist and give him a tight hug. I kiss his chest and mumble, "Alright. Got it."

He sighs heavily and kisses the top of my head. "Good. Now get your ass in bed. We're going to lie down together, I'm going to wrap my arms around you, and we're going to sleep. We've had a really lousy weekend, and we need the rest."

We settle in and, even though I can tell that neither of us are over it, that neither of us are going to sleep peacefully, at least we do it not angry. At least we do it in each other's arms.

Chapter Twelve

Barrett

If the past weekend wasn't insane enough to begin with, Andy and his boys are moving in temporarily today. While I'm happy to help out, I'm also on edge. Our family hasn't exactly had a great few weeks, and things with Tess and I are just… well, they're not at our best right now. I wish I could go back about five months and remove the damn blinders that both of us were wearing so we could see what was happening, but I can't. It's almost as if our Friday night interruption and then what happened with Grady just amplified everything, set us back by years. I feel so disconnected from her. In all our years together, even when we were young and still new in our relationship, she's never questioned me. Never questioned my faithfulness. She always trusted me. To feel like I'm losing that trust, quite frankly, pisses me off.

Lately, if it's not about the kids or our jobs, then we stare blankly at each other or down at our phones. Allowing the almighty electronic distraction to take over our marriage is sad. But it's way more than that. About four months ago, Tess chose going to a design show over being home and celebrating MaryEllen's years of service with us. If I had to be honest, that's when it changed. I don't blame her. I blame myself for telling her I didn't care. I think, in the end, I hurt us both. I cared. I just didn't want her to miss out on something important to her. And she was hurt that I said I didn't care. So, we both shut down.

And the result?

This.

Our living hell.

> **My Girl:** *Did you get the air mattresses pulled out of the closet in the basement for the boys?*

> **Me:** *Of course.*

I imagine her wince at my short response and it breaks my heart but I can't seem to snap out of it.

> **My Girl:** *Just asking.*

> **Me:** *Ok.*

> **My Girl:** *I'm going to make French dip sandwiches for supper tonight. It's Andy's favorite.*

I stare down at my phone for an absurd amount of time. Pouting like a ridiculous grown-ass man. I can't remember the last time she made my favorite meal. And why the hell does she even know what Andy's favorite meal is. Should I be concerned about that?

I spend the day stewing over her last text to me — again— because I'm pouting and can't seem to snap out of it. I didn't even reply to her because I was just irritated. The fact that she is concerned over Andy's well-being and wants to make him comfortable in our home is, in truth, very considerate and one of the things that made me fall in love with her. However, the fact that she is concerned over Andy and hasn't seemed to be concerned over me for the last few months has me beyond irked. Add that to the fact that I'm still a little raw from her accusing me of basically the same thing with Keri, and I'm in a piss-poor mood, snapping at everyone who crosses my path. By the end of the day, Josh blatantly tells me to get the hell out of the office. It's close to quitting time anyway, but I think he's just had enough of me.

Which was fine by me.

Trying to ignore the fact that Keri had texted us a picture of her boobs — or well, part of her boobs, anyway—was proving much more difficult than we imagined. I walked into the office this morning to find Josh huddled over his computer with a cup of coffee from Christine's coffee shop, telling me one thing. He didn't want to make coffee in the shop this morning, like he does every other day. When I walked in and set my stuff on the desk next to him, he jumped about a foot out of his seat and clenched his heart like he was about to have a heart attack.

"Holy shit, you scared the crap out of me. I thought you were Keri," he breathes out.

I laugh out loud at him while he scowls at me. "It's not funny, jackhole! You try standing out there. It's awkward as hell. Did you see she wore a turtleneck today? Like she's trying to not give us any more visuals than she already did."

"Josh, you ass, it was an accident."

"An accident that we were on the unfortunate end of. I

heard Tess was the one who saw it first," he said, admitting what I already knew — that Tess and Lauren had talked about everything already.

"Yeah, it wasn't good. But she knows it was just an accident and one I'm forgetting ever happened. As in ever. As in, we will never speak of it again," I say with as much conviction in my voice as possible.

"Oh, thank goodness!" The sound of Keri's voice causes me to scream — like a total girl — and almost lose my hold on my own coffee cup. (I brought mine from home, thank you very much. Even though I, too, usually made it at the shop.) I look over and see Josh smirking at me. The ass.

It's early evening and I know I need to go straight home. Yet, I don't. I text Tess and let her know that I won't be home for dinner and not to wait for me. I'll either eat late or grab something on my own. She asks me what's going on, but I don't respond to that text either. I feel so irritated with life, and I know myself well enough to know it's best to just step away for a few hours and sort myself out.

I'm sitting in my pickup in the parking lot at the docks, staring out at the lake. My thoughts are running away from me, and I'm getting myself worked up over nothing. Suddenly, a knock sounds on my window, causing me to jump and let out a very manly scream. I look to my left and see Cole standing there with a giant smile on his face, clearly happy and impressed with himself that he was able to scare his dad. He rounds the hood and opens the passenger door before climbing in.

"What's wrong, old man? Did something frighten you?" He laughs.

"You punk." I laugh in return and lightly hit his chest.

"What are you doing here?"

"Looking for you."

"Clearly, smart ass. May I ask why you're looking for me?"

"You may." He smirks. He thinks he's a funny man.

Normally I would agree. Today? Not sure yet.

"Alright, bud, I'll play. Why are you looking for me?"

"Mom."

I divert my eyes from his intense stare-down. I don't know when my twenty-year-old became the rock of this family, but it's been clear the last few days that's happened.

"Why aren't you back at school yet? I thought you could only stay away from classes today? Don't you need to be back for classes in the morning?"

"Nice diversion, Dad. Yeah, I'm leaving soon. I'll get in a little later, but that's okay."

"I don't like you driving so late this time of year. Especially with Mia in the car with you. The weather can be tricky, you know?"

"Don't worry about that. I'll be fine. And I would never put her in danger. You know that. What I worry about is you and Mom. I've never seen you two like this. And tonight? You don't come home for supper? What gives?"

I wonder how real I can get with my son. He's an adult, but still. Pretty sure he doesn't want to hear that his mom and dad have lost touch, and they haven't had sex in a while, and now his dad's having panic attacks because he can't get his life in grips. All because of sex. As dumb as that sounds, it's part of what makes —or breaks— a marriage, and not feeling physically connected to Tess has made me feel detached everywhere else. It's a snowball effect, and it seems to be building fast.

"Nothing gives, Cole. Just needed to do some thinking."

"About…" he prompts.

"Life," I answer absently, not a total lie, staring out the front windshield.

"Dad. Come on. What is going on? Grady, Maggie… they tell me stuff, you know? They see it, Dad. Hell, I saw it when we were watching movies!"

I try to sidestep everything he's saying. "Oh yeah? And what is it they see? Or think they see?"

"So I see we're gonna play the runaround game, huh? Dad. You and Mom. You're not yourselves. It's not like we think you're gonna get a divorce or anything crazy like that, but we know you're not as tight as normal. Grady and Mags tell me how every morning when they wake up they see that Harper has ended up in your bed at night. They tell me how you guys never sit and cuddle anymore in the mornings when you drink your coffee, and how it's been months since you've been on a date. They never see you guys sit on the couch together and watch movies anymore, or share a bowl of ice cream. Dad, I'm gonna repeat… what's going on?"

My stare out the front windshield never wavers, but I can feel my oldest son's eyes on me. His all-knowing, all-seeing eyes. One part of me is happy that my kids notice a difference in their mom and dad's behavior. It shows that — well, until recently — we've shown the kids what it is to be in love. I'm glad that my kids have seen it from us and recognize the difference. The other part of me is scared shitless that it's gotten so bad between Tess and me that the kids notice it.

"Dad," Cole pushes.

"Cole. Buddy, I don't know…" I sigh then take a deep breath before looking at him. "I wish I did. I'm not going to lie to you. Things aren't normal with your mom and me right now. No, we are in no way even contemplating a divorce or anything close to it but yes, we are feeling a bit… muddled. It's been a long time since we've had time to ourselves, but I don't want you to worry about it. It's just a busy time for us right now. With Grady's football, Maggie's volleyball, and Harper busy with her horse-riding lessons and just being an all-around pain in the ass when it comes to sleeping, we've had much on our minds. Not to mention, both of us have this thing we call jobs. Takes quite a bit out of us old people," I say with a smile I know doesn't reach my eyes but hope it will lighten the mood. It doesn't work.

"I don't understand why Harp isn't in her own bed," he says, going for the most obvious snafu in our dilemma.

"Oh, she starts there. She just runs her tiny butt into our room every single night."

"That ain't right, Dad."

"No kidding," I scoff.

"Dad," he says quietly.

I sit, silent, thinking about everything that I just told my son. My son. I'm a moron.

"Dad," Cole says, louder this time.

"Yeah?"

"Here's the deal. You and Mom need to get away. Not just going to dinner or a movie by yourselves. Like actually get away where you have time to be together."

My son. I'm a moron, and he's a genius.

"Right. And who's going to take care of the kids? Not to mention that we can't just leave with everything going on with Grady."

"Grady's fine, Dad. Bri's fine. Dawson isn't pressing charges because… well, because Bri set his dumb ass straight.

Lauren, Josh... they'll help. You know they will. Just, I was home for three days, and I could see it. You guys need some time together to sort it out. Dad, you've gotta do something to shake it up," he says completely serious before his grin turns mischievous. "And... now that I feel a crazy amount of weird for talking to you about all of this, I'm going to get out here, head home, and grab my stuff to head back to school. You need to get home, too."

"I know, kid, I will."

"Like, soon, yeah? Mom looked broken at dinner tonight without you there." He finished the last sentence in a much quieter, deeper voice than I'd heard from him before. And if the desired effect was to break my heart and wrench my gut, he achieved it.

He gets out and slams the door shut, but a second later the door opens back up, and Cole pops his head in with a shit-eating grin on his face before dropping the bomb of all bombs. "Oh, and do it now. Remember, I'm bringing Mia home for Thanksgiving, and I want you guys all better by then."

My eyebrows furrow in confusion, and my mouth opens, closes, opens, and finally my voice emerges in a whisper and gradually turns into a somewhat girly shriek. "Mia? Mia *Mia?* As in... MIA!? Cole! Mia is who you're bringing home?"

His response? His smile only widens before he closes the door and raps on the hood of the pickup a couple times like he hadn't just told me something epic, as the kids call it. I'm staring dumbfounded, watching as walks to his car, my mouth hanging open. He shoots me a wide grin over the top of his car before sliding in and driving away.

And then I remember that Josh and Lauren are going to Arizona to visit her parents for the holiday. It all makes sense. Mia and Cole make total sense. They're both pre-med — well, sort of, she's going to school to be an OB nurse. And they're both amazing kids. Suddenly, I can't wait to get home. I have some incredible news that Tess will want to hear, and I get to be the one to give it to her. To see her smile at me.

On my way home, I call Tess's brother James to see if he is willing to come over for the week and watch the kids. Of course, he agrees, which I expected. I'm surprised he hasn't just moved back closer to home yet. I think he's fighting off the inevitable. I pull in the driveway and park in my spot in the garage then step inside the house. A plate of leftovers is in the microwave, and I don't see anyone around. In fact, the house seems oddly quiet. But it's almost eight, so I assume the kids are either doing their homework or watching TV in the basement. Then I hear voices coming from the living room. I step closer and realize it's Tess and Andy. They're both sitting on the large, chocolate-brown sectional.

I feel like a creeper as I stand on the other side of the doorway that leads into the living room behind the wall so they can't see me but I can hear them. I don't even know why.

"You're a great guy, Andy. What she did has nothing to do with you."

"I get what you're saying, but what you don't realize is that we completely lost focus on each other. I don't remember the last time we were together alone or made time for one another. We just fell apart, never took the time to be together anymore. Everything was all about the boys or the house or what we needed to do with our jobs.

"We just completely lost focus with each other and, dammit all, I know I'm the one who forgot to treat her like she was still my wife, as if she was still my girlfriend. We forgot how to date each other and how to be there for one another. We forgot how to be just us.

"I don't know, Tess. I don't know if our marriage could've been saved or not, but all I know is that somewhere along the line we forgot why we fell in love with each other in the first place. We forgot that we were a couple before we were parents. We forgot that we were a couple before we had all this other stuff that goes along with getting older and growing up. I don't know if we could've made anything different, or if there is anything that could have changed to salvage our marriage."

"Andy—"

I hear Tess's voice break through. She's crying. *Crying.* My heart breaks a little more than it had been already.

"—I'm so scared."

"Tess, there's nothing to be scared about. What's done is done. I hate that it happened but…"

"No, you don't understand. I'm sad for you, but I can tell you're pulling through. But, what you're saying right now. It's what's happening to Barrett and me."

My heart stopped. Then started beating so loudly that I could hear it pounding in my ears.

"Tess… no."

"It is. I don't remember the last time that we went on a date, cuddled on the couch together to watch a movie after the kids went to bed, had a conversation about anything but the kids or our jobs. He used to plan things for us, surprise me for lunch, or bring me a coffee. I feel like I'm just a partner now. I don't feel like his wife. I used to walk in a room, and his eyes would light up. Now we hardly acknowledge one another. I don't even remember the last time that Barrett kissed me just to kiss me… unless he thinks it will lead to sex…"

Her voice trails off as I take a few staggering steps back, taking in everything that I've just heard. None of this is shocking, I just had this same conversation with my own son. But hearing it from her mouth has a much stronger effect on me.

I stand in the doorway, listening to Andy talk to my wife. Listening to Tess's response. I feel like I am on the outside looking in, and someone is explaining what is happening in our marriage. My gut clenches at the thought of her feeling less than anything but the love of my life. How did this happen between us? Did I pull away first, or did she? Or did it just happen because we both forgot to care? Forgot to put effort into each other and started to take the other for granted?

At that moment, I know. I know I have to do something drastic, and if I don't do something to make a change now, our marriage will crumble underneath us before we can even catch up.

I fell in love with Tess when I was seventeen, and I still am. Always will be. I forgot to show her that I'm in love her, but that ends now.

I notice that I don't hear talking anymore. I look into the living room, and what I see makes my blood boil. All thoughts of calm and reason and understanding fly right out the window.

Andy.

My friend.

Has.

His.

Hands.

Around.

My wife.

What. The. Hell?

In the back of my mind I know nothing is happening. But I'm raw and, quite honestly, sad from everything that I heard her say about how I make her feel.

I storm into the living room and grab Andy by the shoulder with such force that, when I pull him away from Tess, his back hits the wall. Immediately I'm on him, pressing him harder against the wall with my forearm against his chest.

"Barrett, what the hell is wrong with you?!" Tess screams in my ear, tugging me back away from him, but I only move a few steps.

"What's wrong with me? What's wrong with you? And you—" I point to Andy. "What in the ever-loving hell do you think you're doing?"

"Barrett, calm down."

"No. I will NOT calm down, Tess. You and I haven't been together in months! MONTHS! And you make Andy's favorite dinner, which I don't even want to know how you know what that is. And then… then, you allow him to have his hands all over you!? You confided in him!"

I'm beyond pissed off at this point, my own head getting in the way of everything I know to be true.

"Barrett. Man. You know I would never. And I mean *never* step across the line. Tess was giving me a hug. A hug.

That's it. Nothing more. Nothing less. And she asked me today what my favorite meal was. That's how she knew. She wanted us to feel welcome here tonight. I promise you. That's all that was."

I'm having a hard time calming myself down, so I sit on the edge of the chaise lounge attached to the sectional. My elbows on my knees, I take several deep breaths in and out as I try to regain my breathing.

I didn't need to hear Andy's explanation. I already knew nothing was happening. It's just seeing another man console your wife sucks. Hearing it sucks enough, but seeing it threw my heart and head into overdrive.

"Barrett, what happened between Heather and me, man… It's not something I would ever put on another person. I love you guys. I feel so damn grateful to have your friendship and support. If my being here is a problem, I can easily go stay with Lauren and Josh. Truly, no hard feelings. The boys just thought it'd be cool to hang with Grady for the week until our new place is ready."

I look up at my friend and shake my head. "No, man, it's cool. I trust you. I do. I just got a little out of my head for a second. I'm sorry."

"No reason to apologize. I get it. Trust me, I'm such a live wire lately that I get it probably better than anyone."

"Thank you," I tell him sincerely as I stand up to shake his hand.

"You're welcome. I'm gonna head down to the shower and get the beds ready for me and the boys."

"Yeah, okay. I'm sorry again. I meant what I said when I told you I trust you."

"I appreciate that," he says before turning and walking away. "Night, Tess. Thank you for dinner tonight. It was great."

Tess has been standing a few feet away from me, not scared but just taking it all in. "You're welcome, Andy. If you guys need more towels or sheets or pillows, or whatever, they're in the hall closet in the basement. Make yourself at home."

"You got it."

I hear his footsteps fade away before I dare look up at Tess. She's standing in front of me now, looking down at me with her eyebrows raised.

"Care to explain?" she asks me, pointing toward the door that Andy just walked through.

I shrug my shoulders as I sit back down.

"Barrett, I don't tolerate our children responding with just a shoulder shrug, and I won't allow it with you, either. Tell me. What was going through your head just now?" she asks angrily.

"I love you" is my only response.

Her eyes soften, and she takes a seat next to me. I scoot over to accommodate her. She rests her small hand on my knee and squeezes lightly. Her voice softens as she tells me firmly, "I love you."

I look over at her, vulnerability written all over her face.

"I'm sorry, Tess. The last few months are catching up on both of us, I guess. Now I know how you felt when you brought up Keri to me. Man, Tess, I know better. What the hell?" I ask as I pull at my hair in frustration.

She chuckles knowingly. "I know you do. And I did, too. It's just that devil sitting on your shoulder whispering words of doubt into your ear. Trust me, I get it. It's annoying as hell, huh?"

I laugh humorlessly. "You can say that again."

"It's annoying as hell, huh?" she says with the cheesiest comeback known to man.

This time my laugh is genuine. I drape my arm around her neck and pull her in to me and kiss the top of her head then breathe her in deeply. For some reason she smells like bacon. "I'm sorry, pretty girl. I trust you, too. I promise. Why do you smell like bacon?"

She doesn't even flinch at my weird question. "For some reason Andy likes bacon on his French dip sandwiches. I went with it," she says then sighs. "Barrett, we need to fix us," she whispers.

I stand up and walk over to the hope chest that sits in the corner. I reach my hand out to her. "I have an idea," I say. "Will you come over here? Please?"

She stands up and walks over to me. We both have a seat in front of the chest full of memories as I lift the lid. The smell of our past assaults us both, and I smile over at her before I reach in for what I'm looking for.

I pull out several photo albums and prepare to remind her of the life we built together.

Chapter Thirteen

Tess

Seeing the anger in Barrett's eyes when he came in and saw me — completely innocently — hugging Andy took me by complete shock. I've never seen him like that before, and suddenly I can completely picture Grady losing it. Although Grady had a much better reason behind it, I also understand that Barrett has no patience for another man touching me. I don't want another woman touching Barrett, so I need to be understanding.

I also feel awful. Barrett said I confided in Andy, and I had. I told Andy things that I should have been talking to Barrett about — months ago, if I'm being honest with myself. I haven't been up front about everything with Barrett, but now he knows. Not that it was the right way for him to learn that, but still, he knows.

When he walks over to the hope chest, I know exactly what he's planning. A walk down memory lane. And I can't agree more. We need to get back to what made us fall in love and remind each other that nothing is going to get in our way again. No one can come between us.

He pulls out all the photo albums that are in the chest and riffles through them until he finds the beginning.

"You ready?" he asks me. And I know what he's asking. He's asking if I'm ready for the emotional toll that this will take.

"Yes," I reply firmly.

The first photo album he opens is full of us in high school.

"Look at your hair!" He laughs. It was so awesome. The big hair, the amount of Aqua Net we went through, the neon clothes. All the tight jeans, stonewash, jean jackets. The ugly sweaters the guys wore and their mullets. It's so ugly that it's awesome.

"I loved my hair that way. I thought I was smoking hot," I say, smiling at the memories.

"You *were* smoking hot. Hottest girl in school," he says, smiling also.

I gasp as I point out a picture to him of us in the hallway. I remember his friend David was on the newspaper and yearbook committee, and he took it. We were standing in the senior class hallway by his locker. I'm smiling up at him, and he's looking down at me, his hand on my waist and my hands on his chest. I was so happy in that moment. No one could have swiped the smile from my face. "Your letterman's jacket. Remember that thing? Man, I felt like I'd just won a million dollars when you asked me to wear it. I remember walking into school that first day, and I wanted every single girl there to see I had Barrett Ryan's jacket on," I tell him, my voice all swoony.

"You're such a dork. It was so huge on you, remember that? But I loved seeing you wear it. I wonder where it is now?"

"At Mom and Dad's." I smile at him, which he returns, but his is better because it's followed up with a wink.

He smiles again, knowing his wink does it for me, then points to another picture of us, me in his red and black Bobcats football jersey. By the looks of these pictures, I never wore my own clothes. It was after the homecoming game of our junior year. The night that he took me home from school and asked me to wear his jersey for the first time. He looks so much like Grady in these pictures. I'm smiling up at Barrett the same way Bri does to Grady. It may sound dumb, and I absolutely could be wrong considering they're so young, and I don't want it to happen for several years, but I see their future plain as I saw ours in those days. I never had love for any other man but him. Once we began dating, neither of us looked any other way but forward. Together.

"That picture right there. I was so damn proud whenever you wore my jersey but especially that first night. When I saw you after the game and knew you'd been in the stands cheering for me, wearing my number…" He shakes his head and grins at me then leans down and kisses me square on the lips before sitting back. "…man, I felt like I was on top of the world."

"When Lauren picked me up for the game that night and I was wearing your jersey, her jaw about fell on her lap. You couldn't erase the smile from my face if you tried."

Lauren's eyes are wide as she points to the jersey I'm wearing. "Tess! Oh my goodness, girl. When did this happen?! You're wearing Barrett Ryan's jersey? Barrett. Ryan! Seriously, this is so. Totally. Awesome! How did you get his jersey? Why are you wearing it? What does it mean?"

Lauren asks me question after question, but all I can do is smile. I can't believe it myself.

"He waited for me after the pep rally and drove me home,

remember? After he walked me to the door, he asked me to wear it and pulled it off his back right there on my door step. I almost fainted, Lauren! He's so-o-o hot!"

"I kept wanting to look up in the stands to make sure you were there and that you were wearing my jersey. I knew, though, if I saw you, I wouldn't be able to focus on the game. I just kept counting the minutes until the game was over so I could see you," he says, the memory surfacing to the front of our minds. "Some days it feels like yesterday, you know?"

"I know what you mean. Time has gone so fast, right?"

"It really has."

We spend the next four hours sitting on the area rug that covers the floor of the living room, pouring over old pictures of our lives together. Whoever says that teenage love can't last can kiss it. The evidence of our love, that started so young but built over time, is right here in these books, staring back at us.

Our first prom together... that strapless, bright, sequined, purple, tea-length prom dress. There was a huge ruffle of material that went up the side. It was so beautiful then. My hair was enormous... I'm surprised a bird didn't nest in it.

Our first summer together... when we first exchanged "I love yous."

Our senior year of high school... So many memories wrapped up in that year. So many firsts.

Our years in college... Barrett wanted to play college football so badly, but it just wasn't in the cards for him. He ended up going to a two-year junior college because all he could see for himself was becoming an entrepreneur, and he didn't want to *"waste time in school."* I went to the same junior college and studied design. I knew I wanted to be an interior designer, but we both wanted to stay in our small town.

Even though my mom was healthy, I still wanted to be close to her. We were small-town people deep in our hearts, and we just couldn't imagine making our home in any other small town than the one we both grew up in, and fell in love with each other in. I saw marriage and motherhood more than bright city lights or a big career.

Our wedding... My dress was enormous. So. Much. Fabric. And the butt bow? Wow. As much as I would change the fashion of the day, I wouldn't change a single other thing. Our happiness was what I remember.

I am hanging on to my dad's arm behind the closed doors of the church. My dress hangs heavily on my body, but I don't care. I love it. The puffy sleeves sit wide on my bare shoulders, the bodice a beautiful, delicate lace. The satin skirt bells out widely, making me feel like a princess. The train that trails behind me is long and sprinkled with lace and pearl bead detail throughout, giving it a romantic and soft shimmer. Everyone told me that I shouldn't wait to see Barrett until I walk down the aisle. That we needed to have pictures taken care of beforehand so that our guests won't have to wait on us at the reception.

Barrett said he didn't care what is better for our guests. "You're not taking that away from me. I want to be standing at the end of the aisle waiting for her to take my name when I see her for the first time. It probably sounds stupid, but I've imagined it a thousand times in my head, and that's how it's going to be," he said to my parents then walked out of the room like the discussion was closed.

My mom looked at me and said, "Okay then." And,

apparently, the discussion was, in fact, closed.

"You ready for this, princess?"

"You know it, Daddy. Get me to Barrett."

He chuckles. "You know, you could at least make it a little easier on your dad. It appears you can't wait to take someone else's name. I think I made it clear to you when you were younger that you were never allowed to do that." Tears shine brightly in his eyes, and he reaches over and hugs me tightly. "Tess, baby girl, I wouldn't let you take anyone else's name. Barrett is a good man. I'm so proud of you both and can't wait to officially call him son."

I swallow hard several times and pull back away from him, tears gently trickling down my cheeks. "I love you so much, Daddy."

"I love you, too, princess. Now let's make you a Ryan."

I hear the traditional wedding march begin on the piano, going against the traditional organ, and my heart beats wildly.

Daddy whispers, "No more tears. We got this," and I look over at him as he nods his head, his eyes still shining with tears. I squeeze his arm tightly, and he places his large hand over my own as he takes a deep breath.

The church doors swing open to reveal my future. The ends of the pews and altar are decorated with tulle and bright blue flowers. Our friends are standing around the decorations, the girls in their giant blue bridesmaid dresses, the groomsmen in their black tuxes. But that's not what I am seeing. My eyes focus in on Barrett, and I see nothing else. His smile is wide, and I see him shift a few times on his feet. He keeps clasping his hands together only to shake them out at his sides. I speed up my walking as much as I can, but Daddy holds me at a steady pace.

"Easy, princess. I'm gettin' ya there," he whispers to me out of the corner of his mouth.

I smile at him but don't turn my head. I don't take my eyes off Barrett for a single moment. When I step close enough for the preacher to ask who gives this bride to this man, I shift my gaze to my dad for one moment as he and my mom release me to take another man's name.

The wedding goes by in a blur of emotions, Barrett choking up in his vows, me crying through mine. His brother sings "I Cross My Heart" for us, with only his guitar to guide him as we light the white unity candle; my heart feels like it may literally burst. I have to hold back a sob from the happiness trying to break through.

When the preacher announces us as man and wife, Barrett doesn't wait for him to finish saying he can kiss the bride before I am bent over backward in front of two hundred of our closest friends and family, their catcalls and whistles only adding to our happiness. And when he lifts me back up but keeps his lips pressed to mine for a few short moments, he leans in and whispers in my ear, "You have made me the happiest man alive for sharing my name, for starting our life together. I love you now. I love you tomorrow. I love you forever."

Tears stream down my face as he steps back, takes my hand in his, and lifts them up in the air as his happiness shines for all to see. Then we take our first step down the stairs as man and wife. He holds my hand tightly in his own, and we race down the aisle, through the double doors of the sanctuary, and into the first door that we find. It's a baby nursery that has been transformed into one of the rooms we used for changing clothes. The bridesmaids' clothes, makeup, shoes, and handbags are scattered everywhere, but that's not what I care about at the moment. And I'm pretty sure Barrett feels the same.

He takes my face in his hands and kisses me so thoroughly that my lips are tingling before we are finished. "You look beautiful. No. Beautiful isn't even a word to describe you. Radiant, glowing. I just... you're mine. Finally."

"Barrett, I've been yours forever."

"No, now you're officially mine.*"*

Before I could respond, there was a knock on the door. The rest of the wedding party and our parents were waiting outside the door for us. We still had to finish taking pictures, and all the other details that go along with the wedding day. And I knew there would be time for more sappy emotions later. Right now, it was time to show off my husband.

Our reception... where we ate roast beef and marinated chicken breasts, garlic mashed potatoes and green beans, drank champagne, listened to Lauren and Josh, as well as our fathers, toast our new marriage, and danced until we were ready to be sent off. After our friends and family threw rice at us as we ran hand in hand out of the reception hall, we climbed into my grandfather's classic Corvette. Barrett's buddies went easy on decorating, only hanging strung-up cans off the rear bumper. Our first dance as husband and wife was to "Love of a Lifetime" by Firehouse. It wasn't a fancy choreographed dance, we simply held one another as tightly as possible. Grateful to be in each other's arms — for a lifetime.

Tears are streaming down my face from the memory of our wedding, but I can't wait to continue looking through more. Barrett stands up and goes into the kitchen and returns with two bottles of water, a bag of popped microwave popcorn, a small plate of the chocolate chip cookies I had made earlier that day, and a plastic bag filled with peppermint taffies, my favorite.

Our first years of marriage... That first rental house we

lived in… such a dump, but we didn't care. We had hand-me-down furniture, lived on frozen pizza, spaghetti and fried bologna and baked potatoes, but we were happy.

Our first Christmas tree… another hand-me-down from my grandparents. The decorations were minimal — and mostly all hand-me-downs also — but we loved it. I made him listen to cheesy Christmas songs and watch *White Christmas* (which he hated, for the record, but did it once to appease me because it was our first Christmas together). The first night the tree was up, we made love under the twinkle lights and fell asleep there.

The day we became a family of three… Welcoming our first dog home, Oscar, a black lab mix…

The day we *officially* became a family of three… Bringing Cole home and into our world. We still lived at the rental house. The house might not have been perfect, but we made it a home. The bright green carpet in Cole's room was worn and old, so we covered it with a large rug.

Two years later, when my stomach was swollen to the max with Grady, we broke ground on our now forever home.

We looked through photo album after photo album and remembered.

The births of our children…

The loss of the unborn baby who would have come a few years before Harper…

Loved ones who we have since said goodbye to… his father losing his battle, a man we loved so dearly and miss daily.

Vacations and holidays, birthdays and celebrations…

Bad haircuts and junky cars, times when we had fewer wrinkles, times of hardship and times of sorrow…

Happy times and moments of immaturity, bad decisions

and right decisions...

We laughed and we shed tears — well, the tears were mostly on my part.

We remembered.

And when we close the final photo album, Barrett stands up and reaches down for me to help me stand. He wraps me in his strong arms and holds me tight. He blows out a deep breath before saying, "Tess, there is no other person on this earth who I would rather do life with than you. It hasn't always been easy, and sometimes the mess got in the way, but it's been perfect. I wouldn't change a single moment."

"Me either, babe. I've loved every moment of being married to you. Even the not-so-fun moments."

"I figured something out," he tells me, his voice low and hushed.

"What's that?" I whisper, looking in his eyes that have turned a deep shade of green — damn his hazel eyes that change colors like a mood ring.

"You know, we keep wondering what happened to us, why we feel so disconnected. It happened when you went to the design show," he tells me, and I start to pull away from him but his hold on me tightens. "Just hear me out. I'm not blaming you. I promise. I told you I didn't care if you stayed home for Mary Ellen's party. I hurt your feelings when I made you feel like you weren't important enough to be there. You didn't stay home anyway and you hurt me, even though I didn't realize it at the time. I think that's why I hired Keri without consulting you, without pushing for you to meet her. I was pissed that you didn't care enough, and you were mad that I didn't care enough. It's both our faults."

I gasp because the thought hadn't even crossed my mind. "So, we reverted back to high school."

He grins at me, clearly just proud that he "figured it out." "Yep. We behaved like our children. How's that make you feel?"

"Like an idiot stupid head."

He chuckles. "Pretty much defines both of us."

"Barrett, how could we have been so… immature?"

"I have no idea, but that's what happened. Tess?"

"Yeah?"

"I'm sorry. I didn't mean that I didn't care if you were there for our party or not. I didn't mean to not include you from hiring Keri. Or to make you question… any part of us."

"I accept and I'm sorry, too. I should have talked to you instead of Andy, and I shouldn't have been so selfish as to care more about a design show than someone who's been a part of our lives for almost two decades now."

"I accept, too." He smiles. "But you know what else? I know how to fix it."

"Tell me, oh wise one." I smile up to his grinning — albeit a bit smug — face.

"Go away with me?" he asks, his voice both shy and sure at the same time.

"What?"

"Go away with me. For a week. We keep saying we want to go hide away in a cabin up north for a while. I found a place that's right along the lake, small and perfect for us — just one bedroom, but it's all open otherwise. There's a hot tub and fireplace inside and an area set up for fires outside too. It has what we need to be away from it all. I want to do this. I need to do this. With you, obviously. It won't be any fun by myself. Let's do it."

I giggle at his rambling then ask, "Did you talk to

Lauren?" because it's exactly what she suggested to me.

He scrunches his eyebrows at me in confusion. "No. Actually, Cole. He told me you and I need a break."

"Well, that is… unexpected. And scary. The fact that our son, who doesn't even live here, acknowledges that we need a break is a little unnerving," I tell him.

"I know. It scared the crap out of me when he mentioned it. I think it was the kick in the ass that I needed though." He pauses, and I can tell he's thinking about his conversation, which I wish I knew more of but let it go. "Why did you ask about Lauren?"

"She said the same thing. That we need a break, to get away just the two of us. She suggested two weeks — and that James could come stay with the kids."

"You don't want to?"

"I don't know. Can we? First of all, can we afford it? Second of all, what about the kids?"

"It's in between seasons, so things are a little less expensive, so yeah, we can afford it. We can use it as our Christmas gift to one another, if that helps. And James is going to come watch the kids. Cole is around. So are Lauren and Josh."

"You've thought about this, huh?"

"To be honest, I've been wanting time alone with you for months, but we never get it. But it wasn't until Cole mentioned getting away that I truthfully started thinking of it. After we talked, I made a few phone calls before I got home."

"I want that too, but…"

"Nope. No buts. We're doing this. We leave on Saturday morning. We can still see Grady's game on Friday night — even though he won't be playing — and Maggie's volleyball game on Thursday night. Harper might even learn how to sleep in her own bed when we're not around."

"Okay."

"Okay? Really?" he asks with hopefulness.

"Yes. Let's do it."

"Yes!" he says as he does a goofy fist punch. "I kind of expected you to put up more of a fight," he admits.

"No way. I want this. I'll talk to my clients this week and let them know I'll be away. And if we wait, then we'll be getting too close to the holidays."

He spins me around as he whoops loudly, making me laugh. He bends down and kisses me sweetly before dipping and kissing me on his spot then pulls his face away and slowly lowers my feet to the ground.

"Oh, speaking of holidays…" he says with a huge smile on his face.

"Yeah?"

"Cole's bringing Mia for Thanksgiving."

"I thought you said he was bringing his new girlfriend?"

He looks at me expectantly with his eyebrows raised before it clicks.

"Mia!?" I hit his shoulder lightly and he laughs at me, clearly pleased with his news to share.

"I know. He just told me tonight. Cool, huh?" he says then slaps me on the butt and walks down the hallway to our bedroom.

Chapter Fourteen

Barrett

"BYE, GUYS. HAVE fun!" Maggie says as she bounces on her toes. She's so excited to have Tess's brother, James, staying with them that she practically packed our bags for us. Obviously, Grady is old enough to not have a babysitter, but we need someone here for Maggie and Harper, Harper especially.

I look over at James who is leaning against the side of the house, giving us the time we need to say goodbye. His left arm is a sleeve of tattoos, his hair shaved close to his head, and his beard scruffy; his bright blue eyes are sparkling. He looks far more reckless than what he really is, but those eyes are what give him away. He's just a big softy.

I lean down and take Maggie into my arms and hug her tightly, followed by Grady then Harper, who climbs up my legs and links her tiny little arms around my neck. I let go of her after a while, but she doesn't. Her arms are still hooked around my neck, but her little legs are dangling. I swing her a couple times lightly and she giggles. I grab her around the waist, and eventually she loosens her hold on me before jumping down and directly into Tess's arms.

Tess is sniffling, hopefully at the thought of missing

the kids and not at being alone with me for a week. She's a sentimental sap and cries easily. Last Christmas there was a commercial where a young woman decorated an elderly man's house with twinkle lights for the holidays. Every single time it came on, she turned into a weeping mess. Unlike my pretty girl, I'm not emotional in the least about saying goodbye to the kids for a week. I'm friggin' ecstatic. An entire week alone with Tess has me giddy. We may not be at our best right now, but I'm about to make damn sure that we're at perfection again before we leave that cabin.

After making the rounds, going over everything with James and double checking with Cole that he will be back for the weekend, we're ready to leave. I load all our bags into the back of the SUV and drag her by the arm to the car.

We've only been driving for thirty minutes of our five-hour drive when we stop at a gas station to fill up and grab a drink. I feel bad for already having to stop, but I didn't have time to make sure the gas tank was full before we left. She's been sitting quietly in the passenger seat of the car, her shoes shrugged off, one of her denim-clad legs bent so her foot is resting on the seat and her knee against the door. Her dark grey sweatshirt that says *Mama Bear* on the front is slipping slightly off one shoulder. Her curls are down, and her face is almost bare, only a bit of mascara on her eyelashes because she *"feels naked without it,"* and a shimmer of lip gloss that I know will taste like raspberries.

She's the picture of relaxation, but I know she's anything but. She's already eaten probably half-a-dozen peppermint taffies. Definitely one of her comfort foods.

She's thinking too much, probably about Grady, but also I'm sure she's wondering how we're going to spend a week together without the distraction of our lives getting in the way, or as a buffer, depending on how we look at it. I want her comfortable and being able to recognize that no matter what hills we've had to climb, we're still us.

"Want a drink or something?"

"Yeah, coffee, please," she says looking out the window.

"You got it. Anything to eat?" I ask, trying to draw out more conversation with her.

"No. I'm good."

I head inside to the gas station, grab a cup of coffee for her and one for me, then I proceed to the candy aisle. She said she didn't want anything, but I know my girl. If I present her with some chocolate, it might soften her up a bit. I find a Caramello, knowing she can't resist the combination of chocolate and caramel, and make my way to the front to pay. I glance out the window as I walk and see her head rested against the window.

I hate that she looks sad. She looks like if she could allow herself to float up to the clouds and rest her head on the soft pillows for a decade, she would. Between the two of us screwing up and accusing the other of looking at another person romantically, everything with Grady and the last few months of friction, the weight of the world seems to be on her shoulders, and I swear on my life I will take the heavy burden from her and release her from the prison that she's living in.

I had hoped that my surprising her when I asked her to come to the cabin with me would bring her back to me. And it did, partially. But I think she is still letting her head to get in the way and isn't allowing herself to realize that we're back. We're going to be back to us again. We're going to fix us.

The quiet of the car ride ends now. I know one surefire

way to bring her out of her funk, so I dig into my pocket and pull out my cell.

Me: *Hey pretty girl.*

I see her startle from her thoughts and reach down into her purse for her phone. I see her shake her head slightly when she sees my text and a small smile lifts her lips.

Score.

This girl has had my heart since I was seventeen years old. She's the one who taught me how to love. What love even looks like. Never have I felt love when she wasn't a part of it. If I could find an actual picture of love, her face would be the only one I'd recognize. I've never once let her go and don't plan to. Time to break out my wooing abilities and show her back to us.

My girl: *Yes? Did you get lost?*

Smartass little brat.

Woo. I have to remember how to woo her. I take a deep breath because I feel like I'm a stumbling seventeen-year-old again. I feel nervous, and my palms are sweating. I pray what I'm about to type doesn't come out cheesy.

Me: *To you.*

I see her stare at her phone for a few seconds, which, to be honest, feels more like minutes. It's not lost on me that I'm standing in the middle of a gas station, two cups of coffee stacked on top of each other in one hand, my phone and her candy bar in the other. I'm staring at my phone, praying that she doesn't think my super corny line is as cheesy as I think it might be. But I feel like we need corny right now. Sometimes a little corny goes a long way.

My Girl: Barrett...

I take her non-answer as what I need. She doesn't need any more than what I just gave her. That, combined with the fact that I see her head slowly lift as she looks toward the gas station, her face directed right at me, and I wish upon everything that I could see her eyes at this moment. I quickly move to the front counter, pay for our stuff, and walk with purpose out to the car. As I get closer, her window rolls down so I can hand the cups of coffee over to her to place in the cup holders, which I do. But before she can close the window again, I lean my large frame into the open window and take her face in mine.

"I love you, Tess. You need to understand that. You need to feel that. My soul is empty without yours attached to it. My heart, my love responds only to you. Even after I take my last breath on this earth, my love is yours."

Before she can respond, I bring her lips to mine and possess her with all the fire and yearning that's been building deep inside since we started our trip. Her breath hitches slightly and her mouth parts, allowing my tongue to invade and caress her own. I taste her salty tears, her raspberry lip gloss, and a hint of the peppermint taffy she's been snacking on. I lean into the window farther. I pause ever so briefly, her tongue searching mine out in a passion that only she owns. I faintly hear the click of her seatbelt and soon she is on her knees, facing me and leaning out the window.

Chasing my kiss.

That's right, sweet girl. Come to me.

I'll chase you forever.

Chase me right on back.

I'll let you catch me.

I let her catch me. Our mouths whisper our intense and never-ending love to each other, but no words are spoken.

We're making out in the middle of the gas station parking lot, and I couldn't care less. Making out like teenagers might just help us get back to ourselves. Find our roots once again.

Our kiss slows, allowing the ache in my chest to ease.

She's back.

I pull back, and I see it in her eyes. I know it in that moment. She's back. Now we just need to continue on this path and not waver. I look into her smiling eyes; the brightest blue I have seen in a long time.

She kisses me once more and says simply, "I love you."

I grin at her and round the corner of our SUV and slide back into the driver's seat, feeling a million times lighter than I had just a few moments ago. She turns and faces me after I get settled, and I reach into my coat pocket and pull out the chocolate bar I bought with our coffees and hand it over to her. Her excited squeal makes me chuckle and shake my head.

"Ee-ee-ek! I'm not even gonna pretend that I don't want it. Barrett, I so wanted some chocolate, and this is perfect. My favorite. Thank you!"

"So predictable."

She leans over the console and kisses me on the cheek with a loud smack and sits back in her seat with a little bounce. We both buckle up our seatbelts, and I start the car up, put it in drive, and head out for the last leg of our journey to the cabin.

I hear her tear open the package, and she breaks off a square of the chocolate and places the whole thing in her mouth. She moans in delight and sinks farther into her seat, her eyes closed like the chocolate is damn near giving her an orgasm.

"Shit."

She looks up at me completely innocent, even though I know she isn't. She's doing it on purpose. The little minx.

"Hmm, you really know how to eat that chocolate, but you have a little bit of caramel on your lip." I'm driving but still do a quick reach-over with my body and lick her chin up to her bottom lip, not seductive in any way at all.

She laughs out loud and dramatically wipes her hand at the place where I left my mark.

"You're such an ass." She giggles.

"That's what you get, trying to get me hard while driving us to the cabin."

She opens her mouth to rebut but closes her mouth quickly when I grab her thigh, high enough that my pinky finger can graze where I really, really, really want to be.

"I think maybe you need to just drive. Faster."

"On it, pretty girl."

"Barrett?"

"Yeah, baby?"

"Thank you for reminding me what it feels like to be falling in love again."

I take a deep breath through my nose because, dammit all, I'm choked up. I grab her hand and squeeze tightly, which she returns. My reason for taking her on this trip was to remind us both of our love for each other. Getting her to fall in love with me all over again makes my heart beat faster, makes my chest swell with pride. Once was amazing enough. Twice is, without a doubt, a miracle, and I can't wait to see it happen.

As we continue down the road, I pull up the playlist I made especially for this weekend. It's one of three playlists I made. This one is meant to remind us of when we fell in love and in the early stages of our lives together: Full of Firehouse, Journey, Boston, Bon Jovi, Bruce Springsteen, and a few others. It might be cheesy as hell. It might only be a step above a mixed tape, but I know that she'll love it. As Bon Jovi starts singing "I'll Be There For You," our song — being children of 80s — I see her smile begin to glow. She reaches down to where my hand still rests on her thigh and clasps it tightly in her own.

Soon we're both singing at the top of our lungs like of a couple of lovesick lunatics to songs that I chose especially for us. She keeps dancing in her seat like a goofball and completely letting loose, which was my plan. She's waving her hands in the air like she doesn't have a care in the world, and her hips are moving all over her seat. Our car ride club reminds me that no matter what we've been going through, I know we can get back to us.

When "I Wanna Sex You Up" starts up, and I start singing in my best high-pitched impersonation, one shoulder hitching up as I try to reach notes that are unnatural. She laughs so hard that she doubles over and may or may not have snorted. (She did.)

"Barrett," she wheezes, "I'm gonna pee. Seriously."

"Cross your legs, woman! No peeing in the car." I laugh at her and begin looking for a place to stop. Giving birth four times has definitely added interesting elements to our relationship, one of those being we make way more frequent restroom stops on our car trips.

Chapter Fifteen

Tess

W<small>HEN</small> I <small>GET</small> into the car today, I am in a full-blown panic. I know our marriage is more important than anything else, but leaving the kids is never easy. Everything that's happening with Grady right now has me on edge a bit, even though it seems that we've got it all under control. But what I'm most worried about is not having our jobs and the kids around for a buffer. I think I forgot how to be Barrett's wife, his lover and girlfriend. It's been so long since my identity shifted from being that woman into who I am today.

As many times as Lauren told me that I was being ridiculous, it's still something that my mind can't seem to let go of. What if he doesn't like me anymore? What if we find ourselves sitting around just staring at each other, completely forgetting how to be alone without all of life's distractions?

When Barrett stops to fill up with gas, I take the few moments of silence to grab some deep breaths. Just as I am starting to feel relaxed, I hear my phone tweet with a text from Barrett. I ask him if he is lost, trying to be funny. When he says he is lost to me, at first I giggle, because it's such a corny line, but then I look up and, even though the distance between us, I can see the truth in his eyes. He is lost to me. Just as I am lost to him. This is our chance, our new beginning to remember. To remember all of why we love each other, not just the good parts.

We started the process that night on the living room floor when we poured through photo album after photo album before moving to the computer. Digital cameras are a wonderful invention, but I rarely end up getting pictures printed anymore. We laughed and wept — well, I wept anyway; he teased me for weeping — and smiled, looking through all of our memories. Some were long forgotten, some cherished. Some pictures can only be a memory. Some we can't wait to relive the memory of again, and some we wish we could forget.

But at the end of the night… we remembered.

Barrett surprised me and created a playlist for our car ride. It could have been titled "The Best of the 80s and 90s," better known to us as "When We Fell in Love." I can't stop dancing and singing and laughing at all the amazing songs he found.

I'm serenading him.

He's serenading me.

When "Take my Breath Away" comes through the speakers, our dancing and singing comes to a slow end, and we listen. The first time we danced under the stars together was to this song. It was a perfect summer night, and we'd been dating for almost eight months. Since the day he asked me to wear his jersey to the homecoming football game, we were a couple. There was never an official invitation; it was just implied. I didn't need him to ask me to be his girlfriend. I knew from the moment I smelled his cologne invading my senses through his jersey that I was his.

He took me out for a date, and we find an empty field, park his pickup, and he leaves the radio on. Well, leaves the radio playing the mixed tape he made for us. Through the horrible speakers and the light of the moon, we stand in the back of the pickup bed and dance. I lean my head on his shoulder, my arms looped around his neck while his are around my waist, pulling me in close. No words are spoken.

Until they are.

"I love you, pretty girl."

I gasp and lean back slightly so I can look up at him. He doesn't wait for my response before he continues. "Damn, I've been waiting to tell you that for what feels like forever, but you have to know it. I can't hold it in anymore. I love you so much. Every morning I wake up happy simply because I know you're mine. Every night I go to bed happy because I've seen you. I don't just love you. I adore you. I crave you. I crave your existence in my life. I crave kissing you below your ear…" He stops just long enough to give me a kiss under my ear that feels so sensual my knees almost buckle. He pulls back, giving me a knowing smile before continuing, "I crave saying hello to you first thing every morning. I crave you being the last person I speak to every night. I crave taking care of you, holding your hand, protecting you. I crave your heart, your mind, your body. Every single thing about you I crave, adore, and love."

I stare into the eyes of the man who waxed poetic words to me without even trying, just spoken from his heart. The love I feel for him matches the love that I know he feels for me.

With tears in my eyes, I roll up on my toes and kiss him with as much passion and love as I have for him. Which is a lot.

"I love you, too. A whole lot." He smiles broad after my blunt response, but I continue on. "You say you crave me. I know what you mean. I crave your love, your kisses below my ear, your good-

morning phone call, your good-night phone call. I love that you cherish me, make me feel protected, hold my hand and pull me close. I love that you inhale me. I love that you make me laugh every day, help me to feel calm when I'm anxious, and that you listen to me and try to understand my level of crazy." I give him a watery smile and he chuckles in response — not denying I actually have a level of crazy. "I wish you could feel what I feel. The butterflies you give me every day just by simply loving me, and I pray that I give you the same."

We stare at each other for a long time, soaking up our words spoken to each other before Barrett reaches down and picks me up, bringing my face closer to his. I rest my hands over his shoulders as my legs dangle between us. His arms are bound under my butt, holding me securely to him. Our breathing is ragged and our eyes are moving over each other's faces, memorizing every curve and angle.

Barrett takes a few steps backward until his back is against the cab of the pickup.

Our kiss is raw and intense. I come to realize in that moment that kissing is far more intimate than any other physical touch. A kiss is a way to speak without words. Our love is spoken through the kiss, even though our mouths have already breathed the words.

The tape comes to an end but we don't stop our dance. I know without a doubt that I want his last name to become my own. I have known for a while that I love him. That I am in love with him. But in this moment, in the back of his pickup, in the middle of a field in the dead of summer with only the sound of crickets chirping, cicadas singing, and the fireflies flirting around our heads, do I realize my depth of love that I have for this guy. This boy who has been slowly becoming a man in front of my very eyes my entire life. I am going to watch him grow old.

He is going to watch me grow old.

Before I know what is happening, we stop in front of a ski lodge. My trip down memory lane has come to an end, but the feeling of the memory still lingers in my heart. Forever. Knowing we have plans to go to a cabin, I look over at Barrett in confusion.

"Just trust me. This is just a little pit stop, yeah? Before we seclude ourselves from the world." He grins cheekily. It is one of his most endearing smiles and I love it. He doesn't have boyish dimples, but his smile lights up his entire face, and his eyes shine with happiness. A happiness I haven't seen in a while.

He puts the car in park, reaches into the back seat, and grabs our coats. "You're gonna need your shoes on for this," he says with a smile in his voice before he opens the door with the car still running. A young man comes out of the lodge entrance and catches the keys being tossed at him while Barrett rounds the front of the car. He opens my door, takes my hand in his, and looks down at my bare feet and frowns. I'm confused by what's happening, but more than that, just a little in awe. He planned things, from the playlists on the way up to our stop along the way, he's showing a side of him that I haven't seen in a long time.

I didn't realize that I missed dating my husband.

He reminded me that I did.

He reminded me that I loved falling in love with him the first time.

He leans down and grabs my black ballet flats and slides them onto my feet then picks up my purse from the floor. He takes my hand in his and gently pulls me out of the car. As soon as my feet hit the ground, he wraps his arm around me and shuffles me inside. The main lodge is absolutely breathtaking, everything I picture a ski lodge to look like. Oversized, dark brown leather furniture is paired with soft fabric pillows. A large chandelier hangs from the middle of the room made entirely of antlers, and large wooden beams stretches across the vaulted ceiling. What looks like antique skis and poles hang on the walls, and in the far corner there's a large stone fireplace with wood crackling, giving off a cozy warmth.

Barrett guides us through the entrance and into another section of the lodge. He opens the door for me while I'm still rubber necking, not paying attention to where he's leading me. Everywhere I look, it's absolutely beautiful.

"Tess and Barrett Ryan, we have an appointment for a couple's massage," he says with all the confidence in the world. I don't think Barrett has ever stepped foot into a spa, let alone a salon. He gets his hair cut at a small barbershop in town, so to say this is a bit of a stretch for Barrett's comfort zone is putting it mildly, but to look at him now, he's the picture of relaxed. His smile stretches widely across his face, his right hand on my lower back, rubbing small circles with his thumb.

Somewhere along the way, he handed off our coats and my purse, to whom I have no idea.

The woman at the front desk nods her head in agreement that we do, in fact, have an appointment.

"Have a seat right over there," she says as she points to some leather seats along the wall. "Can I get you some tea or water?"

"Water sounds great. Thanks," Barrett says then nudges my knee with his to break me out of my trance.

"Oh yeah, that sounds great for me, too. Thank you."

She smiles in our direction before saying, "Absolutely. I'll be right back with that."

As soon as she's out of earshot, my eyes dart to Barrett in surprise, my eyebrows, no doubt, touching my hairline. His eyes twinkle.

"Babe, this is the start of our week of us. I want you to relax and know that this will be a way to get a head start on that."

"I can't believe you did this. Thank you. You're the bestest ever," I say before I lean over and give him a soft, lingering kiss to the cheek.

He chuckles and wraps me in his strong arms before releasing me back into my seat. "I love you, pretty girl."

"I love you, too. A whole lot."

His eyes flare, and I know he remembers the first time we voiced those words to each other.

"I can't wait to have you alone for an entire week," he growls into my ear, which causes a shiver to wrack my body.

Our masseuses interrupt our moment and announce that they're ready for us. They each have a bottle of water in their hands, no doubt from front desk woman.

"I'm Kate," a petite little thing tells us. She's adorable. Her black hair is in a short pixy cut with streaks of purple. She has tattoos down both her arms and up the left side of her neck, a small diamond pierced into the side of her right nostril, and she's dressed in all black from her tank top and leggings to her shoes.

"I'm Georgie," the other girl says. She, too, is dressed in all black but looks a bit more conservative, though she does have a streak of bright pink through her platinum-blonde hair that's pulled into a high ponytail. Her smile is infectious, and I notice that she has a piercing in the corner of her mouth.

We follow Kate and Georgie down the short hallway and into the room where I assume our couple's massage will happen. The room is almost entirely white, with the beds and even the walls covered in creamy white, satiny sheets. The pin tucks in the center of the sheets that hang from the wall make them look like giant bowties, and sheets drape from the ceiling to create a canopy effect. Placed on the floor at the foot of the beds are large red pots filled with water. The white candles floating atop of the water are lit, giving off a romantic feel to the room.

Two beds sit in the middle of the room, not next to one another, but facing each other, just a little off-set. It looks as though they are close enough that we will be able to touch and… see each other's eyes.

Everything about the room shouts romance and seduction, but it is also calm and tranquil, and I feel myself relax instantly.

Kate turns to Barrett and tells him what to expect while Georgie does the same to me. I barely contain my giggle at Barrett obviously trying his damnedest not to question Kate's abilities. She can't possibly weigh more than one hundred pounds, but she looks totally badass, and there is no way I'm going to question her. She's a masseuse, trained in pressure points. My luck, we may offend her and she'll do something to make us pee ourselves in the middle of the massage. Nothing says romantic couple's massage like pants pissing.

After we tell Kate and Georgie that we don't have any major or specific needs, they let us know we can undress to just our underwear and slide under the sheet. I see Barrett's face go pale before he clears his throat.

"Come again?" Barrett asks, his head turned to the side.

Kate turns to him and politely says, "Just undress down to your underwear and slide under the sheet."

"Any other way we can do this?"

"I'm sorry?"

"Any other way we can do this massage?"

"Well, I guess you can lie on top," she says, looking a tad uncomfortable with that option.

"No. Can't you just like go under my clothes or something? Do I have to undress?"

Kate looks at him with a completely baffled expression and looks uncomfortable but smiles like he just made a joke and walks out the door with a giggling Georgie behind her. No doubt they're laughing their asses off at the moron not wanting to undress.

"Care to explain that?" I ask.

"I think I made a mistake. Tess, do you realize how horny I am?"

Nope. Can't contain my laughter. He looks so serious, damn near scared.

"Should I be worried about the fact you're worried about being horny during a massage by another woman?"

"What you should be worried about is being manhandled in front of the two massage ladies because I won't be able to not get hard when I'm inches away from my almost entirely naked wife."

I feel my eyes widen when I realize what he means, also for the first time realizing he will be naked also. Or darn close to it. Cra-a-ap.

"This may not have been my best plan," he mumbles, looking down at my body.

I murmur back to him, "We'll be fine, right?"

"Right," Barrett says with a firm nod of his head. It looks like he's mumbling something under his breath because I just see his lips moving and his eyes are closed.

"What in the world are you doing?"

"Umm… I'm trying to distract myself," he says, eyes still closed.

"And how are you doing that?"

He slowly opens his eyes and shrugs his shoulders. "I'm reciting the presidents, alphabetizing the states, picturing Josh's ugly mug. You know, stuff to get my mind off it."

I smash my lips together to stop from teasing him, but then I get a better idea.

I decide at that moment to make the best of the situation and to challenge Barrett — and, in turn, me — by starting to strip in front of him. I step out of my simple black ballet flats, and slowly I begin to peel off my sweatshirt before I let it unceremoniously drop to the floor next to me. My black push-up bra is currently doing wonders for my assets, so I decide not to remove it… yet. I move my hands to my jeans and pop the button then slowly drag the zipper down. I — seductively in my mind, but who knows how ridiculous I look — bend over and slide my jeans down my legs.

"Tess," he growls in warning. Maybe it was seductive after all.

"What?" I ask, not innocently in any way, as I continue to remove my jeans.

"Fine. You wanna play, sweet girl? Let's play."

In the blink of an eye, Barrett has his shoes toed off and his dark green Henley shirt pulled over his head — that incredibly sexy way that men do by just grabbing the collar — his strong chest and shoulders looking even bigger in the low light. Before I can react, he has his dark jeans pushed down his muscular thighs. In seconds, he's almost entirely naked, and my eyes can't decide what to feast themselves on first.

I swear the spa has Ginuine's "Pony" being streamed through the speakers because, next thing I know, he's pulling some Magic Mike moves and touching me everywhere — only he hasn't actually touched me. His presence, so near to me, is like a thousand tongues licking at my body, making me pant and almost come unglued right there on the spot. He's moving around me in ways he's never moved before, whispering sexiness into my ear as he leans close enough that I can smell the mountain air scent of his body wash.

"Do you feel what you do to me, Tess?" he grinds his hips against me and I moan in response. "This is only from you. Only ever from you." Swiftly he unhooks my bra and throws it in the corner with the rest of our clothes, taking over the striptease that I had initially intended to do for him. He nips at my ear and takes me by the upper arms before spinning me around so his chest is to my back. He runs his hand down my front and cups my center, and I know he can feel how ready I am. "This? Is only for me."

His hands make a blazing trail up my front and palms my chest, squeezing and pinching with just the right pressure. His hips are still gyrating, causing both of us to do a slow grind against each other. His movements have slowed… painfully so. Now "Ride" is filtering through my mind, and I'm about ready to tell him to grab one of the candles and drip hot wax on me.

Before I can get too deep into my fantasy, Barrett spins me around and wraps me up in his arms, his tongue invading my mouth in a drunk hunger. His hands glide into my hair, keeping me close to him. It's a hurried race for who can touch each other more quickly. His black boxer-briefs sport an impressive tent that I can't wait to get my hands on.

Before we can get anywhere we want — and need — to go, we hear a knock on the door, bringing us back to reality. That reality being that we're in the middle of a massage room, about to get a couple's salon. Not in a bedroom. Or alone.

"Are you both ready?" one of the two ask.

"Just a minute!" Barrett hollers, his voice — or growl, rather — a mix of frustration, irritation and panic.

"Oh! All… alright. Just let us know!" she squeaks out.

Embarrassment floods over me, and I squeak also, dropping my face into my hands even though no one but Barrett is in the room with me.

He takes a deep breath through his nose and blows it out his mouth. "Well lying down on my stomach is going to be loads of fun."

I giggle and give him a kiss on the cheek. "Relax, babe. All. Week. Long."

He takes a few deep breaths and then pulls me close once again, my arms going around his waist. "Damn right," he murmurs and kisses me below my ear. "All. Week. Long. You're mine. Mind and body. Every single part of you is mine."

Then the jerk lies down under the sheet and puts his face in the pillow hole thingy, like he didn't just send erotic starbursts through my entire body.

"We're ready!" he shouts at the door then looks up at me. "Lie down, babe. Relax," he says teasingly.

Surprisingly both of us do. Relax, that is. The massage is exactly what we both need. We stare into each other's eyes, reach over the space between the tables and hold hands, rub each other's arms, and come to a sense of complete calm. The oils they have diffusing in the air and the soft tranquil music being piped through the room help create a romantic atmosphere. One hour later, we're both jelly, our bodies fully drained of all the stress that we brought in with us. We stumble out of the room looking like we just spent an hour boozing it up, rather than getting a massage.

James told him the tavern on the resort property has some of the best burgers in the state. And neither of us can resist a good burger. Sweet potato fries for me, regular for him, and each of us enjoy a tall chilled glass of their house brew. It's the perfect lunch. We haven't had a dinner out with just the two of us in so long that we forgot how relaxing it can be. Looking out at the resort that will be bustling with people in ski gear in a few short weeks, we both sigh in contentment.

Somehow Barrett knew that this was exactly what I needed before we got to the cabin. I finally feel ready to start our week.

"Wanna get out of here?" Barrett asks, pulling my eyes away from the windows, a look of heat in his eyes that's unmistakable.

"Abso-friggin-lutely."

Chapter Sixteen

Barrett

I SLAM THE SUV into park, making it rock back and forth. Tess lets out a loud laugh and shakes her head at me before unhooking her seatbelt. She reaches down to the floor by her feet and gathers her belongings, but I have other ideas. She's moving way too slowly. I have my wife alone with me for the first time in months, and I'm not going to waste a second. The couple's massage was the perfect way to start our week away, but it also gave me a visual reminder of what I had waiting for me, and I've had to control myself for long enough.

I round the hood of the car and open her door. She looks up at me in surprise then lets out a cute little shriek when I grab her by the waist, pull her out of the SUV, and hoist her over my shoulder before I head toward the cabin. I reach into my pocket to grab the key and somehow manage to get it into the door handle and twist before I kick open the door with such force it hits the wall and starts to bounce back at us.

"Barrett! Put me down!" she squeals and wiggles.

I slap her ass and smile. "Not a chance in hell. I know you. You're going to want to unpack, go through the cabin, see everything, get settled…"

She huffs in response and starts to say something, but I interrupt her.

"I know you, darlin', so don't try to deny it."

"You're annoying," she says, but doesn't mean it. I know she loves it that I can read her so clearly, just like I love it that she can read me.

I make my way down the hall of the small cabin and easily find the only bedroom. In an effort to tame my caveman tactics, I lay her gently on the bed and hover over her. I stare into her beautiful expressive eyes that are filled with excitement. My eyes move to her mouth, naturally pink and lush, and it causes me to lick my lips in response.

"Hey."

"Hey back," she says, her eyes shining so bright.

I shake my head slightly and close my eyes briefly before opening them up and stare into her eyes. I want her to see the truth in mine when she hears what I'm about to say. "Tess. I love you so much. You're so beautiful, you take my breath away. I can't believe you're still mine after this many years, and I swear — on my life, I swear — I will never let you forget that again. Not for a single second. Not for a single moment in your life will you not feel the love I have for you, will you not know that I adore you with everything that I have. I want your heart, your mind… your soul. I want everything you can give me."

Her eyes well with tears and, as much as I hate seeing her cry, she needs to hear it all.

"When I heard you and Andy talking, I went a little crazy," I admit.

"Ya think?" she says jokingly, her voice watery.

I smile slightly. "I know. But hearing what you felt — it

was hard to hear. That's not to say I didn't need to hear it, but it still sucked the life out of me and knocked me back a bit. I can't believe how selfish I've been to not realize it."

"Barrett…"

"I know you're going to try to play it off and make excuses for me because that's exactly what we've *both* been doing. But it ends now. Letting our jobs consume us. This crap with Grady, Harper still being the biggest cockblock in the history of cockblocks, us forgetting that we were husband and wife first… it's all stuff we've let happen to us, and it's not going to continue. We're going to keep dating each other. Somehow we forgot that important step in our marriage.

"I want you to know that you matter. That your opinions matter. I want you to know that I don't see any other woman but you. My heart has always been and will forever only be yours. I want to gross the kids out by making out in the kitchen while I grab your ass. I want them to see us cuddling on family movie night. I want them to see us dancing under the stars together. I want to date my wife again."

The tears are streaming down her face in rapid progression. I can't swipe them away with my thumb fast enough.

"Barrett, I swear I want to say something sappy and beautiful because that's what you just gave me, but you stole all my thoughts. You read my mind perfectly, and, gah, I just love you!" she cries out then grabs the back of my neck and brings my mouth down to hers with such force our teeth nash together. We both pull away, laughing, before I softly bring my mouth down to hers again and kiss her the way she deserves to be kissed. With love, passion, and forever.

Our hands are everywhere, slowly and quickly at the same time. I want to touch her freely, openly… loudly. I want to reclaim her body as mine and remind her that she has always and only been mine. As we manage to get each other undressed, my rough calloused hands a sharp contrast to her soft skin, I relish in every moment.

Seeing her naked and open for me with no risk of a distraction has me hard and aching for her. I can't wait to sink into her. I also can't wait to taste every single inch of her incredible body, but that is all going to come later. Right now, I plan to fit myself with protection so I don't explode on contact and become one with Tess once again. I reach down into my jeans and pull out a condom, and she bursts into a fit of giggles.

"I'm sorry. It's just so… it's just so funny to me."

"Darlin', you have no idea how badly I want this. I even took care of myself this morning in the shower in hopes it will make me last longer, but seeing you laid out before me now, I don't know if it made a difference or not." I smile down at her, completely unashamed.

The look of heat in her eyes at my admission has me even harder than I was to begin with. The smile gets wiped away from my face as the heat zaps between us like we're both holding onto a live wire.

"Oh shit, it looks like you're going to eat me alive."

"I just might," she admits. "Hearing that you took care of yourself. You don't know what that does to me."

I have a good feeling I know exactly what it does to her. That's why I reach down and stroke myself as I watch her reaction. Her eyes drift down my body and land on my hand wrapped around myself, and she shudders in response.

She.

Physically.

Shudders.

Her eyes are glued to me, she's licking her lips, and her breathing gets heavier. I can't stop. The look of pure lust in her eyes has me more turned on than I think I've ever been before. Until she reaches down and slowly starts rubbing herself.

Nope. Now I'm more turned on than I've ever been before.

She's watching me, and I'm watching her. I hear her soft moans, I watch her fingers become slick with her wetness, and I'm so close to exploding. But I don't.

I quickly fit myself with the condom and climb over her. Her legs open wide for me, but her fingers are still between her thighs. I reach down and remove her hand, pull it up to my mouth, and suck on her fingers. Her eyes flare with lust, and she takes a shaky breath. She pulls her fingers out of my mouth before she uses her hand to guide me into her.

Heaven.

"Shi-i-it… Tess. How. How are you so tight?" I groan into her neck as I take a moment to relish being inside her again, completely still. Part of me wishes that we didn't have the barrier between us, but I also want this to last. We may have all week, but I intend to get my fill of Tess the entire time.

"Barrett," she says breathlessly, "can we have this conversation later? Right now, I just need you to move."

"Yeah. Yeah, I will. But holy… you're tight. I can't… it's just too much."

My hips start moving slowly, but soon the sensation takes over, and I can't control myself any longer. Our bodies slap against one another in a fury that I've never experienced before, the sounds of our love rekindling echoing off the cabin walls.

"Hold on."

"What?" she asks in a lust-filled daze.

I don't answer her though, my response not needed when she realizes what my words mean. I grab her knees and raise up on my own, bringing her legs over my shoulders. Her hair is a mess on the white pillow case and her blue eyes are shining brightly. Her lips part as she cries out when I hit her most sensitive spot, a spot only I've ever touched and with an animalistic growl, my hips move back and forth wildly, her hips meeting me thrust for thrust.

"Still. Damn Tess, you're still so beautiful."

She moans in response, reaching up to grab my shoulders and squeezing tightly. Sweat beads on my forehead, and my fingers dig into the flesh at her hips. Her breasts are bouncing wildly, and our breathing is erratic. Her arms are raised over her head, gripping the slats in the headboard, giving herself leverage.

"Love you," I grunt.

She nods. "Love. You." Her words are quiet. Breathless. "So much. I'm… can't hold on, babe."

"Go."

Soon I feel her clench me tightly, her walls rippling around me. She soars, crying out my name. And I roar out through my release, and she screams through hers. I collapse on top of her, and we both lie wrapped in each other's arms, breathless and completely sated, and once again… us.

"Maybe Lauren was right about being re-virginized." Tess's voice cuts through the quietness of the room as she giggles.

"I have no idea what that means, but get ready."

"Huh?"

I answer by ripping off the condom and tossing it on the

floor, grabbing her by the waist and flipping her over, kissing her over every square inch of her body. Finally.

Chapter Seventeen

Tess

I'M SITTING ON one of the chocolate-brown leather barstools next to the kitchen island. Barrett's back is to me as he whips up some omelets for breakfast. He's not much of a cook; he's just never enjoyed it like I do. He grills, makes excellent tacos and fajitas, but breakfast is his thing. When we had Cole, he was trying to help out in little ways and breakfast became it. I ate so many different types of eggs, dishes with ham or bacon or sausage, and pancakes in Cole's first year of life that, for a while, I couldn't even look at it.

Now, though, the kids and I beg him to make breakfast. He's the breakfast master in our home. He seems to love it, too. After sleeping in this morning, being exhausted after a long night of finding each other again, he woke me up the same way he exhausted me, then told me he was making breakfast.

We brought enough groceries to get us through a couple days, and last night, after we came down from our high and cleaned up, we got ourselves together long enough to unload the car and bring everything in. Barrett helped me unpack the clothes into the closet and dresser, put away the few groceries we brought in coolers and bags, and made a quick and easy dinner of tacos.

I watch the bulge and contract of his back muscles as he prepares the eggs wearing only his low-slung, navy-blue-striped pajama pants — sans boxers. I know this not only because I saw him slide them on but also because I can see his incredible butt cheeks through the thin fabric. I can also see that the jerk just flexed said butt cheeks, clearly knowing that I'm staring at one of my favorite parts of him.

He has bacon baking and sizzling in the oven and is sautéing onions, peppers, and mushrooms for the omelets. Men cooking is sexy as hell. Men cooking shirtless is even sexier. I can clearly see the tricep tattoo on his right arm from here. The tree he had the kids' names engrained into makes me smile and happy every time I see it. He has a few other tattoos, too: an eagle with the Bible verse Isaiah 40:31 stretching across his left bicep, a cross on his chest, on his left wrist the date in which our unborn baby was due to be born, and on his left shoulder, a compass with my name over top of the *N*. They all mean something special to him. He doesn't want to be covered in tattoos, but when he feels led to add more, he does.

He turns around and smirks in my direction. The oven timer beeps, and he whips back around and removes the bacon from the oven. He puts the meat on a plate lined with a paper towel, and then pours the eggs into two small skillets to start cooking. He rotates back around and leans his body against the counter, bracing himself with his hips and hands resting against the countertop. Looking over his shoulder, he raises his eyebrows in my direction, and I return the expression. We stare silently at each other for a few moments before he turns his head back once again and silently finishes cooking the omelets, adding in the vegetables and cheese.

Once he's got them ready, he plates up our breakfast.

Normally our mornings are filled with chaos, even on non-school days. Before we left, I was afraid I wouldn't be able to relax and enjoy the quiet, or that I would miss the chaos, but I was so wrong. The quiet is amazing, and the lack of chaos just adds to the tranquility of our getaway.

He slides a plate in front of me and places another one beside it. He walks around the island and takes a seat next to me. We eat in silence, glancing at each other every few seconds. He widens his stance on his seat so his thigh is touching mine.

"Good eggs," I tell him.

"Thanks," he replies, still with his damn smirk. He knows his chest and shoulders being bare are too much for me to handle.

"I love the vegetables sautéed first," my stupid mouth says.

"Yup," he says as he takes a drink of orange juice. The muscles in his throat contract as he swallows. Cocky bugger.

I decide to play his game. I have a grey sweater cardigan on over my light blue camisole which I slide off and drop to the floor next to me. I stretch my arms high above my head. He glances over at me and looks down, no doubt noticing my body's reaction from the cooler temperature — or maybe from the eye candy he's presenting me. I won't admit to that, though. He takes a deep breath in through his nose before putting another bite of eggs into his mouth, sliding the fork out slowly, drawing my attention to his mouth.

I pick up a piece of bacon off the plate and take a bite, taking my finger into my mouth and slowly sucking the bits of bacon from it; he watches the movement. The ridiculousness of what we're doing almost makes me giggle.

We're eating bacon and eggs and acting as if we're doing some sort of weird burlesque show. He reaches for a piece of toast, brushing his arm against my chest, muscles flexing on contact. We continue our song and dance of trying to out-seduce each other for several moments before he's had enough. The food long forgotten, he picks me up under my knees and places my arm around his neck as he pulls me onto his lap. His tongue immediately begs for entry into my mouth, and when he pulls back away from a knee-weakening kiss, he says with a smile, "You taste like bacon."

I smile widely. I love seeing him happy and smiling. I love seeing his playful behavior.

PART OF THE agreement to us getting away was that we would remember how to relax. It's nearing dusk, and he and I have been lazy all day long, always touching each other in some way, never far apart. Except for right now. He got up off the couch about ten minutes ago, kissed me on the forehead and left the room. I was so engrossed into the book on my Kindle that I didn't ask what he was up to.

But now I feel a little cheated at not having him close anymore. I close the flowery cover on my Kindle case and set it on the couch beside me. I sit up and look around the room and find it's as empty as I expected it to be.

"Barrett?" I call out but receive no response. I stand up and bend over, stretching my fingers to my toes, and call for him once again, but still nothing. I start to walk down the hall to the bedroom just as the sliding door that leads to the back yard opens up.

Barrett strides in with a Cheshire smile on his face. "C'mere," he says simply.

I move toward him and notice that he has my jacket in his hand. He helps me into it and looks down at my slipper-covered feet and says, "That'll do."

I furrow my eyebrows in confusion and have no idea what that means, but I trust him completely. I take hold of his hand once I get my jacket on, smile at him, and walk outside into the dusky evening sky.

I stop abruptly when I notice that he has a couple of outdoor heaters running and his phone set up with a portable speaker. He presses a button on his phone, and the sounds of Florida Georgia Line singing "H.O.L.Y." starts streaming through the quiet, peaceful night. He holds his hand out to me, and I move quickly to his side, not second guessing a single moment.

Barrett pulls me tightly into his arms, and his large chest crushes to mine. His right hand holds one of mine tightly against his heart; his left wraps around my waist. His face buries in my hair, and my head rests close to his shoulder. We sway slowly together, one song fading into the next. Whispering words to each other of the fond memories we have of our past, promises of the future, and how much we love one another.

I take a moment to look around and see he has Mason jars with white candles placed inside them lit all over the patio. I have no idea how he got them all here without me seeing. I look back up at Barrett and notice he's staring down at me, his eyes looking back and forth between each of mine, an intense look on his face that makes my breath catch and lips part.

"Tess, I'm not going to promise you the moon and the stars, but I am going to promise you that I won't forget to dance with you under them anymore. I won't forget to grab a blanket, put it in the back of my pickup, and lay out underneath the night sky and watch the stars light it up. I won't promise you wishes, but I do promise that I'll wish upon every falling star with you."

And that was all I needed to hear. I don't need empty promises. I don't need him to tell me he'll make all my wildest dreams happen, because it's just not possible. What I need to hear is that he'll be by my side, walking with me through our crazy life, remembering that we are in this together.

I stop swaying long enough just to roll up on my toes and kiss him on his jaw, then move my lips to his mouth. I take his face in my hands and look into his eyes and tell him what I know he needs to hear, what I need to say. "I love you more than all my wishes. You're the only wish I will ever need."

Chapter Eighteen

Barrett

I REMEMBER THE day I saw her differently. It was homecoming Friday in 1990, and the entire school was in the gym, waiting for our coach to come give us a pep talk. I sat in the stands with the rest of the varsity Bobcats football team. We wore our game day jerseys and gave each other hell for no other reason than the fact than that was what teenage boys did. My favorite ball cap sat low on my forehead, the curve done just perfect. I enjoyed the bending of the rules that allowed us more freedom to wear hats during school because of homecoming.

I'm sitting next to Josh, my best friend for as long as I can remember, laughing at something he just said, when I see Tess walk through the gym doors. She has a streak of bright red in her blonde curly hair, the same color red that is on my jersey, and a red ribbon-thing that is tied in a bow on top of her head. She's dressed pretty low-key with tight, light-washed jeans, which I could tell fit like they were made for her, a pair of white Converse All Stars, and a blue-and-white-striped tee. I can see a tiny sliver of her stomach peeking out from under her shirt. It's just tight enough to show me that she definitely isn't the young girl she once was. Even though she's dressed casually, she somehow makes it work. She looks like the All-American-Girl-Next-Door who, surprisingly enough, is basically the girl next door. She grew up three blocks away from me. I've known her my entire life, yet today, I see her in a whole new light. When the hell did Tess become that?

Holy hell… she is beautiful. She's walking with her best friend, Lauren, and a bunch of other girls. As they walk past us smiling, I find myself willing her to look my direction. I can't take my eyes off her. She has me mesmerized.

Do you see me, Tess?

Do you see me the way I now see you?

Her laughter floats up to me and I hear it… everywhere. I see her glance up at the stands out of the corner of her eyes, smile still in place, and our eyes meet. My breath catches as her bright blue eyes sparkle with mischief. Her smile widens, and her eyes twinkle when they land on mine, and I feel like my entire world has forever changed. Lauren whispers something in Tess's ear, and she shakes her head slightly and giggles. I want desperately to know what Lauren just whispered to her, jealous that she is so close to her. I've never looked at Tess this way before. And as I glance around at the other guys, I notice a shift. They're all watching her. Her. She turns heads when she doesn't even realize it. Every eye seems to be on her, and I feel this insane desire to run down the bleachers, shield her from their gazes, and declare her as mine for the entire school to hear.

How long has this been going on? How long has she been turning heads? Have I been blind this entire time, or have all our eyes been opened at the same time? It isn't that I thought she was ugly before — it's just that I never noticed her. Sitting there, watching her walk through the gym until she and her group of friends climb the bleachers and take a seat, I have one thought running through my mind. I'm going to marry her someday. Crazy? Probably. At that moment, I don't give a flying turkey. I can't think of a single thing other than how to make her mine. I have always liked Tess. We got along well, and her friends are friends with my friends. I know her. But in that moment, I realize I want to know her in an entirely different way.

After the pep rally, I waited for her outside the gym doors. My palms are sweating, my heart racing. I can't understand why I feel so nervous. I just know that, even though I've had a thousand conversations with Tess before now, this is the only one that matters. This is the big one. The one that will change my life forever. I take off my ball cap and turn it backward so I won't miss her walking past. I don't want anything shielding my eyes from seeing hers.

I see Lauren first and know Tess will be right behind her. I stand a little straighter, thankful that the guys haven't noticed that I stayed behind. Miracle of all miracles there. Except for Josh. But I know he doesn't have eyes for my girl. He has his sights set on Lauren. At least that's what he told me when he noticed my attention drawn to the bleachers rather than the coach on the gym floor trying to get us keyed up for tonight's game. And when he made the varsity players — including me — come down to the floor with him to help get the students pumped up, I was able to flick my eyes in her direction. I probably looked like an insane person, not being able to stop my eyes from drifting over to where she was sitting. Again, I didn't care.

The second she walks through the gym doors, I touch her arm. It wasn't the first time we have touched. Growing up together, we've played on the playground together, had recess together, been on field trips and already had a million other memories together. But none of them were together. And this touch? It felt like the first. The first time I touched my forever.

I don't have some crazy electrical shock. I don't have tingles. I have the thrill and knowledge that I am holding the arm of the person I want around for the rest of my life.

I want to be the reason her heart beat faster.

I want to be the person she looks at with stars in her eyes.

"Hi." That's my opening line. Apparently, my tongue has forgotten how to form actual words. My brain has forgotten how to function. And that's what it came up with.

She smiles a beautiful smile. A smile that is directed only for me. "Hi, Barrett."

"Can I give you a ride home?" I ask her.

It's then that I know I want to forever be her way home.

"Yeah." Her smile is still in place. She didn't hesitate. It's like she expected it, or hoped for it. I'm banking on the latter.

"Yeah?"

Her.

Smile.

I am done for. She smiled at me and that's all it took. I follow her to her locker while she gathers her things. I'm not a bit ashamed to admit that I check out her butt as often as possible. She follows me to my locker while I get my things. We walk out the front door and through the parking lot to my pickup — my dad's pickup, that is. It is only a couple years old, a maroon Chevy. Dad let me take it often. I never understood why, but I didn't question it. I open the passenger door and grab her hand to help her into the seat. Such a simple act, but it feels so... good. She lays her backpack on the floor beside her feet, and I find myself ridiculously grateful that she didn't put it on the seat next to her. I didn't want a barrier between us. I round the front and climb into the driver's seat, then throw my backpack into the small back seat of the extended cab.

We don't talk much on the way to her house. But it isn't

weird. It's comfortable.

"Are you coming to the game tonight?"

"I go to every game."

"You do?"

"Of course."

I love that she goes to the games.

I smile.

She returns my smile.

"Good."

She smiles.

I pull up to her house, put the pickup in park, and get out at the same time she does. I walk her to her front door.

"Would you do something for me tonight?"

"What's that?"

I take off my cap, grab hold of my jersey from behind my neck, and pull it off, leaving me in just my white V-neck T-shirt. I put my cap back on, backward again so I can see her clearly. I hand her my jersey.

She smiles.

"Wear it tonight?"

"Yeah?"

"Yeah. And after the game. Wait for me, okay?"

"Okay."

She smiles.

Her smile is what I fell in love with first. Because when it is directed at me, it means something. It means she is happy because of something that I have been involved in somehow. I brought her happiness. I wanted to bring her happiness forever.

I play my best game that night. And every time I think about Tess cheering in the stands wearing my jersey, what I'm assuming looks like a goofy-ass smile spreads across my face, and I play harder because I want to impress her. I want her to be proud to be wearing my jersey.

After the game, I sit through our post-game talk in the locker room but don't hear a word of it. I shower, and then I come out of the locker room. To Tess. She waited, just like I asked her to.

She's leaning against my pickup, hair in a ponytail.

She's smiling.

I smile back.

And that is that. From now on, we will no longer be Tess. And. Barrett. We are Tess and Barrett. Barrett and Tess. And I love it. She loves it.

I didn't think life could get better. The day she allowed me to change her name to match my own, I knew. Life could get better. It could be the best. I looked into her eyes and promised her forever and in the deepest parts of my heart I meant it. She looked into my eyes and promised me her forever, and I knew in the deepest part of her heart that she meant it also. On that day, her beauty was unmatched. Unwavering. But it was more than her outside beauty. I fell in love with Tess's heart, her caring and loving nature, the way she laughed easily, allowing me to tease her. I fell in love with the way she loved me.

Our time here is about getting back to the way we fell in love. Last night we danced together by the light of candles and moonlight. Tonight, I plan to remind her of something else we used to love to do together, before life got too busy. After I get everything set up outside, I send a text to Tess.

Me: *Come outside.*

My Girl: *Huh? Where are you?*

Me: *Outside. Duh.*

My Girl: *Dude. Did you just say duh?*

Me: *I did. Did you just call me dude? That's kind of hot.*

My Girl: *SMH — only you.*

Me: *Get your cute ass out here.*

My Girl: *Why? It's cold!*

Me: *Because I said so. Now be a good girl and get your ass out here.*

My Girl: *You know it's not nice to be so bossy.*

Me: *Don't lie. You're so turned on right now from my bossiness and from me calling you good girl.*

My Girl: *Whatever. Where outside?*

Me: *I'm on the dick.*

My Girl: *Ummmmmmm*
Me: *I meant dick.*

Me: *DICK.*

Me: WTH? DECK!

My Girl: Awww, autocorrect hates you too! ☺

Me: Well, if I'm honest, I'd take you coming out on my dick too.

My Girl: You're such a weird horny ass.

Me: Weird horny ass, huh?

My Girl: Yup. Ok, if I don't come out there, what are you gonna do? Shank my ass for being a bad girl?

Me: I don't think I'll go to that extreme.

My Girl: But bad girls get shanked.

Me: Oh, pretty girl, just stop texting and get your ass out here already or I will SPANK your ass — not SHANK it like you're asking me to, bad girl.

My Girl: Oh my gosh. Damn you autocorrect! **shakes fist**

Me: Just get out here before I come in there and lick you up and throw you over my shoulder to bring you out here.

My Girl: *A good licking isn't so bad.*

Me: *I give up. Just come outside please?*

I'm standing outside on the deck waiting for her when she comes outside, a blanket wrapped around her shoulders. She's giggling at our texting snafu and looks calm and relaxed, the same way she's been for the last few days since we arrived. I grab her hand as soon as she gets close to me and lead her down the stone path to the back yard where the fire ring is sitting, deep set and surrounded by landscape rocks. The sun has almost set, the last of the day's rays reflecting off the lake water, making the night take on a mysterious form. The hot tub that sits off to the side we haven't had the pleasure of enjoying yet, but we plan to. Even with the cooler temperatures of Michigan autumn biting at our backsides, it's serene, beautiful, tranquil even.

We sit next to each other in the dark-stained Adirondack chairs that are set around the fire ring. She's still wrapped in her big, fleece, red-plaid throw blanket, and she stares at the fire, seemingly content.

I've been sitting out here for a while, thinking, going over in my head what I want to say to her. What to say to make the past few months go away, to make it better. But maybe I already have. We're back to ourselves. Or getting closer every minute, at least.

"You know, I don't remember the moment we met," I tell her.

"Me either. I was thinking about that earlier too. So many people have these great when-we-met stories, and you've just… been there… my entire life. I'm not complaining, but I know what you mean."

"I guess. I do remember the day I saw you differently though."

"You do?" she asks.

"I do," I say, looking straight into her bright blue eyes. The flames from the fire are making her blue eyes shine even more, shine brighter. I go on to tell her about the pep rally, my feelings, what I remember about the following few weeks. How I fell head over heels in love with her when I was still a teenager — barely able to comprehend what love was at that age, but still old enough to understand that what I felt wouldn't change over time.

By the time I finish with the story, she has silent tears slowly trickling down her cheeks, and her breathing is coming in a little heavier. But what I notice most is that she's radiating with love. For me.

"Tess. That moment that I saw you walk through those gym doors at the homecoming pep rally, my world was turned on its axis. No longer did I think of tomorrow, but I thought about forever. Of how you would be part of my forever. I no longer cared if I crossed everything off my teenage bucket list. I didn't care if I went on to play college ball, if I traveled all over the world, or if I gave people a reason to remember my name. You were all that mattered — and still are. I knew, without a doubt knew, that if I could get you to smile my way, shine your eyes in my direction, give me your love, that I would do anything and everything in my power to treasure it, to keep it. I wanted to show you every single day what you mean to me. I failed you."

"Barrett, no. You didn't fail me."

"I did. I know that you understood in your head that I still loved you. But you weren't seeing it. You weren't feeling it. At least not in the capacity you deserve. I should have never let you feel like I wasn't continuing to fall in love with you. I might be a selfish son of a bitch for saying this, but I want to be the one that puts the spark in your eyes every day. I want to be the reason your heart beats faster, the cause of your bright smile. I sat on those bleachers that day and willed you to look my way, and you did. You looked my way. And that's all it took. I felt it when you let me drive you home from school that day and agreed to wear my jersey. But I forgot that feeling. I forgot that you made me feel like the king of the school that day. I wanted to get on the speaker at the football field and tell everyone that you were mine, even though you weren't yet. I felt like I had won the best thing in the world, just by you agreeing to wear my jersey.

"And I did. I discovered the best treasure that day. I discovered you. But I got wrapped up in my own self, Tess. I neglected to remember you changed my world for the better. In all the mundane normalcy of our lives, I let it ruin us. I let the day-to-day stuff lead and used it for an excuse. I won't do it again. I promise you."

"Barrett. I love you so much. I failed, too…" she starts saying, but before she can continue, I reach over and pull her into my lap. I can't stand another moment of not having her in my arms. I lean down and kiss her, showing her that I don't feel like she failed me. And maybe she doesn't feel like I failed her either, but she needs to hear my words. Deserves to hear them. I know we'd just gotten a little lost, but we are finding our way back to one another. I hold her close and begin shifting her so she is straddling me. I didn't plan on the kiss going this way. Hell, I didn't plan the kiss at all. I planned on us sitting around the fire, talking, hashing everything out.

But those plans changed the moment I had her in my

lap.

Now the plan is for kisses. Lots and lots of kisses. Kisses of all kinds.

Butterfly kisses.

Cheek kisses.

Neck kisses.

Eyelid kisses.

Throat kisses.

Open mouth kisses.

Passionate kisses.

I feel a raindrop hit the top of my forehead. And soon another. And another. It didn't stop us from kissing each other though. Nothing can make me tear my mouth from hers. I stand up, awkward as hell, from the Adirondack chair, with her still wrapped around me. We laugh around each other's mouths at the klutziness of trying to stand still linked together, but we don't part.

"Hold tight — don't let go."

She holds my face in her hands and looks into my eyes, through the rain that is coming down even heavier now, a steady shower of cool raindrops. Her legs are still wrapped around my waist with her ankles hooked tightly. "Never," she says with such confidence and happiness in her voice that it makes me shudder.

We walk through the rain, back up the stone path and into the cabin. I fumble for the knob and twist. The door opens, and I kick it back closed; the fact that this is the second time we have walked into the cabin lost in each other's kiss isn't lost on me. And I won't change it for the world.

We only make it to the couch before we stumble and fall, still linked together by our mouths, our hands, our legs.

I tug and pull until her clothes are a wet mess on the

floor.

She stands over me on the couch, blue eyes shining, lips red and swollen from my kisses. Completely naked. Completely unashamed. She snaps her fingers once. I sit up instantly, smiling up at her.

She tugs and pulls until my clothes are in a wet pile on the floor beside hers.

I flip her over onto her stomach and continue my kisses.

Shoulder kisses.

Back-of-her-neck kisses.

Between-her-shoulder-blade kisses.

Small-of-her-back kisses.

I kiss her everywhere.

She kisses me everywhere.

We kiss and kiss and kiss. We touch. We caress. We remember. We make love on the couch. We make love in the claw foot tub. We make love in the bed, and, when we are sated and have had our fill of each other, we lie wrapped in each other's arms, bodies exhausted, hearts happy, souls complete. We listen to the rain and thunder until we fall asleep holding one another. We are finally once again… us.

Chapter Nineteen

Tess

"I REMEMBER SEEING you in the bleachers that day. For some reason, my eyes were drawn to you. I couldn't stop glancing up at you. Lauren whispered to me something about how hot you and Josh looked then told me you were staring at me. I didn't know what to do. I'd never been nervous around you before. But right then, I was. I desperately hoped that you were staring at me, and that it was for the same reason that I wanted to stare at you. When Coach called you guys up front, I saw your eyes flick over in my direction," I tell him after we had both woken up from a rain-induced nap, and he gives me a huge grin, not ashamed at all that I saw him looking my way. Of course, this isn't the first time either of us have revisited this story, but it always makes me smile remembering those first few days, weeks, months of loving each other. Finding each other, discovering each other in an entirely different way than we had before.

"Man, Barrett. I fell so hard and so fast for you. It's kind of crazy since we had known each other our entire lives. It was like a switch was flipped, and I saw you in an entirely different light. I remember feeling like the luckiest girl in the entire world that your eyes only found mine. That you had picked me. We were so young. Can you imagine our kids having that kind of love already?"

"Yeah. Look at Grady. He only has eyes for Bri. Only her. He reminds me so much of the way I was with you. When he sees her wearing his football jersey, it's like his chest swells with pride. I know the feeling. The first time I saw you in my jersey, I had the same reaction. I don't know how he has the self-control to not take things to the next step with her. I couldn't wait five minutes." He chuckles.

I smile, remembering how he grabbed my arm the second I walked through the gym doors. I couldn't wait until that pep rally was over. I wanted to find him afterward so badly, but he found me first. From that touch on, he didn't waver. I was his. He made sure I knew it in the little things he did.

"When you were driving me home that night, I was so nervous." I grin at the memory. "I still don't know why I was so nervous. I think it suddenly occurred to me that I wanted something more to happen between us, and I didn't know what I would have done if you weren't thinking the same thing. Then you asked me to wear your jersey, and it was like I had just won the lottery. The hot guy lottery," I say with a grin.

He laughs at me but otherwise stays silent as he lets me continue walking down my own memory path.

"Life is funny, isn't it?"

"What do you mean?" he asked.

"I guess just that neither of us really thought much of each other. You were always just Barrett Ryan to me. My buddy. The kid who used to always bring cold lunch to school because you hated the school lunches. You always had a bologna and cheese sandwich and a Hostess chocolate cupcake. Every single day. You were the kid who always smiled at everyone, who dominated the playground with your mad kickball skills, who got in trouble for mouthing back to Mrs. Kaplan because she made Eric feel about an inch tall when his parents couldn't afford to buy him new snow boots." I stop talking and look at him. "Do you remember that?"

"I do. I was so pissed at her. His parents both lost their jobs that year — I remember hearing my parents talk about it. I got a blue slip, so I went home and told my parents about what happened. They didn't even care about the blue slip. Dad took me to Walmart, bought Eric and his siblings each a pair of snow boots, and shoved some cash in an envelope. He had me drop them off at their door and run. He didn't want them to know who it was from."

"Sounds like your dad. Such a good man. He always put others before himself. You remind me of him, you know? That way, I mean. You're always helping people, willing to help someone move. You even keep those gift cards in your wallet for emergencies when you see someone who needs it more than us. You don't think I know about that, but I do. And the kids have seen it. You do those things not for people to see it, but because you have a big heart."

He graces me with one of his small smiles, and I continue my story.

"Then suddenly you were Barrett Ryan. Still all those things but more. So much more. Why we both started thinking differently at the same time is beyond me, but I know it was meant to be."

His eyes go soft as he takes all of me in, but his voice is gruff, "Yeah, it was. It is."

"I won't let it happen to us again."

"You won't have to worry about that because I won't either."

This man.
He's far from perfect.
But he's perfect for me.
Our dream is wide awake, and we are living it.

Chapter Twenty

Barrett

I wake up slowly, body completely spent and exhausted — in the best way possible — from our activities the day before. Two nights ago we played strip poker… kind of… which turned into naked Sorry, naked Checkers, naked Twister, naked… well, let's just say it became our Reign of Nakedness that lasted until… now. Yesterday morning, we woke up and decided it was a good idea to spend the entire day naked.

We slept randomly, played more games, and cooked (things that didn't splatter). We ate ice cream sundaes, and we talked. Actually talked. About things other than the kids, other than promising each other we were still in love with each other. I'll spend the rest of my life making sure she knows that, but for this week, we've said it enough. We both get it. Now it's time to show each other. Actions do speak louder than words, after all.

Not a single scrap of clothing was placed on either of our bodies for a second of the entire day. It. Was. Awesome.

Tess has a glorious body. I've loved it every minute of our years together. It always turns me on, makes me want to beat my chest and shout with pride to the world that this hottie is mine. So given the chance to see her all day in her favorite outfit of mine, I definitely took full advantage. I couldn't keep my hands off her. Even if we were eating or resting, I was touching her in some way. It gave me peace. A peace to remind me that we survived the crap we put ourselves through. And a reminder that we will always survive, as long as we turn toward one another rather than against one another.

The fact that I'm not touching her now is probably what woke me up. I don't feel her near me. I'm not touching a part of her body and, quite frankly, that annoys me. I lift my head, eyes still adjusting to the soft light that comes through the fabric-shade-covered windows. I roll over and see the other half of the bed we have been sharing empty, which also annoys me.

I let out a growl and groan, "Tess?! Get your ass back in here!"

Silence.

Okay, that's weird.

One quick look to the side where the bathroom is attached to the bedroom of our small cabin, I see that the door is wide open and the room is dark, which in my half-asleep state of mind, I'm vaguely aware means that she's not in there.

"Tess! Baby, where are you?" I shout once more.

Silence.

What. The. Hell.

Where is Tess? I quickly make my way out of the bed, much quicker than my body likes, considering how worn out it is, not that I mind the exhaustion. But what I do mind is the fact that I haven't figured out where she is.

I find a pair of blue, plaid pajamas pants draped over the arm of the chair that sits in the corner of the bedroom and pull them up my legs as I make my way into the main room of the cabin. The cabin is not huge, only around a thousand square feet, and the fact that the main area is just one large room that contains the TV-watching area, a dining table, and the kitchen just off the side of it, tells me that there's not places for her to play hide and seek.

"Tess?" I ask to the silence once again.

I don't know why I keep calling her name. Clearly she isn't here.

I stop abruptly when I spot a medium-sized gift-wrapped box with a card leaning against it. The envelope has my name on it, written in Tess's handwriting.

I grasp hold of the envelope and scrunch my eyebrows at the gift, more than a little curious where she can be. Still holding the envelope, I walk over to the front door and open it up. I stick my head out the door and a quick check outside tells me that she's gone. As in, car is gone. A million thoughts and questions race through my mind, but one thought never does. I know she's not left me.

I glance into the kitchen and notice that there's an almost-full pot of coffee, and it's still warm, which again, tells me that she didn't leave too long ago. Just call me Sherlock Holmes.

I grab a mug from the cupboard — still annoyed that I didn't get my normal wake up by nuzzling my face into her neck and stealing a sip of her coffee — pour myself a cup, and sit down at the kitchen table next to the gift.

I open the envelope and slide out the handwritten note that was folded neatly and placed inside.

Barrett—

I love you.

I love you.

I love you.

I love you.

I could repeat it a million times, and it still won't be enough. You're the reason I am who I am to this day. Every day for us is crazy.

And my love, my respect, my adoration for you somehow got lost in the shuffle of our lives.

I never lost the feeling. I'm so happy in our life, darling. Having you to share everything with means everything to me. Your love for me has never wavered, I know this. In the deepest part of my heart that only you've reached.

I love that you love our family fiercely.

I love that you push our boys to be men.

I love that you tell me I'm beautiful, even when I'm not.

I love that you tell me I smell good.

I love that you don't hesitate in telling me when I'm moody.

I love that you let me be moody then make me snap out of it.

I love that you tease me.

I love that you catch my tackle hugs.

I love that you put your phone down for me. (usually)

I love that you bury your nose in my neck when you need me.

I love that you allow me to be a goober.

I love it even more that you're willing to be a

goober with me.

I love that when I get a wild hair up my ass and decide I'm going to learn something new, you embrace it and laugh at me as well as with me when I'm a fumbling kickboxing disaster.

I love that you let me cry when I need to.

I love that you have to wake up every morning by giving me a kiss on your place.

I love that you grow a beard when I want to see your scruff.

I love that sometimes I catch you staring at me.

I love that you dance with me even when I know you hate dancing.

I love that you protect our daughters with incredible passion.

I love that you don't kiss my ass.

I love that you let me eat chocolate cake in our bed.

I love that you want to take selfies of us together.

I love that you make me laugh every single day.

I love that you embrace our text fumbles.

I love that you still jam to our 80s music.

But most of all…

I love being yours.

There's not a single person on this earth who I'd rather do life with.

You have my heart forever.

We fumbled.

We picked ourselves back up.

xoxo
Your pretty girl

Well, damn. I actually have tears in my eyes. And a few may or may not have escaped.

I take a deep breath and let it out and sip at my coffee. I stand up and walk over to look out the large picture window in the living area. All we see behind us is woods. Much like our own home, but it's even denser here. Flurries are coming down from the grey sky. It's weird that just a few days ago it was raining, and now it's turning so cold that it's snowing. It makes me itch for Tess to be back here. I trust her driving in the snow, but it still doesn't make me feel any less nervous to have her out there in it.

I walk back over to the table and pick up the note she wrote me, straight from her heart to mine. I read it again and once more. Then I start to tear the paper off the box.

A basket is placed inside filled to overflowing.

First I see a soft-book photo album. The note attached to it reads:

The special times meant just for me and you

What I see inside makes my pulse race. It's full of pictures we've taken of each other in random times that I thought we had long since deleted. But more than that, there's a whole section of pictures I've never seen before. Seems my little minx had some boudoir pictures taken without my knowledge. Pictures of her in just a sexy bra and panties with my tool belt around her waist. Some in one of my button-down shirts, open and barely revealing some of my favorite fun parts of hers to play with. Her eyes are dark and smoky and her lips light pink and glistening. Her hair is all curls. I can't help but feel a little cheated that I didn't get to be there for those pictures. Although, I'm pretty sure if I had been standing in that room the photographer (who had damn sure better been a female) would have gotten an eye-full.

I start going through the contents of the rest of the basket. One of the corniest T-shirts I've ever seen, but I'll wear it loud and proud, is rolled up in one of the corners. It's a dark grey, short-sleeve shirt with black letters. She saw it at a novelty shop last Christmas and joked that she was going to get it for me. She followed through.

Tatted Up Bearded Dudes Do It Better.

A six-pack of my favorite craft brew was under the shirt, one that we are rarely able to buy, or find, for that matter. Several cards that look like coupons for things ranging from breakfast in bed to date-night at my favorite steakhouse to some date-nights that will happen after the kids are tucked away safely in their own beds. And finally, a wooden watch. It's cool as shit, to be honest. I've been wanting one for years but never spent the money on it. I flip it over and on the back is engraved:

I've Loved You Every Second

I pick up my cell phone and quickly shoot off a text. I have no idea where Tess is, but after going through this box and reading her note, she needs to get her cute butt back here. Now.

Me: *You need to get your ass back here.*

I wait impatiently for the ten seconds it takes for her to text me back.

My Girl: I take it you liked my present?

Me: Wrong. I loved it.

My Girl: I'm glad.

Me: Now get back here. The pictures in the album aren't humping my current situation.

My Girl: LOL

Me: It's not funny!

My Girl: It totally is.

Me: So, it's like that, huh? You don't want it genital when you get back here?

My Girl: DYING! Oh, B— AC hit you again.

I scroll back up and bust out laughing. Although, humping and genitals is fairly spot on for what I'm feeling right now. When I tell her to get her ass back here now, I'm totally serious. Between her words and the boudoir photo album, I'm ready to go… again.

Me: This damn phone.

My Girl: Right. It's the phone. Not your thumbs.

Me: It totally is. I meant to say the album isn't helping my situation and that you don't want it gentle.

My Girl: …

Me: Whatever. Good thing I embrace our texts, yeah?

My Girl: LOL

Me: So, when are you coming back from wherever you're at?

My Girl: Just checking out. Went to get more hookers then I'll be home to the cabin soon. XXX

Me: So, hookers and kissing. A good day for all!

My Girl: Ok, we're done. Clearly texting is just not meant for us today. I meant FOOD! How does food turn into hookers?

Me: Just hurry up — no hookers necessary ;)

My Girl: Ok. These lines are so slutty compared to what I'm used to.

Me: That's because they're hookers. Geesh.

> *My Girl:* Done. I think I should stop texting for a while.

> *Me:* LOL This entire thread made me so happy.

> *My Girl:* Ugh. Ok, I'll see you soon. I promise. Even with the SLOW lines.

> *Me:* Drive safe. Love you.

> *My Girl:* Love you!!!!!!!

Well, that was fun. At least our texting keeps us both entertained. I figure I have at least thirty minutes until Tess gets back. The nearest town is about twenty minutes away, and it sounds like she is just out grabbing some groceries. I hop in and out of the shower quickly, pull on a pair of jeans and a dark blue flannel shirt, and start a fire in the wood-burning stove that sits in the corner of the room. While I'm twisting newspapers and strategically placing logs in the woodstove, I call James to check in on everything at home. Tess and I may be away from home to reconnect with each other, but we've still made sure to keep in contact with the kids.

It's about nine o'clock, so I know the kids will be at school already, but we talked to each of them last night, so now is simply my time to checking in with James to make sure there isn't anything he needs to tell me that he can't when the kids are around. I find his name in my recent calls and press send.

After just the second ring, he picks up, "Hey brother!"

"Hey there. How was your morning?"

"Oh, the typical. Saving lives by finding Mags' missing algebra book, making Harper the best eggs she's ever eaten in her entire history of ever eating eggs, her words, not mine, and feeling like a total wimp after watching Grady work out on his torture chamber."

"Yep. Sounds about right." I laugh.

"Seriously, Barrett. Grady is getting huge. Maybe there's something to that thing."

"I know. Every time I go out there with him, though, it totally kicks my ass."

He busts out laughing. "I can see that. It's hell."

"Yep." I laugh again. "So, how are things going? We talked to the kids last night, you know, but I figured you'd be able to tell us more when they're not hanging on your every word."

"You know them well. I bow to you."

We both laugh lightly. He's such a smartass.

"Honestly, it's going well. Maggie is Maggie — you know. She always just lets life roll off her shoulders. I can't believe how carefree she is. She definitely got that from you. Tess was never that way growing up."

"No, she wasn't. Still isn't. She has gotten more easygoing as I've forced it on her by being around my awesome self," I say, only to be interrupted by James.

"Yeah, yeah, yeah. Anyway, as I was saying. Maggie is great. Easy peasy. But Barrett — you're gonna have trouble soon. A few of Grady's buddies were over after practice last night. Fair warning. It does not go unnoticed that Grady's little sister is gorgeous, easy going, athletic, and a generally happy girl who's able to just hang as one of the guys and doesn't try to show off for them all the time. It also doesn't go unnoticed that Grady would rather cut his left arm off than watch his sister date. So, I think you're safe, for now anyway, but the minute Grady is off to college, it'll be like open season."

I groan in response and drop my head into my hand. This isn't news to me. She's a replica of her mother. She is gorgeous, and I don't just think that because she's my little girl. "I know this, but thank you very much for the reminder. I told Brandon that he needed to somehow infiltrate back into the school next year so he could take over in Grady's absence."

James laughs loudly. "Good plan. Probably better than you stalking the halls."

"I'm not above it. So, what else? Grady? How is he doing with everything that happened?"

"He's managing — seems to be doing well, actually. Like I said, he kicked some butt out there on his torture chamber this morning. I almost I threw up for him. He's been working especially hard since he had a two-game suspension for the fight. Even though he still goes to practice, I guess he just wants to prove to Coach Mac that he's still the same guy. You know him better than I do."

I place another log on the fire and use the fireplace poker to move the wood around. The flames begin to build, so I slowly close the glass door then move over to the couch and settle in with a cup of coffee, propping up my sock-covered feet on the low table.

"I know the suspension about killed him, but I think he's worrying the most over what this could potentially do for his scholarships. According to his coach, he doesn't have anything to worry about though."

"He talked to me about that the first night I was here,"

he tells me.

"That doesn't surprise me. I hate that it happened, but I do like that it knocked him on his ass a bit. Knowing that there are consequences for your actions is a hard lesson to learn."

"For sure. I don't blame him for what he did though."

"Nope."

"How about this for a development only about eight years in the making. I think it's safe to say that he and Bri are officially out of the friend zone, though. About damn time, if you ask me," he mutters the last sentence.

"Yeah? Good," I grunt.

"Yeah. At least Maggie told me that the whole school is talking about how they're BF and GF now — her words not mine, obvs." He laughs at his use of Mag-Speak. "Actually, he did tell me that he was taking her out on a date on Saturday night. Don't tell him I told you that, though. I think he wants to be the one to tell you guys when you get home on Sunday."

"That's awesome. I'll play dumb when we talk to the kids tonight."

I hear a vehicle pull into the gravel drive and quickly remember that I was only talking to him to keep my mind busy while waiting for Tess.

"Listen, Tess just got back from getting groceries — or slutty hookers — one of the two. Not entirely sure since she left before I was even awake this morning."

"I'm going to go out on a limb here and guess that the slutty hookers thing was another texting blunder?"

"Absolutely."

He laughs loudly. "Alright. Tell her to text me later. It's always my favorite part of the day. But I'll let you go. I don't need to be on the phone to hear you two greet each other," he says with a fake, exaggerated gag, as if he hasn't grown up one single bit. Makes me love him even more. He's a good brother-in-law but an even better friend.

Even still, I laugh at him. "I would deny it, but… yeah. Oh — how's Harps sleeping?"

"Good. Surprisingly enough. Two nights ago she woke up a couple times, but last night she didn't at all."

"Awesome. Man, if she was out of the habit of waking up in the middle of the night when we got back home, I'd owe you. Big time."

"Working on it. The little twerp." He chuckles. He loves Harper like his own baby girl, so I know his words are teasing.

"Thanks again for staying with them. It means a lot."

"Are you guys… I mean, is it helping?"

"It is. I don't think either of us knew how badly we needed time away."

"I get it. I'd rather see you two have that time together."

"Thanks, man. Tell the kids we love them and we'll call tonight."

"Oh, I almost forgot. Don't call tonight. I promised the kids we'd meet Cole halfway for pizza. There's this little parlor that is going under that contacted me a few weeks ago. Thought we'd do a little drive-by eating and see what's up with it. Lily's meeting us, too."

Lily is James' daughter. James' wife, Nicole, had a bit (or a lot) of a breakdown when Lily was just three years old. She took off, never to be heard from again from anyone. Lily is the light of James' life, since it was always just the two of them. He never remarried. We never pushed it; he dated a few ladies here and there, but his main focus was always Lily.

"That's great. Alright, so we'll talk tomorrow. Later."

"Later," he says before he hangs up.

I put my phone down on the coffee table and walk over to the front door. I peek out to see if it looks like Tess has enough bags that she needs my help or if it's just a couple.

"Hey, pretty girl!" I shout out to my bride as I step out on the front porch.

"Hey, babe!"

"Are the slutty hookers coming in their own car?"

"Yep! I told them they'd need to have their own way out of here when we were done with them, so they couldn't ride with me." She grins cheekily at me then reaches into the back seat and grabs what looks like three bags of groceries before shutting the door with her hip. Since it seems that's all there is, I let her get it, knowing she'll wave me off anyway.

"Nice," I say with a smile as she gets closer. She's wearing one of my old plaid flannel shirts. And by old, I think it might have been around in the early 90s. It's rolled up at the sleeves and hangs low on her body. I might have to spank her for not wearing a coat. Her long legs are covered by another pair of skinny jeans that I'm pretty sure were somehow made for her body. With a couple of tattered holes strategically placed, they're perfectly distressed, as I've heard Maggie call it on more than one occasion, (a little shoulder pat for my fatherly listening skills on that one). Her hair is pulled back in a messy ponytail, her natural curl making it messy whether she wants it to be or not.

But her smile aimed at me is what has my gut clenching. It's an infectious smile, one that our children all inherited from her. It's always been infectious. As I got older, I recognized this about her. I remember it lighting up a room, even before we became a *we*. It always pulls me in, it always pulls everyone in. Over time, I also came to realize that it isn't only her smile that draws everyone to her, it's her entire demeanor. She has always been happy, even in times that she probably didn't need or want to be. I asked her once if it was exhausting to always be the one to cheer others up. She told me it's more exhausting to complain and be unhappy than it is to just allow the goodness of life to soak in. Looking at her happy smile now, even after getting up early, grocery shopping with the slutty hookers, and driving home in the snow, all evidence points to that being truth. She's happy. Genuinely happy.

I lean down and take the bags from her hands and walk back into the cabin. I place them down on the counter in the kitchen then turn and wrap my arms around her. I dip my face close and kiss my spot, because starting a day without it just plain sucks. "Morning, babe."

"Mmm…" she says.

I don't lift my face from her neck. Instead I inhale her sugary scent and continue kissing her neck. I lift her up and place her on the counter, my lips never leaving her skin.

She wraps her arms around my neck and weakly says, "Ice cream."

"Yep. No. What?"

She giggles. "Ice cream. In one of the bags. We need to put groceries away, and I know from the past few days that if we don't stay on task we'll definitely stray from what we need to do."

"Is that such a bad thing?" I ask, grabbing the fleshy part beneath her butt.

She squirms at my touch. "Nope. But I want that Ben & Jerry's."

I smile at her and shake my head before chuckling. "Fine. You win. I won't be the one to stand in the way of your

Chocolate Brownie Batter. What else did you get?"

"Oh, you know, just the basics. Plus, I may have gotten the ingredients to make your favorites."

"You did?" I ask.

"I did. Tonight, we're having BBQ ribs, though we'll have to just bake them since we don't have a grill, homemade coleslaw, and mac and cheese, and some Peanut Butter Fudge Ben & Jerry's for dessert. Their pickle selection isn't what we have at home, so you're just gonna have to deal."

"Everything you just said just gave me a boner."

She bends over laughing then stands up quickly and runs to the bathroom. After a minute I hear the toilet flush then the water turn on and off. She comes back into the kitchen area wiping her eyes. She takes one look at me and bursts into a fit of giggles all over again.

I pull her into my arms and look down into her crystal blue eyes that are glistening at me with love. "Thank you for the gifts. I love them. Especially the spank bank material." I smile down at her.

And another fit of giggles.

"You're welcome," she says through a wide smile.

"I loved the note the most," I say, my voice low and husky even in my own ears. I take a curl that fell from her ponytail and tuck it behind her ear and drag my finger down her face.

"Yeah? It wasn't corny?"

"Oh, it was corny. But I loved it anyway," I say knowing that she'll know I'm teasing. Not about the loving it part, only about it being corny.

"So just the right about of corniness, then?"

"Just right."

"I love you, Tess. I know we've talked about it several times this week, but I do. Some days I wake up and I'm still in shock that you're mine. I love the life we've created. I even love that we disconnected for the past few months."

"Why?" she asks, her eyebrows bunched together.

"Because it led us here. This week has been so amazing. And not just because I've gotten some hot sex. Oomph." She hits me in the stomach and we both laugh. We've been laughing this past week. More than is probably normal, but that's all right. I won't trade it for the world.

I straighten back up and study her face. "Do you know what I mean, though?"

"I do. I guess I hadn't thought of it that way. Us forgetting our way only led us to finding our way again. And the journey has been fun, and probably what we needed even before we got a little lost."

"Exactly. Now, before we drop everything for some more hot sex, let's take care of this…" I point to the groceries. "… and eat some late breakfast."

"Good plan," she says then lifts up on her tiptoes and kisses me square on the mouth. It's one of my favorite kisses from her.

As I help put away the groceries, I let her know that I talked to James and filled her in on everything that was happening at home, including Grady's secret but not so secret date with Bri. She's thrilled with the idea and excited to hear about it from Grady but she understands that he wants to be the one to tell us himself. After we get everything put away, we prepare the ribs so we can start slow-roasting them a little later. We get the rest of the meal ready and put it in the fridge, then make breakfast.

We spend the day in each other's arms, watching the snow fall outside the windows, keeping each other warm by both our bodies and the fire. We venture out for a bit to sit in the hot tub, which is so awesome that I'm thinking we need to do again. As in, I might have ordered a hot tub to be delivered as soon as possible. And then we feast on my favorite meal. Because she knows my favorite meal, without having to ask. It was another day of perfection.

Chapter Twenty-One

Tess

I'M STANDING AT the kitchen counter, looking out the window that sits above the sink. The trees that line the property behind the cabin are covered in frost, making it look like a winter wonderland. My hair is in a ponytail, and the black leggings and off-the-shoulder, camel-colored tunic sweater I'm wearing make me feel warm, cozy, and comfortably sexy. I feel strong, warm hands wrap around my stomach, and I smile while leaning back against my husband's muscular, bare chest. The instrumental music playing from Barrett's third playlist he made for the weekend is filtering through the sound system. It's a sensual, tantric, and damn near erotic soundtrack to what we were both feeling, what we've been feeling since we stepped foot in the cabin, only fueling the desire and fire that is building in my core.

His mouth descends upon my neck. I can feel his firm lips open before his teeth graze the soft skin just above my bare shoulder. He wraps one hand around my ponytail and tugs just hard enough for my head to tilt backward, opening me up for him completely.

He bites down on my earlobe before his tongue sneaks out and soothes the delicious ache the nip caused. The hand that isn't wrapped around my hair snakes up my body and wraps loosely around my neck, holding me in place for him to do with as he pleases.

My body is a livewire. I can feel his kiss everywhere.

My fingertips.

My toes.

My stomach.

My core.

Everywhere.

He continues nipping and sucking, biting and licking while the music pulses through my body. Between the delicious combination of his mouth, hands that seemed to be everywhere — tugging my hair, grazing my throat, skimming my stomach, squeezing my breasts — and the sound of his ragged breathing in my ear and hot breath on my skin, I feel like my entire body could go up in flames.

I lean back and turn my head so I can feel his lips on mine, but he holds back, only allowing me a soft tease and taste of his mouth on my own. After what feels like hours of his delectable torture, he spins me around hastily then slams me against the counter and assaults my mouth with such force it almost takes my breath away.

He reaches down and grips my butt in his hands and squeezes tightly before he lifts me up and wraps my legs around his waist. He quickly moves us and presses my back roughly against the fridge, causing it to rattle and shake. It's frantic and frenzied, hands and mouths and legs and heavy breathing and kissing and tongues and so many other things that my mind is having a hard time catching up with what I want and need first.

Moving from the fridge, he lays me back on the kitchen table before pushing my sweater up around my neck then pulling it off completely. Swiftly and quickly yanking down my leggings, he quirks his mouth up when he sees that I'm commando under my leggings, and my chest is bare, having obeyed one of his rules of the cabin: no panties or bras allowed. He leans down and takes my breast into his mouth, nipping at the already oversensitive bud. My back arches up to meet his mouth as he gives both breasts equal and extensive attention.

After he has brought me to the brink of orgasmic insanity, he drops to his knees in front of me and places my feet on his shoulders, opening myself up to him completely. I look down my body into his eyes that are blazing with heat, his cheeks a bit flushed, and I can only imagine what my own face looks like. My body burns like an inferno. He skims the tip of his nose along the inside of my thigh, his tongue sneaking out in a touch so light it sends my once-blazing skin into a fit of shivers. He continues his way up my body and without hesitation, he leans forward, his mouth pressed to my center, licking and sucking in such a perfect rhythm it makes me come unglued almost immediately. I cry out, a string of unintelligible sounds, my nails dragging, clawing at his back, his hair, anything I can reach.

I'm still riding my high when he stands abruptly, strips himself of his jogger pants, and plunges inside me, deeply and unrefined. He groans at the intense contact but doesn't let up on his movements. I lean in and press my lips to his chest, leaving sloppy open-mouth kisses over every inch of him I can get my mouth on. My mind is a blur, and my body wants everything. All at once. He leans over and takes my hands in his, stretching my arms above my head, leaving me incapable of movement. His breath is hot and heavy on my cheek then by my ear.

We're both so keyed up from our kitchen show, our bodies are performing in sync with one another. The sensual music playing through the cabin's sound system is replaced by our heavy breathing, grunts, and groans. Soon we're both calling out each other's names loudly, struggling to regain our breathing. An erotic mix of sweat, lust, and heavy pants fill the cabin.

No words were spoken.

No words need to be spoken.

Just our love for each other and proof that we still wanted each other on a deep and visceral level, so in tune with one another that our bodies speak the words our mouths can't.

Chapter Twenty-Two

Barrett

I CAN'T BELIEVE we have to leave this place, our cocoon, in two days. It doesn't seem possible that almost a week has already gone by, and I find myself thinking that Lauren may have been right — scary thought. Two weeks would have been awesome. But, we already miss the kids.

We've reconnected and loved every minute of our time together. We've made the most of it, and I know, without a doubt, that we'll never let distance like that come between us again.

Outside, the ground and trees as far as our eyes can see is covered in white. It's been unseasonably cold already, and a storm of this size isn't typical. The past two days we've had light snow, but this is the real deal. Luckily, my pretty girl is a genius and thinks of everything and packed our gear. I also think she secretly was hoping for a light winter storm. She absolutely loves the first real snow of the season, when it's more than just flurries or a dusting. Her weird, cute little self loves scooping the sidewalks, making snow angels, having snowball fights, sledding. It's like she's still a kid when snowstorms come. Of course, her tune starts to change around springtime, when winter just won't release its hold on us.

I know she'll be so excited to see the snow, and I want to be there when she sees it. I wake her up by bringing my lips to my favorite spot just after I set a cup of coffee on her nightstand for her.

"Morning, babe," I whisper huskily.

"Mbwdkng," she mumbles.

"Babe, wake up. Look outside."

"Sleep" is her only response.

I chuckle and bring my lips to my spot again before I whisper in her ear, "Babe, it snowed. Come look."

That gets her attention. Her eyes pop open, her blue eyes shining with excitement. She smiles widely at me before leaning up on her elbows and kissing me square on the lips, morning breath and all.

"Coffee's on the nightstand. Let's go work up an appetite," I say with a smile.

She doesn't miss a beat and waggles her eyebrows out me.

"Get your mind out of the gutter. I meant let's play outside."

She quickly jumps to her feet, her excitement over playing in the cold Michigan weather making me laugh. "Fine, but only if you promise me that we can work up an appetite for lunch after we're done with breakfast."

"You got it." How could I deny her of that?

After we each chug down a cup of coffee, we work up a sweat just getting into our gear. She looks adorable in her maroon-and-grey Volcom snow-pants and winter coat. She can barely move but manages to wedge her feet into her new Sorel boots that she splurged on last year. She loves them so much I've even seen her wear them with leggings to the store.

As adorable as she looks, I probably look like a walking LL Bean ad — construction edition. But it's all about warmth, so I could care less about what I look like wearing the camel-colored overalls because they're warm as hell. Ten minutes later, we're both dressed — although a little sweaty from how much exertion it takes to just bundle up — and ready to go outside and play, like kids. She's so giddy that she bounds out the door before I even have both my gloves on.

Luckily, the cabin has a snow shovel, and I woke up earlier and shoveled a pathway out the door leading to the back yard. I'm just closing the door behind me when I hear Tess squeal at the top of her lungs and see her dive back first into a big pile of snow that I shoveled off the back deck. She disappears almost completely. I bust out laughing at the cloud of white that puffed up around her and trudge through the snow, seeing her foot prints much smaller than my own. When I get to her, a black glove-covered hand shoots up, and her beautiful, tinkling laughter fills the air.

"Little help?" she asks, still laughing.

I reach down a hand to her and grasp her hand in mine. "What's wrong, my little snow bunny? Was it a little deeper than you expected?" I say, chuckling, but my laughter is cut short when the little brat pulls on my hand rather than allowing me to do the pulling. The combination of standing in the snow and laughing causes me to lose my balance quickly, and the next thing I know, I'm face first in the snow next to her.

The two of us struggle to sit up, both of us laughing hysterically — me spitting out snow — which makes it that much harder to move in the dense white powder. She eventually gets up and sits on her butt, and I am next to her on my knees, both of us covered in head-to-toe white, but I notice she has one distinct difference compared to me. She doesn't have snow all over her face… yet. I do what any loving husband in this situation would do. I discreetly make a soft snowball and then smash it in her face, much like some people do with wedding cake.

She sputters and laughs and thus starts one of our most epic snowball fights yet. This isn't by far the first time we've ever had one together. In fact, we've had one every single year that we've been together. But it still doesn't take away our enjoyment of the moment. We're trying to run through the deep and heavy snow, both of us out of breath from our laughter and the exertion of the fun.

Finally, we call cease fire, after I get one more snowball thrown, which she, of course, returns, because she's a brat. But I suppose that makes me the male equivalent.

"Wanna go for a walk before we go back inside?" I ask her.

She beams up at me and nods her head. "I really do."

I grin widely at her joy and love for the winter snow, knowing most women — or people, rather — would prefer to give the middle finger to Mother Nature when she releases heavy snows onto the earth.

"Come on, then. Maybe we can go find that little creek that lady at the grocery store told you about."

"Yes! I've been wanting to find it!" she says, almost shouting.

I shake my head as we decide to take a short walk through the woods. The densely populated trees prevented much of the snow to fall on the ground, so we're able to walk much easier than we are through the yard. But still, the snow has blanketed the area, enveloping us in our personal haven where we've lived for the last few days. It makes me want to hole up here forever, not letting the outside disturbances in again. We've rekindled our love for each other, remembered why we fell in love with each other when we were just kids. Our love runs deep, so deeply that I know those outside disturbances won't blacken our days again.

We come to the small bridge we were looking for beyond the thicket of trees. The creek below, partially snow-and-ice-filled, partially still flowing, looks like the scene out of a Norman Rockwell painting. We stand on the bridge and look down at the flowing stream and each take a deep breath of the early winter's hold. The fresh air is wonderful, and the serenity of nature's stage has me feeling lighter than I have in years.

I pull my phone out of my pocket and open the camera app. I take a few pictures of Tess leaning over the bridge and looking out at the landscape before she catches me. She smiles and shakes her head.

"Come here. Let's get one of us." She smiles.

I stand next to her and flip the camera around, and we take a couple different selfies before I lean down and kiss her cheek, taking a picture of that as well.

"Ready to head back?" I ask her, ready to return to our cabin and its warmth. Besides, the woods aren't necessarily a safe place for us to be walking in the winter. Although not super common, we could encounter a grey wolf or moose. I know it will be more likely to see a squirrel or owl, but I still don't want to take any chances.

"I am. I'm starving."

"Me too."

After walking for what feels like miles, our cheeks are rosy, our breaths are short, and we're both exhausted and even hungrier than we were before. I promised her we'd work up an appetite, and I delivered.

We get back to the cabin and hang up our snow-soaked winter clothes. Tess moves to the kitchen, sexy as hell in her black leggings and light grey, wide-necked sweater, perfect for me to be able to still kiss her on my spot. While she starts breakfast, I build us a fire.

Soon we're sitting side by side on the couch in front of the fire, eating plates full of spinach egg frittata, crispy bacon, and hash browns. Slowly we're thawing out, the food helping.

COFFEE CUPS AND bellies full, kitchen cleaned up, we cozy up in front of the fire once again and slide in the Season Two disc of the *Sons*. They have us both completely hooked — even if we are a little late to the SOA game. I'm also pretending that it has nothing to do with Jax, and it's just that intriguing of a show, but by the way she gasps and yells at the TV every so often, I think it's safe to assume the show is truly that kick-ass.

We've been watching SOA for hours, our minds completely morphing into the motorcycle club world. I am pretty sure I should buy a Harley when we get home, and Tess thinks she could easily be my Old Lady. The sun is starting to set outside, and our stomachs are growling, reminding us that we haven't eaten anything since our late breakfast.

"Hungry?" I ask her, snickering when I hear her stomach gurgle loudly.

"Sounds like it, huh?" She giggles, but at the same time

she makes no motion to move, just burrowing in closer to me. I'm about to playfully shove her when my phone rings on the end table next to me. Usually, we talk to the kids after supper, which has me a little worried as to why I see James' name lighting up my screen a little earlier than normal.

"Hey, man, what's up?"

"Don't freak out, but there's been a… bit of an, well, an accident," he says instead of greeting me. For the record, whenever a conversation starts with *"Don't freak out,"* typically most people's brain goes into freak-out mode without delay. I instantly sit up and gently lift Tess's head that had been lying on my lap. I swing my legs off the big square wooden coffee table where they were resting before bringing my feet to the floor. I look at Tess. Her eyes are wide and staring straight into me.

"A bit? What's… a bit?" I ask, hitting pause on the DVD.

"Barrett," Tess whispers, her hand resting on my arm and her eyes full of fear and confusion. It isn't lost on me that once again, for the second time in as many weeks, I hit speaker on my phone so Tess can hear everything that's being told to me about something that happened to one of our children, so I don't have to relay information to her.

"Harper kind of fell. Off her horse. Today," he says, his voice a little shaky and staggering. Like he's trying to figure out the best way to tell me what happened.

"What do you mean she fell off her horse? Did Shadow buck her off or something?" Tess asks but looks at me with doubt in her eyes. Neither she nor I can imagine he would. He's the tamest horse we've ever seen. We wouldn't have her spending time with him if we thought he was dangerous.

"I don't know what happened, to be honest. It was like one minute she was on, riding the ring like normal. The next she was on the ground, crying."

"Is she alright? Hurt? Is anything broken?"

He's silent for far too long.

"James," I bark.

"Yeah, um, her left arm. Not bad," he quickly puts in, his voice sounding a little surer than before. "She won't need pins or anything, but she has a pretty bright purple cast decorating her arm right now. She's asleep, which is good, but she'll want to talk to you both when she wakes up. Tell you all about it."

"Wait. Why are we just now hearing about this? You didn't think we should have found out as soon as she fell!?" she yells at her brother.

"Well, sweet sister of mine, I didn't realize it was broken. I didn't want to make you guys panic over nothing. She cried when she fell, but then she was giggling and said she was alright. She even went over to Shadow and gave him a hug and told him it was okay. He bent his head down low like he felt bad, too. It was pretty sweet," he tells us, but I am more interested to hear how she went from giggling to broken arm. Fortunately, James can read us like a book and continues on with the story without us even having to ask. "We actually went back home first. But then she got on the floor and was playing with the dogs. When she said it hurt when she put pressure on her wrist, I thought we'd better go in. She had an X-ray, and they did a quick cast. I honestly only took her in because I didn't want to risk it, which, as it turned out, I'm glad I did."

"Her arm is broken, and she said she was okay and told Shadow she wasn't upset with him?"

"Yup. Tough girl, huh?" he says with some pride in his voice.

"I guess," I mumble, slightly distracted. I'm scared for our little girl who had to go through that without us, and I feel nervous that Tess will blame herself, or me, because we weren't there. I know our week has come to an end. Not that either of us want to be anywhere else when our baby — or any of them — has been hurt, but it's still somewhat disappointing.

I look out the window and back to Tess who nods her head, knowing what I'm thinking.

"James, we'll be home tomorrow morning. It's snowing. Again. And pretty heavily, so we'll head out during the daylight."

"Guys…" He starts to protest, but it's weak.

I'm positive that she's been asking for us and will be happier if we were there with her. "It's not a big deal. We can come home two days earlier. We won't be able to relax up here, and I can only imagine how Harper feels. She'll want her mom and dad."

"You're right," he says, sighing and sounding disappointed in having to agree to it. "I'm sorry, you two. I wanted you to have your time together."

"James. It's fine. Not like you threw her off the horse yourself. Besides, there's no other place we would rather be. We'll be home as soon as it's safe enough for us to drive."

"Sounds good. I'm so sorry. I know how important this was to both of you," he tells us. Ever since Nicole walked out on him, he's been overly protective of his siblings' marriages, helping out whenever and wherever he can. He doesn't want the same thing to happen to any of us.

"Hey, stop it. We're fine. I promise. I'm not going to lie and tell you that I don't want more time at the cabin with your smokin' hot sister," I say, chuckling when I hear him gag and say "Dude." "But, it's been good. We… we're good, right, babe?"

I look over at Tess, and her eyes are shining, her head slightly tilted to the side a little bit, and she has her signature beautiful smile lighting up her face. "Yep. I promise, big brother, this was just what we needed. Barrett's right. We would love to have more time, but what we had together… it was perfect. Thank you for being there. If we couldn't be there for her, I'm glad you were."

"I'm glad to hear that. And I am happy to be here any time. You know that."

"We do. Thanks again, and make sure Harps calls us as soon as she wakes up. She can tell us all about how she conquered the great Shadow and came out on top," I say, snickering, knowing that this story is going to be her monster fish story of all time.

"I will," he says. "Hey, Grady's buddies were going to be coming over a little later. Do you care if they sign her cast? And Maggie's girlfriends, too?"

"Nah, that's fine. Just make sure they leave room for us."

"Got it. Alright. Christine just dropped off Maggie from volleyball practice. We'll talk in a bit."

"Christine?"

"Uh, yeah. She called as soon as she heard and said she could help. I assume that's not a problem? We've never met, but you guys have talked about her so much that I know you trust her, right?"

"Not a problem at all. Thanks again for being there. Love you," Tess says.

"Love you guys, too."

"Later," I say before hanging up and tossing my phone on the couch beside me.

I lean my elbows on my knees and look over my shoulder at Tess, who's sitting on the couch cross-legged facing me. She gives me a sad smile and wipes a stray tear. I reach over and grab her hand and squeeze tightly. "I'm sorry," I tell her.

"What are you sorry for?"

I shrug my shoulders and give it to her straight. "Are you mad that we weren't there for her?"

"Would it have made a difference if we were home for her when she fell?"

"I suppose not, but I just assumed you would be upset."

"Of course I'm upset that she fell, but not at you. It would have happened regardless. I want to be there for her, but I know James has this. She has her brother and sister, Lauren, Josh. Sounds like Maggie and Grady's friends are going to cover her in love tonight, so she would have ignored us anyway."

"You're sure? I can start packing up, and we can drive home tonight."

"In this snow? No. It's not safe. It won't do any of us a bit of good for us to try to get there if we run into trouble because of weather. The forecast shows it's supposed to stop snowing in a few hours. By morning, we'll be in a better place to head out."

I sigh deeply, way more relieved than I expected I would be. I feel so grateful that I married a woman who is understanding, calm, and easily goes with the flow.

I lean back into the couch and turn my head in her direction. "I love you. So much."

"I love you, too. A whole lot." She smiles.

I love that she remembers the way she told me she loved me the first time she blessed me with those words, just as much as I remember it.

"I don't want to leave early, but, if I'm honest, I don't think I'd have been ready to leave on Sunday morning either. I can't imagine either of us will be able to relax knowing she was hurt though, do you?"

"No. I agree with you. I wouldn't be ready to leave our cocoon any time, but now I am eager to get home."

"Yeah. We'll be fine, Tess. You know that, right?"

She smiles at me, her sweet and genuine smile, so I know what she's about to tell me is her complete honesty. "I do. We won't let it get like before. I know this."

I can't help but still ask her. "Do you? In your heart, you know that what happened four months ago will never happen to us again, right?"

"I promise, Barrett. You and I are solid. Nothing could ever separate us."

I lean over and grip her by the waist and pull her over so she's straddling me when I bring her in closer for a kiss. It starts gentle, but as my tongue traces her lips and she lets me in without any hesitation, it becomes more. She tilts her head to the right and moves her hands up to my upper arms, gripping them tightly while my hands rest on either side of her neck, keeping her close.

I love the taste of her, the way her soft lips mold to mine, the way she's both timid and forceful, showing me what she wants, how she wants it. She nips at my bottom lip, and I suck on hers. Our kiss is a slow dance that we've perfected, a private showcase of the love we've built over time. It's not new; it's not sudden. Not a sprint, but a marathon. It's clay that's been molded, formed, cherished until it is in its most perfect form. It's never rushed, never hurried.

As our kiss builds, memories flood my system like an old movie reel of our life together. Of goodnight kisses that neither of us ever wanted to end, lazy summer day kisses that weren't heated from the sun, stolen kisses, wedding kisses, desperate kisses between diaper changes and hurried schedules. Our passion and love for each other has built just as our kisses have, with grace and beauty that only love built from the ground up can provide.

I move my mouth from hers, but only so I can kiss her cheek, her jaw, and then my spot before I tug on her ear with my teeth. She lets out a sexy noise and moans my name, and I know our supper will be delayed. Packing for driving home will be delayed.

But our love for each other will never be delayed again.

Chapter Twenty-Three

Tess

IT'S EARLY MORNING, barely light out, and Barrett and I are both moving around the cabin, packing up our belongings and sipping on coffee. After we spoke with Harper last night, we both felt monumentally better. Hearing her small voice and knowing that she was hurting and we weren't there was hard. But hearing her laughter and bravery as she re-told the story to us about how Shadow got spooked but *"it wasn't his fault, he just got scared and jumped and I wasn't holding tight enough."* Her words.

Our little girl. So strong, adventurous and spirited, so quick to forgive and move on. It's only a very small part of the reason we love her so dearly. As I fold our clothes to put into the suitcase, I can't help but think back to when Harper finally called us last night, putting our worried minds at ease.

"Brandon came over and signed my cast, Mom! Grady pushed him to the floor and they wrestled because they were fighting over who got to sign my cast first. While they were wrestling, Uncle James came over and signed it."

I just bet he did. I bet he looked rather smug when he did it, too.

"Even Coach Mac came over! And ALL of Grady's friends came after practice. Cody, Charlie, Blake, Spencer, Jack, Will…" She went on and on, so happy to have the attention from Grady's friends. Not that she ever lacked of it. They loved her like their own little sister. When the boys were playing football in middle school, Barrett was assistant coach. These boys have known Harper since she was a baby. She has a league of protection around her that rivals the Avengers, so I can only imagine how they reacted when they found out she'd been in a minor accident and broke her arm.

"I'm sure they were excited to sign your cast, baby."

"Uh-huh! They were. There's hardly any room left!"

"Well, make sure there's room for your mom and me," Barrett spoke up, his voice cracking a little. Ever since he heard her voice, he had a hard time not packing up and leaving straight away. His baby was hurt, and while he heard it from James and knew she was going to be fine, hearing her telling us the story made him go board stiff. Her coming into our room and breaking up our peaceful sleeping probably no longer mattered. I knew we both wanted to be home, cuddling our little girl and knowing for certain that she was going to be just fine. Healthy, and not scared.

I placed my hand on his leg, and he gave me a small shake of his head, letting me know he was fine but a little overwhelmed.

"Daddy, of course. I told the boys they had to save the spot right at the top for you and Mommy."

I smiled, imagining that she did just that. She may only be six, but she has a mind of her own for sure.

"We'll be home tomorrow, baby, so make sure you have the Sharpie ready for us."

"I thought you weren't coming home until Sunday?"

"Nope. We miss you kids too much," I said, feeling the words *that I had just spoken aloud. As much as I was loving being alone with Barrett, I did miss the kids. It didn't take away from the love I had for him. Our kids were proof, a gift, a blessing... an addition of the love that we share.*

"YAY! I miss you, too! But tell Uncle James he can't leave yet. He promised he would stay until Sunday, and you know that promises aren't allowed to be broken s-o-o-o... just because you guys are home doesn't mean that he's allowed to leave, and he told me that he'd have lunch with me at school on Friday and take me out for pizza before the game if I slept in my room all by myself, and I did it ALL WEEK LONG, and then Lily is supposed to come here — I think that's what he said anyway — and oh! Cole called right before I called you guys, and he promised to be home and to save room for him to sign my cast, and did you know that Grady and Bri are FINALLY going on a date this weekend? I can't believe it! Maggie told him it was about time he got off the pot, but I don't know what that meant because he wasn't going to the bathroom or sitting on a pot from the kitchen, but I'm really super excited that they're going out. I think they'll go for pizza too because that's what people who go on dates do, and I asked him if I could come along because I LOVE pizza and I REALLY like Bri, and I NEVER get to play with her because he's ALWAYS hogging her, so I think it's only fair that I can go on the date with them, don't you guys think? And I know I'm not supposed to tattle, so I'm not doing that, but I'm letting you guys know that he said NO! Can you believe it? I really don't think that's fair, but Maggie said that it was normal, and that I had to let them go alone, but I think that's only because she wants to go on a date with someone but she won't tell me who, but I bet it's that guy Jack from the football team because he likes her. I heard Blake telling Grady that, and Grady said it wasn't happening and then so did Brandon, but I

don't know what isn't happening, and no one would tell me, but Maggie told him it wasn't fair, and I said see it doesn't feel nice when you aren't included in things, and she just rolled her eyes at me and ugh... This thing is kind of annoying, but it's really pretty because they let me get purple, and that's my favorite color, but it's in my way, and I have an itch. Uncle James! I need you to itch my arm!"

My head was spinning, and my eye had a slight twitch to it from Harper's speech and the abundance of information I learned from our six-year-old. I'm not entirely sure that she breathed the entire time she spoke (or that the doctor didn't slip her a little somethin' somethin') but it was so wonderful to hear her normal self. She was Harper, and a week apart from us and falling off her horse didn't change that.

Before we left, I was so worried about our trip. I worried that we wouldn't be able to connect again. I worried that the kids might fall apart with us gone. I worried that they'd be upset with us for leaving and not understand, but I worried about it all for nothing. Our time away was so wonderful, and we loved every single minute of it. Barrett and I still had it. In fact, I daresay, we had it more than what we did when we were younger.

"Babe, did you hear me?"

"Huh?"

Barrett chuckled, "Dream girl, I asked if you wanted me to make some breakfast before we leave, or if you want to just keep packing and grab something on the road?"

"Oh! Sorry, I was just thinking."

"Got that. What about? You doing alright?"

I walked over to where he was standing in the doorway of the bedroom and wrapped my arms around his waist. I leaned in and held him close, resting my right cheek against his chest and inhaling deep. His natural heady scent washes over me and makes me feel calm, relaxed. Only he can do that for me. I nod my head against him and smile. "Yeah," I say as I pull back slightly and tilt my head up to look at him. "I'm good."

"Sure?"

"Positive."

He stares into my eyes, no doubt checking to see if I'm lying. Whatever he sees is enough for him to relax a little bit but tighten his hold around my waist. He bends down and brushes his lips against mine, which starts out brief, but a slight taste has us both reaching for a bit more, before standing up straight again and smiling down at me. "Alright."

I smile back up at him and repeat, "Alright."

"Babe?"

"Yeah?" I ask, a little distracted by how incredibly beautiful my husband is.

"Breakfast?"

"Oh!" I say a little too loudly and then laugh at my own ridiculousness. "Let's make something. That makes for fewer groceries we have to cart back home with us."

He smiles at me and nods his head once, "Good plan, baby. I'll get started." He kisses me once on top of my head, swats me on my butt, and walks back out of the bedroom toward the kitchen.

I hear him moving around and soon a "Babe?" is hollered through the small cabin.

"Yeah?"

"Any requests?" Again, hollered.

"Cheesy scrambled eggs and ham!" I yell back, knowing that will use up the last of those items. And it's his specialty.

Well, sort of. I just know he makes excellent cheesy eggs.

"Sounds good!" he shouts back, even though he could just speak in normal tones because the cabin is so small. I know he's doing it just to mess with me, or maybe he's doing it to get me used to the loudness that will come back as soon as we enter our house. Either way, I love him for it. He's a giant dork most of the time, but that's one of the things I love about him the most. He owns his dork.

THE SNOWSTORM LEFT its magical wake, making our trip home quite… interesting. But after seven lon-n-ng hours in the car — which should have taken us five if the weather had cooperated — we are pulling into our driveway. The second I open my car door, I see three beautiful heads pop out of the door that leads from the house to the garage. We got a much later start than expected because of the roads not being cleared, but still managed to get home at around five in the afternoon. I didn't expect to see Grady here, so this is a wonderful surprise. Behind the three of them, I see James towering over them, shaking his head and smiling.

Harper pushes through the door as I round the front of the car and I, carefully, considering her arm is casted, hoist her up and hug her tightly. "Mommy! You're home! It's been nearly years!" she says in her dramatic flair that only six-year-olds exhibit — well, teenagers too, I suppose.

I hug her close and inhale her sweet scent. "Hi, baby girl. How ya doing?"

"I'm so great! Uncle James had lunch with us at school

today! And guess what?"

"What?!" I ask her, in my own dramatic flair.

"He. Brought. Subway!"

"No. Way!"

"Uh-huh! A ham sandwich, some apples, and a cookie, and it was in one of those awesome bags!"

"Well, sounds like Uncle James scored some major points!"

"How'd you know that? He scored like a hundred points playing soccer at recess after lunch!"

"He did, huh?" I giggle, just picturing my big brother chasing Harper and all her friends around the playground.

"Yeah huh! I asked Ms. Hanson if he could stay, and she said he could if he wanted to, and he said he wouldn't miss it for the world!" She's so excited that almost everything out of her mouth is screamed, and I wonder if her voice will go hoarse pretty soon.

"I just bet he didn't say no to Ms. Hanson," Barrett snickers, but I hear James laugh.

Ms. Hanson used to be Mrs. Hanson. From what I understand, a few years ago, her husband of twelve years decided he needed to downgrade to a much younger version of her. Given the fact that Ms. Hanson looks like the definition of the girl next door, with her naturally blonde hair cut in a blunt shoulder-length bob and deep brown eyes to match, is also a yoga instructor, middle school tennis coach, and all around gorgeous person inside and out, not only is her ex-husband a complete moron, but the parents of her students (and some of those that aren't her students) are constantly trying to set her up. Even the few brave single dads have asked her out on their own. This isn't to say that I haven't thought of James one of the many times she and I have spoken.

We all step inside, and Barrett and I continue to give hugs. When I greet Maggie with a big squeeze, I whisper in her ear, "I hear there's someone who's caught Jack's eye, hmm?"

I hear her gasp before she whispers back, "Mom?! How'd you hear that!?"

"Harper had quite a bit to tell us last night. We'll talk later?"

"Yeah, of course. It'll never happen though, Mom," she grumbles quietly, and if I'm not mistaken, there's a hint of disappointment in her voice. "Grady freaked. So did Brandon. Cole will too. Not to mention Dad."

"We'll talk," I promise her as I pat her on the arm

I turn around and see Grady is still talking to his dad. Barrett has his hand clamped on Grady's team-jersey-clad shoulder, but when he sees me looking his way, he turns and walks straight into my arms.

"How are you, my sweet boy?" I ask him as he lifts me up and hugs me tightly.

"I'm good, Mom. Missed you," he murmurs into my hair.

"Missed you, too, bud," I tell him as I step back a little and look up into my handsome son's face. I know he will need to be heading over to the field in a few minutes. I also know he'll be anxious to not be late as he's still trying to prove his worth to Coach Mac and the team, even though he needn't do that. I'm sure they have full faith and trust in him, regardless of his flub a few weeks ago.

"How you feeling about tonight? You gonna make it?"

"Yeah. It sucks. I hate sitting there while the team is playing, but it's my penance. I can take it. After tonight, I'm free."

"Good attitude, kid. Love you."

"Love you, Mom."

"Gotta go?"

He grins cheekily at me. "Kind of. Sorry, I told coach I wanted to see you guys, so he said to come as soon as I could."

"No problem, bud. We'll see you after the game."

"Yeah. Oh, I have something I want to tell you and Dad, but it will have to wait until after the game. I'll come straight home."

"Everything alright?"

"Oh yeah. Everything's great," he says walking backward toward the garage. His smile fills his entire face, and I'm so glad that Barrett and I remembered to let him be the one to tell us about his date with Bri. His excitement is infectious, and I can't wait for him to tell us in his own words. It makes me a little disappointed that James spilled the beans to us, but at the same time I'm happy.

Harper runs up with a black Sharpie in her hand and points to the spot she wants us both to sign. Her tiny cast is already covered in signatures, with Grady's in the middle, followed by *My Favorite Person On Earth* scrolled in his handwriting.

Maggie and Harper tell us they're going to get ready for the game tonight, still not willing to miss it, even though Grady isn't playing. They're completely over the excitement of seeing their parents who've been gone for almost a week. While this could make me sad, it makes me feel completely happy. Knowing that they're growing up to be well-adjusted humans who can adapt and not break down when we're not around makes me proud. It also makes me realize that we can spend more time focusing on each other without feeling guilty.

After we sign Harper's cast, the girls trudge off to the hall closet and grab their coats for tonight.

As soon as they're out of sight, Barrett launches in on James. "So-o-o… Ms. Hanson, huh?" Barrett says, teasing.

He punches him in the shoulder lightly and chuckles. "Shut up, man. She's your daughter's teacher," he says like he's repulsed, but the gleam in his eye says that he is not immune to the beauty that is Carly Hanson.

"True. But you can't deny that she's beautiful. Even I'd hit that."

Two sets of wide eyes swing to me. "Tess!" James guffaws while Barrett raises his hand and says, "I'd watch," then laughs like he's the funniest person on the planet, like a total idiot. Good thing I know he was just being a complete goober and teasing.

I roll my eyes at his immaturity but still reach over and give James a tight hug. "Thank you, James, for staying with them. For helping everything here to stay rolling along, for keeping the kids happy. For taking care of my baby."

"Nowhere else I'd rather be."

"I know. And I love you for it. Stay through the weekend?"

"Yeah. I was planning on it. Anyway, I wanna see Grady's panic attack tomorrow night. He's so sure of himself now, but I can't wait to see the nerves settle in," he says, grinning widely.

"It's killing me that he hasn't told us yet!"

"I honestly can't believe that you didn't slip up and say something."

"Barrett coached me on the way home," I admit. Barrett's eyes are gleaming, and his smirk is sure. I roll my eyes and shake my head at his cockiness.

"Mom! Dad! Why aren't you ready?!" Maggie's voice breaks in. She's standing in front of us with her hands on her hips and a stern expression on her face. She's eager to get to the game, just as we are. Only one more game remains before playoffs begin, and Grady is no doubt feeling even more eager for missing these last two weeks, knowing that.

"You just want to get there in time to watch Jack warm up," Harper says in a bored tone.

"Quiet, Harps!" Maggie shrieks, her face flaming bright.

"Alright, let's go change and head over to the game," Barrett says, not wanting to hear about his daughter's sudden crush.

"So, what is it you wanted to talk to us about?" Barrett asks Grady casually because he's probably certain my voice will come out squeaky and excited.

We got home from the game about forty-five minutes ago, and, despite our weekly tradition of our home tailgates, we chose to hang at home tonight after the game. After being gone for a week, we needed to catch up with the kids and weren't ready to fully socialize quite yet.

Barrett and I are seated on the couch, next to each other, and Grady is on the other end of the sectional.

"Well, you know how Bri and I have been friends forever, right?"

"Yeah," Barrett hedges.

I swear if he doesn't just spit it out soon, one of us is

going to explode. As it is already, Barrett keeps having to squeeze my knee because my leg won't stop bobbing up and down.

"And I know you guys already assumed this, but yeah, I kind of have a thing for her."

"Kind of?" I ask, my voice staying surprisingly steady.

Grady grins at me, completely reading into my struggle. "Yeah, Mom, kind of. Or more than kind of. Actually, I asked her to go on a date with me tomorrow night."

"And? Spit it out, man!" Barrett says, making both of us laugh.

I seriously thought I'd be the one who broke down first.

"She said yes," he says. His grin is split so wide. His happiness is radiating off him. In fact, he starts laughing at nothing in particular, either his excitement or nervousness catching up with him — maybe both.

But no matter what, it's easy to see what this night means to him.

James pokes his head around the wall that separates part of the living room from the rest of the house, looking like a total creeper but funny, nonetheless.

"Tell them yet?" he asks, his own grin splitting his face. His interruption comes so early into our conversation we hadn't even had a chance to weigh in with our thoughts yet.

"Yes, Nosey Noserson. I just did."

"About time. That secret was killing me," he says with a wink in our direction.

He's so subtle.

I shake my head and roll my eyes at my brother. He's seemed happier than he's been in a long while. I don't know if being around the kids has helped his overall mood, or if something else is going on, but I'll take it, whatever it is.

I turn my head in Grady's direction and speak truth to him. "Grady, neither of us could be happier. You know we love Bri and have felt for a long time that you two are perfect together. You also know that your dad and I have been together since we were younger than you guys are now."

"Mom, it's one date."

"No, son, it isn't. Trust me. This might be the first official date between you two, but you know as well as we do that it's been more than that for a long time. There's a reason neither of you have ever truly dated anyone else. There's a reason Bri is the one who wears your jersey every Friday night. And there's a reason you point to her in the stands after every touchdown," Barrett says, his voice full of authority but loving sincerity.

Grady blows out a deep breath and looks us each in the eye before nodding his head in understanding.

"Grady, bud, what are you so afraid of?" James asks him. It's a question we've all been wondering, so I'm glad to hear it finally asked aloud.

He shrugs his shoulders and shakes his head a bit. "I don't know. I guess first I don't want to lose focus. I plan to play college ball. I plan to get a degree. Bri plans to get a degree. I don't want us to settle and regret settling down when we're so young. I don't want to go through life wondering if I just fell in love with the first person to come along."

All the breath is whooshed from my lungs, and my eyes instantly well with tears. Is that how he thinks of us? Does he think Barrett just settled with me? Does he think I just settled with Barrett? Does he think we have regrets or that we just fell in love with the first person to come along?

"Grady," Barrett says in a voice that is scarily low. Clearly, he has the same questions rolling around through his head and isn't pleased.

Grady's eyes widen with recognition as he looks from my tear-filled eyes to Barrett's anger-filled ones. "No. I didn't mean…" he trails off.

"Grady," Barrett says again, this time his voice back to his normal tone.

"I'm sorry. I promise that's not what I meant."

"Be that as it may, kiddo. You need to understand something. Your mom and I didn't settle. I fell in love with her. I never fell *out* of love with her. Were we young? Yeah. Are we one of the few lucky ones who don't have to date many people to find our one? No doubt about it. Do we still have to work our asses off to make our marriage work? Absolutely. But everyone does. Not a single marriage is easy. Look at this past week. Obviously, we needed time together. It happens. That's what marriage is about. We forgot that. We stopped putting each other first and focused too much on the young punks who invaded our home decades ago." He grins. It takes a punk to know a punk.

Grady laughs. "Nice. I know, Dad. I guess it just freaked me out. That's why I said something to Cole in the first place. It just wasn't like you guys. And I guess I assumed some stuff or maybe panicked a little bit."

"I get that. I promise you we're good. We're better than good. We're great. There's no one else on this earth for me but your mom, and I think she would say the same." He looks at me with his eyebrows raised, to which I roll my eyes and agree with him.

Grady chuckles, but Barrett isn't finished. "You also need to understand that you're just in high school. Yes, your mom and I are high school sweethearts — her words, obvs…" He grins at his use of words because he's the biggest dork on the planet. "…but that doesn't mean that just because you date someone in high school you're automatically going to get married."

He clasps his hands together and leans over, elbows on his knees. "I know that. But also, if I'm being totally honest with you guys, and myself, I guess, I think I've always just been scared of admitting what I feel for Bri. Keeping her as a friend always seemed easier, because if I ended up screwing something up with her and then we weren't friends anymore, I don't think I could handle that."

James, who has been oddly quiet this entire time speaks up. "I was married to a woman who I was not friends with first. Despite what I thought when I said 'I do', I didn't know her at all. Bud, whether this thing between you and Bri is long-term or whether you guys date a bit and decide you are better off as friends, I guarantee that you're in a better place than most marriages. You two have a foundation that most people only dream of. And seriously, you haven't even gone on a date yet. Relax."

"Alright, I get it. I may be overreacting a tad bit."

"You think? It's Bri, kiddo. You two have hung out hundreds of times. Don't put so much pressure on yourselves. Not everyone is as perfect as your mom and I." Barrett snickers.

We all laugh and spend the next few minutes listening to Grady tell us his plans for his date, nothing too crazy. Just dinner at a Mexican restaurant that James told him about a few towns over. After a bit, we all head to bed. Harper went to bed shortly after we got back home, and miraculously, she's still there. Obviously, James is going to live with us forever, given the fact that a few days with her he's kept her in her own bed at night.

Chapter Twenty-Four

Barrett

Tonight can't come soon enough. Between Grady's continuous pacing and overall anxiety over his date tonight and the plans that I've been making, we're both pretty much live wires. About fifteen minutes ago, I walked into Grady's room and really wish I hadn't. He was looking at himself in the mirror, making faces. Only thing I can assume is that he's practicing how he's going to greet Bri. I had no idea he would ever be so nervous about a date with her, but it only proves to me just how deep his feelings are for that girl. I turned on my heel and exited just as quickly as I'd entered, without saying a word. There was simply nothing to say.

Tonight, I'm taking Tess on a date, too. James said he was staying through the weekend and was cool with staying home with Harper tonight. I plan to give Tess the gift that I had intended to give to her while we were at the cabin, but since we came back early, it just never happened. Now I'm glad it didn't. This way is better. Much better.

Her mom called this morning and asked Tess to come over and do some baking with her. It's been a holiday tradition for the two of them for years now. I can't remember a year when they didn't do it. It's just that it's usually scheduled after Thanksgiving. I may or may not have called her mom and asked her to get together today. She agreed and said she will tell her she wanted to hear all about our trip to the cabin. Hopefully she doesn't tell her all about *everything*.

Right before lunch I took Grady to the flower shop in town. He wanted to get some flowers for Bri, wanted to make tonight perfect. I decided to copy my son's brilliant idea, hoping it will bring back memories by sending Tess flowers to her at her parents' house.

In fact, the entire night I want her to remember. I plan for tonight to be another walk down memory lane. After making dozens of phone calls, picking up everything I need from just as many different places, I think I have everything in place.

The past week we got back to ourselves. Our week was cut short, but that doesn't mean that we're going back to the way it was before. Ever. I plan to continue to date the love of my life. And it starts tonight, reminding her of what the foundation of our love was built on. It was easy while we were alone, but now that we're home, I'm so afraid that we're going to let our world cut into our marriage. I'm determined not to let that happen, so even though I had this planned for while we were at the cabin, it actually works out better to do it tonight, here in our home town.

After getting Grady relaxed, I head to our bedroom to get ready to pick up Tess for our own date. My only fear is that she will be upset with me for not being home before Grady's date, but I hope that tonight's events make up for it.

After showering and dressing with the clothes I picked up from Josh, still not entirely positive why he had them at his ready, I head out into the living room where Maggie, Harper, James and Grady are sitting watching a movie, relaxing their way to a perfect Saturday afternoon. The second I walk into the room with my arms spread wide and a grin on my face to match, James and Grady both burst into laughter that doubles them over. James falls off the couch, clutching his stomach, and wipes his eyes as he takes another look at me, only causing him to laugh harder.

Maggie is giggling but smiling wide, and Harper is looking at me funny with her nose scrunched up. "Daddy, why are you dressed like that?"

"Because I love your mommy, sugar. And I plan to woo the crap out of her tonight."

"Huh?"

"He's taking Mom on a date tonight, Harps. This is what old people do. Dress like weirdos and hope that their wives don't laugh in their faces," Grady tells her.

"Aw, come on. This is cool, right, Mags? Mom will get it, yeah?"

"Yeah, Dad. It's cool. It's totally sweet, and Mom is gonna love it."

"I'm still confused," Harper says as she turns her head back to the TV to continue watching *Home Alone,* entirely over the conversation and her dad's epic surprise for her mom.

James, whose laughter finally subsides, turns and looks at me with a smile still on his face. "Maggie's right, Tess is gonna love it. She'll cry, you know, because she cries at commercials, but this is perfect for her. Thanks, man. I couldn't ask for a better guy to love my sister."

"She makes it easy," I tell him. Not to suck up, but because that's the truth. It's never been a hardship to love Tess. It's been what comes most natural to me. Even though I may have forgotten to show her that over the last few months, it never left me. It will always be easy to love Tess because my heart won't let me ever stop loving her.

"They're right, Dad. You look like a giant dork, but Mom is gonna flip," Grady says as he has his phone up and aimed in my direction. "But that doesn't mean that I'm not gonna send a picture to Cole, since he missed this epic display of your dorkiness, or that I'm not gonna use this against you some day."

"Picture it up, dude. This is your dad showing you how to date a woman, even when you're old and decrepit," I say, completely unfazed by him calling me a dork. I don't deny that. "Besides, your dad can totally rock the Dylan look. Admit it."

"Who's Dylan?"

"Man, it makes me so happy that your kids have no clue who Dylan is."

"Right?" I grin at James.

"Bye, Dad," Maggie says while she's gently pushing me out the door to the pickup waiting for me in the driveway. It seems, she's just as anxious as I am to get this date started.

Twenty minutes later, I'm pulling up to Tess's parents' house. The memories of our past hit me in the face like a Mac truck.

On our first official date on the night after homecoming of our junior year when she wore my jersey for the first time… I still remember knocking on her door, my stomach feeling like it could drop out from underneath me at any moment. Her dad opened the door with a scowl on his face that had me almost turning around.

"What the hell do you want?" Tess's dad, George Cole, says when the door is open fully.

"Uh, hi, Mr. Cole." I clear my throat. "I'm Barrett Ryan?" I ask, rather than say, my nerves shining through like a jackass.

"Are you asking me or telling me, boy?" he says in a voice that scares the crap out of me.

"George! Leave Barrett alone!" Tess's mom, Deb, comes into the room and pushes George out of the way.

A bright pink scarf-thing covers her head because of the chemo treatments I know she's been going through. My mom told me about her cancer, so this doesn't really surprise me but is still sad to look at.

"Come in, Barrett. Tess is just about ready for you," she tells me, her smile as bright as can be.

"Ah, Debbie, I was just having fun with the boy," George says and grins at me. He claps me on the shoulder and squeezes lightly once. "Come in, kiddo."

"Thank you, sir." I tell him, still completely terrified of the man. I know he's protective of his only daughter. I'm just glad that her older brothers aren't here, too.

"Daddy, were you being rude?" Tess says as she descends the stairs. My breath catches in my throat, and my jaw drops to the floor. She is beautiful. Her blonde hair is full of curls and down around her face. Her bright purple long-sleeve shirt is just short enough that I can see a tiny sliver of her stomach poking through, and her jeans fit her perfectly. Her tall black combat boots give her a couple inches of extra height, but she's still way shorter than I.

"No, princess. Just welcoming Barrett into our home," George says, clearly not wanting to be in trouble with his daughter.

"Good," she says to him with a smile before turning that gorgeous face to me. "Hi." Her voice is shy and sweet, and the slight blush to her cheeks tells me she's just as nervous and excited for tonight as I am.

249

"Hi. You look, um…" I cough. "…you look beautiful, Tess. Like, really beautiful."

"Thanks," she says, as her head dips down a little bit. "You look really good, too."

"Ayyy, get out of here!" George says, apparently not able to listen to much more, causing Deb to choke on her own laughter.

Tess giggles and lifts up on her tiptoes to give her dad a kiss to the cheek. "Bye, Daddy. I love you."

"Bye, princess. Love you, too. Midnight. Not a minute later, got it?"

"Got it," she tells him even though he was looking at me when he said it.

I nod my head at him, letting him know I understand, while Tess gives her mom a hug goodbye.

As soon as we're out the door, I take hold of Tess's hand as if it's the most natural thing in the world, because it feels like the most natural thing in the world. How I went seventeen years without holding her this way I'll never understand, but I take this moment to relish in the comfort of it. We make our way down the sidewalk to my waiting pickup, and I open the door for her to get in.

After crossing to the driver's door, I will my heart to stop beating so hard against my chest and slide inside. As soon as I get settled, I look over at my forever and smile her way. She smiles back and, in a whoosh, all the nervousness is gone. Only excitement remains between the two of us.

"C'mere," I tell her. And she immediately slides over the seat and nestles in next to me. Right where she belongs.

"Ready?" I ask her. But it's not just ready for our first date. It's ready for the first date of the rest of our lives.

She looks up at me from under my arm that's resting on the back of the seat behind us. "I am." And I feel it. I know, *in my soul, that she feels it too. She knows this isn't the start of something little. This is the start of something huge.*

I knock on the door, shaking my head of the memory that completely assaulted me. I'm surprised at the level of detail I can remember from that night. The night that started it all. The door swings open, and I see her dad staring back at me, a man who I've known for decades, have come to respect and love as if he's my own. A man who's held me as I cried over losing my own father. A man who handed his daughter's hand over to me to take care of forever. A man who trusted me with that honor. I find myself fighting my knees from buckling beneath me. If I manage to be half the man that he is, I'll be lucky.

"What the hell do you want?" George barks, making me laugh hard.

I can't believe he remembers the first thing he said to me. Or, at least, the first thing he said to me as a boy who was desperately wanting to date his daughter.

"Uh, hi, Mr. Cole, I'm Barrett Ryan?" I say in return, causing him to grin right back at me.

"Get in here, boy. I don't want the neighbors seeing you looking like a giant jackass."

"Hey! Don't deny it. I've got game tonight." I grin widely.

"You've got somethin', alright." He chuckles at me. He knows my plans for tonight but still can't resist giving me grief for it. But I'm good with that. I can handle it. I know I look like a dork, but I am willing to look like a dork in the name of love.

"Where did you find those clothes?"

"Josh. My guess is he thought the 90s were going to make a big come back and kept a bunch of his old clothes."

"Ha! I wish I could say I'm surprised."

"I know. He always was a little more concerned with his clothes than the rest of us. Did you find the jacket?"

He nods his head. "Debbie did. She said it was in Tess's old bedroom closet. She hung it in the coat closet right there," he tells me, pointing with a smile on his face.

"Awesome." I open the closet and pull out the hanging time capsule. All the memories I've been walking through over the past few weeks have my normally unemotional-self feeling like a walking emotion. I'm not real hip on that.

Just as I hang the jacket back up, wanting it to remain a little bit of a surprise, I see Tess walking down the stairs. She's not a walking time warp like I am, but she still looks hot. And yes, my wife of twenty-two years is still hot.

"Hey," she says, completely shy, which makes me smile remembering that's how she greeted me for our first date too.

"Hey, yourself," I reply.

We're staring at each other like a couple lovesick idiots when her mom and dad interrupt and start shuffling us out the door. As I hand her my old letterman's jacket, her eyes light up and fill with tears. She dips her head and lifts up the corner of it, smelling the collar, as if time has stood still and she can still smell the old me in it. Funny thing, she can. I snuck some Drakkar Noir over to Deb, and she made sure to get the jacket ready for her sniff test that I anticipated happening.

After saying our goodbyes to her parents, I walk her to the pickup that's parked by the curb. I wait for her reaction and am not disappointed in the least. I got lucky finding this thing. The guy who bought it off my dad when he sold it barely drove it. When I called him up and told him my plans for tonight, he didn't hesitate in the slightest. He was a close friend of my dad's and knew what this pickup meant to Tess and me.

I open her door and help her in, then as soon as I get seated, I tell her to slide over, just as I did the first night we went on a date together. Having her next to me, nestled up closely to my side, makes every nervous feeling I have for tonight vanish immediately. I love and adore this woman and can't wait to show her that I remember everything about our decades' worth of love together.

The drive-in went off without a hitch. Josh's aunt came through and made it just as perfect as I remember from our first time we went on a date. I hope she's having memory flashbacks just like I am. I hope she's falling all over again.

I pull into the park that we went for a walk in after our first date, and I feel the smile stretching across her face as we climb out and head for the bench that we sat on when I first placed my lips on hers. And suddenly I'm nervous again, wishing I had a pen to flick around like I do when I'm on an important call at the office. Not for her reaction, but because I want to make this right. She deserves this night to be perfect.

Chapter Twenty-Five

Tess

My mom called me today to see if I would come to her house to help her do some Christmas baking. She also wanted me to tell her about our trip to the cabin. Not that I plan to give her all the details, but I know she was concerned. James had them over for supper one night while we were gone, and even though I had told her we were leaving and why, James said she seemed worried. The past several weeks haven't been the easiest — well, except for this past week — with way too many stresses than I care to ever rehash.

I may be slightly nervous about tonight, so I think I've eaten about a half pound of peppermint taffies to try to calm my nerves. I am also just as excited. I think back to the note I received from Barrett today, along with a bouquet of purple roses, and I can't help the smile that graces my lips of their own accord. It's surreal to think that we're going on a date tonight. Alone. Finally. We may have had our week together, but tonight feels different. I don't know if it's because we're back home or if it's because of the flowers he sent reminding me of when we were dating or in the early years of marriage, but it feels bigger somehow.

*I can't wait for our date tonight, Tess, just
you and me.
You make my every day brighter.
Thank you for saying yes.
-Barrett*

That simple note, just a few words, gives me chills. *Thank you for saying yes.* I know there is so much more meaning behind that statement, and it makes my heart feel so full it could burst. He's everything I ever dreamed of, and whenever I'm around him, I feel safe, loved, cherished. Knowing that he's excited to spend time with me, too, makes it even better.

I'm in the middle of rolling cookie dough and peanut butter balls in melted chocolate when I hear the doorbell ring at my parents' house. Either my watch and the house clocks are broken, or he's an hour early, which tells me he's just as eager to get this date going as I am. I don't feel nearly as ready as I should, though. My hair isn't done the way I planned; I'm still in black leggings, a button-down winter, plaid, flannel shirt and some warm brown boots. Not exactly date material, but he's here now, and I hear Dad yelling that he'll get the door.

"I'll be right back! Be nice!" I holler.

My dad chuckles at my nervous demeanor. "No worries, princess. I'll go easy on the kid."

I shake my head as I run upstairs to the bathroom to see if I can at least get the extra chocolate off my fingers and ugh… from around my mouth. Why do I always have to taste test everything? I know I don't have time to change clothes, too, and he did say to dress warm tonight, so I suppose my clothing choice is fine. I touch up my makeup and fix my hair as best as I can, then sprint toward the stairs to greet Barrett before my dad can embarrass me more than I'm sure he already has. Being the only — and youngest — daughter of a family of five has made my brothers and dad overprotective, no matter my age.

When I get to the bottom of the stairs and turn the corner, I stop short and have to hold in a giggle. There stands Barrett, looking gorgeous as usual, even in his extremely dorky and colorful sweater that looks like his shoulders could bulge right out of, the relaxed-fit, light-colored jeans that hug his thick muscular thighs, black boots, and bomber jacket. He looks like he walked off the set of *90210,* and it takes everything in me not to laugh out loud. Despite his attire, his presence alone makes my entire body relax. He does that to me. He calms me when I didn't even know I needed calming before. This is, by far, not the only date I've ever been on with Barrett, but for some reason, it seems like it is. The smile he shoots my way from his position standing next to my father makes the butterflies take flight like they're battling their way to Mexico.

"Hey," I say when I see him. My voice comes out shy, though I'm not sure why.

"Hey yourself." He smiles and winks at me. Damn that wink. When this man winks at me, it's like he's telling me a secret, something that's special for me and me alone. I'm sure he knows what it does to me, but I don't care.

"You're early." I grin. I know Barrett, and I know he's probably been pacing at home, twirling a pen with his fingers while he walks around, until he couldn't stand it any longer. We haven't had an actual date alone in a long time, and I think we're both anxious and nervous at the same time.

"Am I? If anything, I think I'm late." And I know what he means. This date is a long time coming.

"Maybe right on time. How's that?" I ask as I sidle up to his side.

He pulls me in closer and kisses my cheek lightly.

"All right, geez, get on out of here, you two. Y'all are gonna make me gag up my dinner, and I'd prefer to keep it down," my dad says slowly, making his way into the room. He's a well-spoken Southern boy with enough charm to still make my mother swoon. He never fully lost his southern accent, and it seems to get thicker when he needs it to.

"All right, we'll go. Bye, Daddy. Love you."

"Love you too, princess. Make smart choices," he says as he raises his eyebrows at the two of us. This makes me almost break out into laughter, but no matter how old I am, I know not to laugh at my dad.

"We will," I promise him instead. "Bye, Mom," I say as she emerges from the kitchen, chocolate still on her fingers and a brush of it on her forehead. And I wonder where I get it from.

"Bye, you two. Have fun tonight."

"Thanks. Love you guys," I say again, because I've learned never to miss an opportunity to tell someone that I love them.

Barrett reaches into the closet and retrieves my jacket. Or, his jacket, rather. His bright red and black letterman's jacket from Liberty High School, showing his devotion to our beloved Bobcats. Last time I knew, the jacket was hanging in the closet of my bedroom, so I'm not sure how it got down here. I glance over at my mom, who has a huge smile on her face, and my un-asked question is answered.

It's been a few years since I slid my arms into this jacket. I smell the collar, hoping it still smells like Barrett like it used to. I still remember when he asked me to wear it, and I put it on for the first time. Embarrassingly enough, I slept in it. I couldn't escape his smell if I was sleeping in it, and it gave me such an incredible comfort.

"Get a good sniff?" Barrett asks, a knowing smirk gracing his lips.

"I had to check," I tell him.

"And? What's the verdict?"

I make a big show of inhaling deep, and it does, in fact, smell exactly how he smelled when I first put it on. In fact, I'm pretty sure he snuck in and sprayed cologne on it. Sneaky man.

"Smells like some guy I met once."

"Must be a stud to have smelled that awesome that you remember it."

"Or stunk. You never know."

"Ha ha, funny girl. You ready?"

"I am now." I grin up at him.

We walk out the door and Barrett immediately reaches for me. I look down at our laced hands slowly swinging between the two of us and feel such peace. I glance up into his dark hazel eyes and momentarily feel lost in the depth of love I have for him.

"Me too."

"Huh?" I respond.

"Me too. I feel it, too, Tess. Whenever I'm in your presence. I feel it. Always. Forever."

Tears spring to my eyes, and I let out a breath I could feel I'd been holding. I smile at him because, honestly, that's all that he needs. He knows my inner thoughts just as I know his.

And he's right.

Always.

Forever.

My smile widens when I see the pickup parked on the street in front of my parents' house. A dark maroon, late 80s-model Chevy pickup sits waiting for us, looking immaculate. I look up at Barrett with wonder. It's exactly what he drove the first time I rode in a vehicle with him. "How did you get this thing?"

His smile is wide, and eyes full of mischief. "I have my ways," he says. I have no idea what he has going on right now, but this certainly surprises me. He opens the passenger door for me, and I slide in before he closes the door behind me. I take a deep breath, the smell permeating my senses, memories of all those hours spent in here washing over me in waves.

The driver side door opens, and he climbs in behind the wheel. He looks over and quietly says, "C'mere."

Without hesitation I slide over the velvety cloth bench seat until I'm nestled in close to his side.

"Close enough?" he asks with a smile on his face.

I shake my head as I try to burrow in closer, and he chuckles lowly. He throws an arm around my shoulders and leans down to place a kiss right below my ear. Heat blossoms all over, just as it does every single time he kisses me there.

"Hi." He smiles at me. "That was the proper greeting I wanted to give my girl, but not with her daddy breathing down my neck," he says, mock teasing me for my use of the word daddy. He knows I'll never change no matter how old I am, and he doesn't expect or want me to.

"I like that greeting. And you're right. Daddy probably wouldn't have enjoyed that particular greeting. I'm never allowed to grow up, according to him. What's the plan?"

"Well, maybe you'll have to wait and see. It's a long

overdue date night with my girl, and I have no intentions of wasting a single second," he says as he shifts the pickup into drive and pulls out into the street.

Since the moment Barrett picked me up at my parents' house, the memories have been flooding through me. Between seeing him in his ridiculous outfit, climbing into the pickup that held so many memories, wearing his letterman's jacket that even smelled like I remembered him smelling when we were first dating, the perfection of our time at the drive-in… it's all come to a head. And now sitting here, on the bench that holds the best memory of all, tears begin to prick the back of my eyes. This place has become special to us. For every special occasion, we come back to this place. Pictures on our wedding day… pictures with each of our children here shortly after they were born… It's become a place that holds such value in our hearts but brings such comfort as well.

As Barrett slowly stands up and then lowers himself down to one knee, the emotions that have been sitting at the surface all evening begin to bubble over, and I can't hold back the tears that begin to trickle down my cheeks. My right hand goes to my mouth, my left being held by Barrett as he smiles up at me. With his free hand, he brushes away the tears with his thumb.

"My emotional sap," he murmurs and smiles lightly at me.

I smile back at him and sniff unattractively as I wipe the

rest of the tears from my face with the back of my hand, not wanting to miss a moment of what is about to happen.

My mind is racing, shifting back and forth between past and present when this same beautiful man dropped to one knee in front of me so many years ago, dressed quite similarly, but with far more nerves radiating off him then. He spoke so clearly, so sure of himself, even though his hands and mine were shaking.

"Te..." His voice shakes and cracks before he clears his throat and squeezes his eyes shut tightly. When he opens them up again, he stares straight into my eyes, *"Tess. My pretty girl. I don't remember a time when you weren't in my life, but I remember a time when I considered you only a friend. I also remember a time when I sat in those gym bleachers back at Liberty High and noticed you for the beautiful woman you had become. We were just kids. Are just kids. But I fell in love with you then. I fell in love with the idea of us."*

"Tess, my pretty girl, I fell in love with you so many years ago. It seems there hasn't been a day on this earth that I haven't had you a part of my world. We started so young. I had the pleasure of considering you a friend, then one day my eyes, thank goodness, were opened. You walked into the gym that day, and my heart no longer was mine. It was forever yours."

"There's nothing I won't do for you. I will lay down my life for you. I want to give you all that I have. I want to give you the good. I want us to go through the bad together. I want us to stand by each other for all of our lives, building our lives together."

"I love you more than anyone else on this earth. That might sound terrible considering that we have four examples of our love, but it's true. I'd do anything for you. So many years ago, I told you I'd lay my life down for you, and it's still true. I asked you once to walk with me through the good, through the bad, building a life together."

"Tess, I want you to build a life with me from the ground up. Will you do that? Will you let me show you what love is, that love is more than just a feeling? It's showing you that I'll serve you, give to you, that I will prove to you what it is to be loved your entire life. Will you let me continue to choose you above all others for the rest of our lives? Will you allow me to give you my name for you to carry for the rest of our lives? Will you do me the honor of becoming Tess Josephine Ryan, for as long as we both shall live? Marry me?"

"I want to be given the honor to continue to walk alongside you for the rest of our lives. I used to think that I was given the choice to love you. But it's not the case. I was given the choice to protect you, to show you that you mean more to me than anyone else. My heart doesn't know any other way but to love you. When I asked you to marry me, I asked you to build a life together from the ground up. We did that. But I wanna do it again. We're building our lives together again because it was friggin' fun as hell the first time around, and I can't wait to do it again with you. Marry me? Again?" His smile is so bright, but his voice is slightly shaky, like he's fighting back his own emotions.

My gaze has been solely fixed on his eyes that I didn't even notice the round-cut, floating diamond eternity band that he has slid onto my ring finger. The same finger he's placed a ring on two other times in our life: the first time when he proposed to me in this very same spot and the second time during our wedding. I'm full on crying, have been since he dropped to his knee, the ugly hiccup sort of sounds coming out of me, tears streaming down my face, and I have to keep sniffing up (completely unattractively, I might add) the snot trying to make its way out of my nose.

"Of course I'll marry you all over again. Any day of the week," I manage to squeak out.

"Man, I love you. So. Damn. Much."

"I love you, too. A whole lot." I smile at him.

Suddenly he stands, bringing me with him. His large hands are cradled around my face, and his mouth is covering my own. His lips both soft and bruising at the same time. His hands travel down my sides until they're settled on my waist. He circles his arms around my body and pulls me in close as he dips over us just slightly. My arms are wrapped around his neck, my back arched.

The passion I still feel for this man is overwhelming at times. I look at him and can't fathom how I was blessed in the way I am. How was I given the opportunity to love and protect and cherish this human standing in front of me, holding me in his arms as if I'm the most precious of gifts? We stumbled and fell, and we'll probably do it again, because that's life. Life isn't easy. It isn't gentle or perfect. Sometimes life is full of beauty, and sometimes life is full of ugly. But that's what makes it so much fun, stumbling and falling and brushing our dirty selves off and getting back up again to fight through it.

I feel us walking and shuffling through the fallen leaves crunchy underneath our feet. Or his, rather, since he's picked me up, and my legs are wrapped around his waist. His strength has never failed, nor waned, over time. Our mouths are still connected, kissing each other in feverish movements, not willing to part even for a moment. Before we dated each other, I had kissed a few other boys, and he had kissed a few other girls, but our bodies... our bodies have only fully connected with one another's.

We reach the pickup, and we both start laughing into each other's mouths as Barrett tries to get the tailgate down. After a bit of bumbling, neither of us admitting it's because we're a few decades older than when we first did this, he manages to get it unlatched and lays the gate down before turning and placing me on it. The moment my butt hits the frosty cold tailgate I yelp and jump at the contact.

"Maybe this flashback portion of my first proposal will have to be put on the side burner until it's warmer out," he says, eyes twinkling and a beautiful broad smile stretched across his face.

I'm sitting on the lowered tailgate, my butt an icicle, and the tears start once again. From start to finish, he's managed to recreate the moment when he asked me to take his name. His words were different, but the actions were the same. He asked me once to give him my entire heart for the rest of my life, but what he didn't realize then — and still doesn't realize — is that it was never mine to give. I never had my heart in the first place — he had it the moment it first beat, and every thump, every skip, it's all been for him.

"I love you. A whole lot doesn't even cover it."

"I love you, too, my beautiful, emotional girl," he says, wiping away the tears again, and places a firm kiss to my lips. "Let's get you home. I'm sure Grady is back to the house from his date by now, and I know the kids are dying to know how this all played out."

After climbing back into the pickup, me sliding over right next to him again, this time without him asking, he drives us home. A home we've built together, just like he asked and promised so many years ago. We're barely through the door when we're assaulted by not three, but all four of our kids. Cole couldn't stand being away, knowing what was happening between his parents and Grady tonight. Harper, of course, loves having him home and shows us where he signed her cast right away.

We spend the next half hour telling the kids and James the entire story, the boys in the house all giving Barrett grief at appropriate times for being corny. Maggie, being Mags, gets a little emotional as well as, sighing with happiness. Harper is her typical oblivious self, completely unaware of most everything happening around her. Grady tells us about his date, how the restaurant was killer and Bri looked so gorgeous, and it wasn't awkward at all, even when she fumbled and spilled Cherry Coke all over the table from her nervousness. He is one smitten kitten and finally able to show it.

Our family is happy. Our family is healthy. Our family is together, and tonight we are able to remind ourselves that we did that. We built our lives together, and the bumps and detours along the way that took our time and stole our focus only brought us closer together.

We've been home for a few weeks now, and things are basically back to normal. The normal, being, before the four-month dark place we ventured into. Our focus is back on one another while making sure our family is steadily chugging along. As Lauren put it, *"Stella got her groove back."* It's been fun making time for each other once again.

Grady's and Maggie's seasons are complete, Grady's team

taking home second at State. He, of course, would have preferred to win at State for his final year playing for the team that helped mold him into the person he is today, but he's happy, nonetheless. College scouts are still calling and knocking on our door, giving him options and lots to think about.

Two nights ago, Harper came into our room. It was a day that had exhausted both of us and it would have been easy to let her have her way, but we stood firm and Barrett carried her back to her room. It seemed to be taking a little longer than it should have, so I crept across the hall to see what was taking so long. My steps faltered when I heard the low timber of Barrett's voice softly singing "You Are My Sunshine" to Harper as she, no doubt, laid her head on his lap while he played with her hair. When he finished the song, I heard her ask for him to pray then sing it one more time, and his quiet response of "Sure, baby girl, then it's time to go to sleep, alright?" … well, it was all enough to completely melt my heart. When he came back into our bedroom, I jumped him. Hearing him softly singing her favorite song to our baby girl, giving her the time she needed to relax once more in her own bed, hit me everywhere.

I met Keri a few days after we got home from the cabin. I surprised Barrett with lunch from his favorite deli in town and made sure to introduce myself to her, bringing her a small —and much belated — welcome gift. I also made it a point to apologize for not meeting her sooner, and she assured me it was totally fine, that she felt she knew me already because of how much Barrett spoke of me. We have since had lunch one time and plan to again. She's soft spoken, but when it comes to the guys in the shop, she's hard core. She's relentless with making sure they're where they're supposed to be, filling out the right paperwork. I can see how her office managerial skills are a blessing to the guys and, after pulling up my big girl panties, getting over myself, and hauling my ass into the office, I feel nothing but contentment over her being there.

It's the day before Thanksgiving, and James has yet to leave our place. He's taken over Cole's room and isn't showing signs of heading home any time soon. Not that it bothers me, but it has both Barrett and me curious. Cole and Mia are due to arrive any minute. James and I have been cooking most of the day, prepping all the food for tomorrow. My parents are coming over. Dean, my oldest brother, and his wife Meredith along with their kids, alternate every year between the families. This year is her side of the family, so they won't be joining us.

Not that we'll be lacking for people. Between James and Lily, our family, Bri and Christine joining us this year, as well as Mia and Brandon, we'll have a house full. When I told James that Bri and Christine will be joining us, his reaction was one I wanted to dig into at a rapid pace, but Barrett pulled me back and told me to let it go. Right. Because that's my MO. Andy and the boys have been staying at Josh and Lauren's and will be joining us tomorrow as well. The house will be full, and I'll love every single minute of it.

Years ago, Barrett gave me the best gift he could have ever given me. His heart. When he took me to the cabin, he gave it to me all over again. And I'll never take a beat of it for granted.

Epilogue

James
Day before Thanksgiving

W̲e̲'̲r̲e̲ ̲a̲l̲l̲ ̲s̲t̲a̲n̲d̲i̲n̲g̲ in the kitchen of Tess and Barrett's house, the delicious smells circling around us like a wonderful, food-coma hug. A college football game is playing on the TV in the living room, but the food and snacks are keeping everyone centered in the kitchen. Tess and I have cooked Thanksgiving dinner together for years now. It's become a tradition, and I won't have it any other way. Today we're working on the dressing, pies, and getting the rest of the sides prepared. The turkey is sitting in its brine in the fridge.

I hear Cole and Mia walk into the house from the garage. They're holding hands, and both have enormous smiles on their faces, although Mia's is a bit more timid and shy.

"Well, well, well. What do we have here?" Barrett teases.

Mia's face goes beet red, and she looks down at the ground beneath her. She's been around this family her entire life, but now she's showing signs of shyness. I get that. I also see why Cole suddenly fell hard for her. He likes adorable. He likes shy. He's had the assertive girl, and it burned him. Mia complements him well. He's always so sure of himself, but she grounds him, it seems. At least, that's what I get from the phone conversations I've had with him recently.

"Well, if it isn't the two star-crossed lovers," Grady teases too. So much like his dad, it's creepy at times.

"You just wait, little brother. When Bri gets here tomorrow, all bets are off." Cole grins, not really caring at all, but pulls Mia into his side in a protective manner that has me chuckling.

My own nerves about who's showing up tomorrow will no doubt be coming through soon, so I'm not about to join in on the teasing.

Grady's return grin is unashamed. "Bring it on. I've been taking this family's sh…" He catches himself as he looks at his parents. "…crap for years about Bri. I've built up a tolerance to it."

"Welcome, Mia. Barrett and I are so happy you're here with us." Tess interrupts their good-natured sibling quarrelling.

"Thanks, Tess. Thank you for having me."

"Of course, sweetheart. We couldn't be more excited to have you in our home. We'll catch up soon, but for now go ahead and bring your stuff to Maggie's room. You can sleep in there with her, if that works for you."

Maggie doesn't give her a chance to respond before she's dragging her off to her room by the arm, Mia's bag in Maggie's hand. She could have just stayed at home this weekend, but she wants to be around family, or so Tess told me. I wonder if she wants to be around Cole, too, but if Tess and Barrett aren't bothered by it, who am I to argue?

I hear Tess's phone ring, and a huge smile lights up my baby sister's face.

"Is my baby girl there yet? Where's my handsome son-in-law?" I hear Lauren's voice come through the FaceTime speaker call.

Tess's laughter bubbles out of her, and I shake my head. I've dealt with those two for so many years now I decide to leave them to it. I don't need to be around to hear their squealing. I learned to tune them out years ago. I walk into Cole's room, the room I've claimed as my own but will do him the honor of sharing with me for a few days, no doubt crimping any plans he may have to spend some extra time with Mia. I hope to have a few minutes to catch up with my oldest nephew.

We're making homemade pizza together. I'm not nervous to tell them my news. They wanted me to move back home for years now. Over the last few years I've been thinking of it more and more. When I stayed with the kids while Barrett and Tess were at the cabin, an opportunity came up. An opportunity I put out of my mind as even an option years ago. But this restaurant is perfect. I've always wanted to find a space where I could claim the kitchen as my own.

I'm excited to move on, to move forward. To get into a better place than where I've spent the last several years. I put my life on hold while I raised Lily, and I don't regret a single moment of it. I wouldn't change anything, but it's my time now. And I have my sights set on more than just a new restaurant and conquering my own kitchen.

James' story will continue in *A Better Place,* coming soon!

A Better Place

James Cole has been alone for most of his adult life. Alone to raise a daughter who was the light of his life. Now, he's ready. He's ready to take what he wants. He's had his sights set on owning his own restaurant for as long as he can remember. After the perfect opportunity arises, he can't deny that it's meant to be, for more reasons than just the restaurant.

He's kept his heart closed off for more years than he cares to count. He's never found someone who he thought was worth it. But one look at her, and he knew. He couldn't deny himself her, too. He's no longer standing still. He's moving forward and has no plans to stop until he has it all.

He's finally in… A Better Place.

Acknowledgements

NEVER IN MY dreams did I think I would get to the point where I could write these books. It's surreal and humbling, and if you've read to this point, my humbleness just shot up about a thousand points. Thank YOU! Also, I like to talk, and write, so bear with me because I have a lot of people to thank.

Always first is God. I am so grateful to have Him by my side every day. His blessings are abundant, and His grace is never-ending. For Him to allow me this opportunity, there are truly no words. His love is enough.

Travis. You're my rock. You're the only person who can calm me down, make me laugh every single day, and love me the way you do. Thank you for choosing me twenty years ago (holy crap!), and never wavering. Thank you for loving our family and caring, guiding, and protecting us with everything in you. I love you, baby. A whole damn lot.

Joey. Bud. Just writing your name brings tears to my eyes. Thank you for being just as excited as I was when I finished writing this book. I wish I could show the world how awesome, uplifting, and encouraging you are, but I have a feeling they'll find out from you. Honestly, when I think of the places you'll go, the person you'll be, I'm overwhelmed. Never change. I love you beyond words. #thisisawesome

Jake. Kid. You're the best brother, sweetest and most gentle soul out there. Thank you for being kind to everyone, for being happy for me, for loving me like only you can. For giving me hugs for no reason at all. Your beautiful heart blows my mind. I'm so proud of who you are and who you will become. Never change. I love you beyond words.

Riley. My beautiful little sweet and spicy. Girl, your willpower, perseverance, and strength amazes me. Thank you for loving Jesus with your entire heart, for devouring sweets, trying new things, for encouraging me and loving me. Thank you for being such an enormous treasure. Big things, girl. Never change. I love you beyond words.

To the rest of my family, you all swell my heart. For my parents and in-laws, you encouraged me and cheered me on, and I can't thank you more for it. Thanks, Mom and Aunt Deb for reading my story, even though I made you blush!

Julia. You read it first. You gave me the courage I needed. You're my constant sounding board. I'm so grateful to call you sister and best friend. Thank you. For always being real. For everything. I love you!

Matt. Thanks for coaching me on Grady and Cole! I bet you cringe when you see your screen light up with a text from me. *I need help. Again.* Ha! Thanks for never laughing at me. At least to my face.

Jill. Thank you for encouraging me, for being a true friend and such a beautiful person. For talking me down when I go nuts. You amaze me. Every day. I love you.

Michelle. My #SoulSister and fellow mama bear. You probably already know what I'm gonna say without me writing it. Our friendship is cherished. Thank you for being wonderful. I love you!

Deann. You are one of my favorite mamas out there and

I'm so lucky to have you as a friend and be in your village. I don't know if I'm more grateful our boys have each other, or we have each other. Love you.

Erin. Thanks for always listening, and most of all for telling me, "I swear to you, I would never let you publish crap." I know you meant that with your whole heart. I got you. You got me. For life. Big love.

My ladies. My every day smiles. Michelle, Alison, Allison, Erin and Stacy. Every. Single. Day. I love us. I really do. I will never ever be able to look a single one of you in the eye after all that we've shared, but that's what makes us so great.

I have been so incredibly blessed by many authors cheering me on along the way. Some who read early versions of *From the Ground Up* and some who simply told me to keep at it and supported me to keep at it. It's an incredible feeling to have someone who I've looked up to in the book community tell me that I should continue writing. Elizabeth Lee (our fantasy lives are the best), RS Grey (that tackle hug IS happening), Yessi Smith, Rachel Van Dyken (girrrrll!), Erin Noelle, Kristin Vayden, Stephanie Rose, Alison G. Bailey, JL Berg, Anissa Garcia and Jessica Prince, thank you for being someone who I can trust and call friend.

My beta readers: Alison, Allison S., Ella, Yessi, Elizabeth, and Rachel. I couldn't wait to get this baby in your hands, then I wanted to reach into my computer and yank it back. Ha! Thank you for sticking by me and for your honest opinions and time. It's so precious to us, and I appreciate you taking the time to tell me what worked for you and what didn't. Every one of you gave me incredible feedback.

Paula, my editor (Eeek! I have an editor!), girl you are beautiful, amazing and incredible. Thank you for taking your time on my story. Thank you for giving it attention and love and helping me to make it great.

Amy, my proofreader, you polished it to greatness and I am so appreciative. I loved your notes and working with you. Thank you for giving From the Ground Up your love.

Jena, my cover designer, you are brilliant. Brilliant, I say! Thank you for FaceTiming me, having a ton of patience, and letting me get my vision out of my head and into yours. Thanks a million!

A special thank you to the Language Arts teachers, librarians, study hall monitors, reading coaches, tutors and everyone else who stands up and encourages our generation and our children to pick up books and read. Your work does **not** go unnoticed. My children have been incredibly blessed by some of the best in the business. Your time you give and love for expanding their world (and ours) through the eyes of literature is both beautiful and selfless.

Thank you, especially, to Blue Tulip Publishing for taking a chance on me. I am forever grateful and feel beyond blessed that you loved Barrett and Tess as much as I do.

And finally, the readers! Thank you for reading *From the Ground Up* and taking the chance on a new author. I know it's not your typical escape. I know it's real. Marriage isn't easy. Marriage (with or without kids) is sticky and dirty and hard work but so worth it. I hope you enjoyed reading about Tess and Barrett and their very real marriage. I remember very vividly, when our kids were 6, 4, and 2… a wise friend said to us, "These years feel impossible at times, but the rough parts will smooth out. Hang in there, and never stop dating each other." See? Wise. So, while this story may not be entirely based on my life, I, and SO many others, can relate to many parts. #missionkeeprileyinherbed #neverstopdating #lovefromthegroundup

About the Author

FROM THE GROUND UP is Jennifer's first published novel with the hopes of many more to come. Jennifer makes her home in small-town Iowa with her high school sweetheart, three beautiful and amazing kids, and one crazy Jack Russell terrier. This is where her love for all things, reading, baking, and cooking happen. Jennifer's family enjoys camping, fishing, boating, playing board games, and spending time outside as much as possible. When she's not writing or editing/proofreading manuscripts for the many talented authors she's come to love, you can find her sipping coffee or iced tea with her Kindle in her lap or binging on Netflix with her husband.

Also From
Blue Tulip Publishing

BY MEGAN BAILEY
There Are No Vampires in this Book

BY ELISE FABER
Phoenix Rising
Dark Phoenix
Phoenix Freed
From Ashes
Blocked

BY STEPHANIE FOURNET
Butterfly Ginger
Leave A Mark
You First

BY MARK FREDERICKSON & MELORA PINEDA
The Emerald Key

BY JENNIFER RAE GRAVELY
Drown
Rivers

BY LESLIE HACHTEL
The Dream Dancer

BY E.L. IRWIN
Out of the Blue
The Lost and Found

BY J.F. JENKINS
The Dark Hour

BY AM JOHNSON
Still Life
Still Water
Still Surviving
Now & Forever Still

BY A.M. KURYLAK
Just a Bump

BY KRISTEN LUCIANI
Nothing Ventured
Venture Forward

BY KELLY MARTIN
Betraying Ever After
The Beast of Ravenston
The Glass Coffin

BY NADINE MILLARD
An Unlikely Duchess
Seeking Scandal
The Mysterious Miss Channing
Highway Revenge
The Spy's Revenge
The Captain's Revenge
The Hidden Prince

BY BRITTNEY MULLINER
Begin Again

BY MYA O'MALLEY
Wasted Time
A Tale as Old as Time

BY LINDA OAKS
Chasing Rainbows
Finding Forever
The Way Home
Fighting For A Chance

BY C.C. RAVANERA
Dreamweavers

BY KV RIDER
The Real Winner

BY GINA SEVANI
Beautifully Damaged
Beautifully Devoted

BY ANGELA SCHROEDER
The Second Life of Magnolia Mae
Jade

BY T.C. SLONAKER
The Amity of the Angelmen

BY K.S. SMITH & MEGAN C. SMITH
Hourglass
Hourglass Squared
Hourglass Cubed

BY MEGAN C. SMITH
Expired Regrets
Secret Regrets

BY CARRIE THOMAS
Hooked

BY LORI THOMAS HARRINGTON
The Point

BY NICOLE THORN
What Lies Beneath
Your Heart Is Mine

BY RACHEL VAN DYKEN
Upon a Midnight Dream
Whispered Music
The Wolf's Pursuit
When Ash Falls
The Ugly Duckling Debutante
The Seduction of Sebastian St. James
An Unlikely Alliance
The Redemption of Lord Rawlings
The Devil Duke Takes a Bride
Savage Winter
Every Girl Does It
Divine Uprising

BY KRISTIN VAYDEN
To Refuse a Rake
Surviving Scotland
Living London
Redeeming the Deception of Grace
Knight of the Highlander
The Only Reason for the London Season
What the Duke Wants
To Tempt an Earl
The Forsaken Love of a Lord
A Tempting Ruin
A Night Like No Other
The One
How to Silence a Rogue

BY JENNIFER VAN WYK
From the Ground Up

BY JOE WALKER
Blood Bonds

BY KELLIE WALLACE
Her Sweetest Downfall

BY C. MERCEDES WILSON
Hawthorne Cole
Secret Dreams

BY GRACIE WILSON
Beautifully Destroyed

BY K.D. WOOD
Unwilling
Unloved

BOX SET — MULTIPLE AUTHORS
Forbidden
Hurt
Frost: A Rendezvous Collection
A Christmas Seduction
Christmas at Brentwood Abbey

BLUE TULIP
PUBLISHING

www.bluetulippublishing.com

Made in the USA
Columbia, SC
17 March 2018